STILL LIFE WITH A VENGEANCE

JAN
TURK
PETRIE

Published in the United Kingdom
by Pintail Press.

Printed in the United Kingdom
First Printing, 2021

ISBN: 978-1-912855-92-6

Author's website: https://janturkpetrie.com
My Twitter handle: @TurkPetrie
(Twitter profile: https://twitter.com/TurkPetrie.)

My Facebook author page: https://www.facebook.com/janturkpetrie

ALSO BY JAN TURK PETRIE

Until the Ice Cracks –
Vol 1 of The Eldísvík Trilogy

No God for a Warrior –
Vol 2 of The Eldísvík Trilogy

Within Each Other's Shadow –
Vol 3 of The Eldísvík Trilogy

Too Many Heroes

Towards the Vanishing Point

The Truth in a Lie

Running Behind Time

Contents

STILL LIFE WITH A VENGEANCE

"Do not cast away an honest man
for a villain's accusations."

William Shakespeare

"Guilt has quick ears for an accusation."

Henry Fielding

Chapter One

Judging the room as a stranger would, she's troubled. White sofas, pale grey rugs, all spotless to a fault. The art, the flowers, every object strikes a harmonious note. Everything looks perfect. Too perfect. Eve checks her watch – and only thirty minutes to go.

Her first target is the magazine pile on the oversized coffee table. It's easy and rather satisfying to knock it out-of-shape, scatter a few open copies on side tables. Those plumped-up, carefully mis-matched cushions need the wind taken out of them. She slumps across one of the sofas hoping to leave an imprint though, back on her feet, it's hard to discern where she'd lain. If she had a magic wand, she'd shrink things down to less remarkable proportions.

And it's not just this room she's worried about. Marching into the kitchen, her fears are fully realised – it's immaculate. Eve opens a few cupboards, their contents all carefully arranged. She grabs a cereal box, then a bowl that will need to look casually abandoned. In half a minute she's created a tableau with an empty mug and a breakfast bowl in which a

1

few lost shreddies are swimming in a pool of milk, the spoon handle sticking up like a paddle. Seizing a chopping board, she hacks away at a random selection of fruits and then leaves the evidence centre stage. Still life with a vengeance.

Like an intruder on a mission, she rushes through the whole house adding signs of casual abandonment here and there. She's tempted to scatter some of their dirty linen on the bedroom floor, but that seems a step too far.

Less than fifteen minutes now. Where the hell's Nick got to? Two people could mess this place up much quicker than one. If he's late for this, she'll never forgive him.

Leanora seems an unlikely name for the middle-aged, poker-faced woman sitting opposite them. She'd waved away their offer of tea and cake. 'Oh – not for me, thank you all the same.' And then patting an approximation of where her waistline ought to be, 'Have to be careful.' Thankfully, she doesn't elaborate.

Each time Leanora asks a question, she tilts her head a fraction to one side putting Eve in mind of a curious wood-pigeon. Although the woman is recording their conversation, from time-to-time she jots a note on the little pad in her lap. It's hard to work out why these particular utterances should merit a specific aide memoir. Belt and braces no doubt.

To begin with, Leanora – she can't get over her exotic name – had been sitting upright, her stout legs in their heavy denier tights crossed at the ankle. Charm at full strength, Nick has succeeded in softening her up a bit; in the last half hour, Leanora's shoulders have lost their stiffness and she's now leaning forward, attentive to what he's saying.

'Tell me about how the two of you met.' This one is aimed squarely at Nick. In anticipation, Leanora's features form themselves into a coquettish smile.

'It's a complicated story,' he says. 'Would you like the long or the shorter version?'

The woman's eyes dart to her wristwatch and back. 'Oh, I think there's time for the longer version.' Her pen is poised.

He begins with how he'd first noticed Eve in the school refectory all those years ago. Sounding a bit too much like a stalker, he goes on to describe how, during previous walk-bys, he'd identified her street and then narrowed it down to her front door. 'Number twenty-one. And that door colour – so defiantly bright compared to the drab shades of all the rest. This may sound a bit fanciful, but it felt to me like a sign that the people inside were different – exceptional.' He turns to look into Eve's eyes. 'Which is absolutely true, of course.'

Blushing a little, Eve says, 'Yellow was actually my mum's choice. I remember her saying it was the colour of liquid sunshine and we all needed more of that in our lives. Mum was an artist; a professional one, though she never made a huge amount of money out of it. That picture over there is one of hers.'

'Really?' Following her line of sight, Leanora gives her mother's work a cursory appraisal. Her silence makes it obvious the style doesn't accord with her taste. 'And now both your parents are deceased, as I understand it?'

Too many memories stirred, Eve can only nod.

Searching her notes, the woman's face clouds. 'Ah yes. And in such tragic circumstances.'

Nick loudly clears his throat. 'Anyway, as I was saying, I found myself drawn to Eve's front door like it was some sort of homing beacon. Had to be a two-mile walk from my house at least and all the way there I'd build up this steady rhythm telling myself I'd do it, I'd knock this time. But then, I'd bottle it.'

Nick begins to tap one thigh to a beat. He's brushed back his hair to reveal more of his face than she's used to, paler edges where the sun hasn't reached. Odd to see him in chinos instead of scruffy denims. The blue shirt she'd left out looks good on him. Plus, the sleeves hide some of his more elaborate tattoos.

All that tapping might make him seem a bit too wired. She puts her hand over his to stop him and he takes the hint. 'Every flipping time, I'd be standing right there on her doorstep and I'd lose my nerve.' Eve's never heard him use the word *flipping* before.

Leanora's eyes can't quite disguise her mounting excitement. 'And so that's when you wrote Yellow, Yellow Door?'

'Well, not straight away.' Another charming smile. 'It was actually a couple of years later. By then Eve was away at uni and I'd moved to London. I'd been doing bar work while knocking around on the edges of the music scene. Not having much luck until Javier – Javier Holden that is – came into the pub one night.' (Eve shudders at this namedrop.) 'We got chatting and Jav told me Twin Barrels were looking for a bass guitarist. I auditioned and then I joined the band.' He gives her the full crinkle-eyed smile. 'Yellow, Yellow Door was a real departure in style for them, but it became our international breakthrough single.'

Leanora looks smitten. 'And such a romantic song.'

Eve takes over. 'All the way through school I'd had the hots for Nick, but I had no idea – never would have guessed – he felt the same way about me. Then someone played that song to me at a party because it had my name in it. I'm not sure what made Nick used my, um, full name – Genevieve.'

He laughs. 'It worked better with the beat.'

'And then there was the door colour – that seemed way too much of a coincidence. It didn't take me too long to discover Nick had written it.'

For a moment Eve is back at that party, in the very moment when, besides the driving beat, the words of the song began to permeate her booze-soaked brain.

Just a yellow, yellow door
between me and the girl
I a-a-a adore,

She'd shouted into Sarah's ear, 'This song – I think it might actually be about me.'

Her friend shook her head. She read her lips, 'Can't hear you.' And then there it was again, her name: *Genevieve*. She'd stopped dancing, overwhelmed with the realisation that someone had written a song about her and not just any song but a passionate love song. All that time she'd been someone special to them without even knowing it. In her drunken state, she was convinced the universe had conspired to get his message to her. The cosmos had spoken.

Eve leans into Nick's body, into his familiar smell and the conviction that is still there – this was always meant to be.

'I was thrilled and a bit overwhelmed when Eve got in touch through a mutual friend,' Nick says. 'And the rest, as they say, is history.' He slaps his thigh like he's delivered a killer punchline instead of a cliché.

'Well not exactly history,' Eve feels the need to add. 'History sounds like it's all over and done with. I mean, that phrase – it implies the past. But, as you can see, we're still very much together; and we're both absolutely ready for this next exciting chapter of our lives.' To emphasise her point, she holds up Nick's hand – their intertwined fingers.

They move on. Eve wishes she could tell him to stop raking back his hair like he keeps doing. Such an obvious nervous tic. 'I guess I should address the, um, obvious elephant in the room.' Nick looks straight at Leanora. 'The whole fame thing – it wouldn't be an issue. Mean to say, it doesn't impinge on our lives here. Things are a lot different for Leon – being the band's frontman he's recognised everywhere he goes. On stage or off, the focus is very much on him; not that he doesn't enjoy all the attention.'

Dropping the grin, Nick clears his throat. 'People hardly ever recognise me – not out of context, as it were. I'm not saying they don't occasionally look twice because maybe I seem a bit familiar. They probably assume they've seen me down the pub or wherever. Don't get me wrong, I never mind being asked for my autograph, but it only happens once in a while. It's never been an issue off-stage and certainly not down here in deepest Somerset.' That said, he exhales. 'So, you see we lead a pretty normal life.'

Leaning forward, Eve gives Leanora what she hopes is a confident smile. 'The people in the village know who we are, but, to them, we're just plain old Nick and Eve. They never treat us like a celebrity couple or anything like that. I'm afraid we're far too boring to sustain much local interest.'

Leanora scans her notes. 'And your family, Nick? I understand your parents divorced when you were twelve.'

'Mum left us – ran off with a bloke from work.' He shrugs. 'My dad became a single parent overnight. Did a pretty good job, though it must have been a struggle at times. My older brother, Pete, manages a vineyard in the Yarra Valley northeast of Melbourne. Haven't seen him since Dad's funeral three years back.'

'And your mother?'

'Didn't want to know. Sent us birthday cards with vouchers until we were eighteen.' A forced laugh. 'Must have decided that was the limit of her parental responsibility.'

'I see.' Leanora decides not to comment further. She gathers her things together, done with them for now at least. 'Right, well, thank you both for answering my questions and for showing me around your, um, *very* lovely home. I think I have all I need for now.' She fishes a buff folder from her large and practical bag and traps the little notepad inside its covers. The click echoes as she presses the stop button on the recorder. Her expression gives nothing away.

Lanyard swinging like a pendulum, the woman stands up, smooths down her tweed skirt and takes a last look around the room. Eve's gaze follows hers to the sharp edges of the table, the blazing log fire Nick lit with only moments to spare. No spark guard in front of it.

They see Leanora to the front door, waving her goodbye with the sort of enthusiasm normally reserved for good friends. The woman's dusty Astra sweeps past Nick's gleaming Lotus though she's forced to wait for the electric gates to open.

They stand at the open door with its view across the fields beyond. A child's paradise, surely. 'Well, that's round one over with.' Nick does his best to lighten the mood. 'You definitely scrub-up well, Mrs Quenington. Can't think of the last time you wore a dress. I'd almost forgotten those sexy legs of yours.' He rests a heavy arm along her shoulders. 'Bloody glad that's over with. Felt like I was up before the head again.' When she doesn't respond he takes hold of her chin – turns her face towards his. 'So, what d'you reckon? D'you think we passed the test?'

'No idea.' She shakes her head, shakes off his grip. 'Let's face it, we were never going to come across as Mr-and-Mrs-Average.'

'Don't tell me you're secretly longing for a life *more* ordinary.'

'In some respects, yes. I mean, I suppose fundamentally I want the same things everybody else wants.' Surely, she doesn't need to elaborate – not to him. And yet she adds, 'Underneath it all, we're like any other animal. The biological imperative – it's hardwired into us.'

'The zoologist's perspective, eh?'

The sun is low on the horizon, already giving up on the day. Shivering, she tells him, 'That was another life,' not quite disguising the wistfulness in her voice.

Eyeing up their front door, Nick says, 'You know, the

conservation people would go spare if we painted this yellow.'

'Then maybe we should move.' She's only half joking.

It's a relief to step back into the warmth of the house. 'Don't know about you but I'm bloody starving.' Nick rubs his hands together. 'Wouldn't mind a spot of afternoon tea by the fire.'

'Afternoon tea?' She laughs. 'Not exactly rock'n'roll, is it?'

He puts on a silly posh voice. 'Would you care to join me in the withdrawing room, my dear?'

Eve threads her arm through his. Patting her stomach, she says, 'I have to be careful. One bite of cake and who knows what might happen.'

He runs a hand up her thigh. 'Sounds promising.'

Chapter Two

Eve strides off towards the stables, the frost-hardened grass crackling under her boots. Reaching the stable yard, she breathes in the sweet-sour smell of hay and manure. There's no one about. Inside, perhaps already sensing her presence, Brandy is kicking at the door to her stall. Catching sight of Eve, the horse's whinnies turn into nickering – a quiet greeting that sounds suspiciously like she's grumbling. Her deep brown eyes are full of accusations. Patting her neck, Eve reconnects and reassures, aware that Brandy instinctively tunes into her moods.

She dares to imagine giving step-by-step instructions to a child; boy or girl – it wouldn't matter either way. *Check the horse over and then lift each hoof one at a time.* Knowing the routine, Brandy lowers her head as soon as Eve picks up the bridle.

Adjusting the throat lash, she's startled by a movement in the shadows. 'Sorry,' Jared steps into the light. 'Didn't expect to make you jump like that,' he says. 'You okay?'

'Yeah, I'm fine.' Her heart is slow to return to its normal rhythm. 'I just, you know, assumed you'd left already.'

'My first meeting got cancelled and, seeing's you're not in the habit of standing me up, I thought I'd hang around for a bit.' Smiling, he turns away to check Domino's stirrups.

'Nick's back,' she tells him by way of explanation.

A grin creases his cheeks. 'So, our lord and master made it home from his travels after all.' An old jibe worn thin – Nick had once drunkenly revealed he could officially call himself the Lord of the Manor courtesy of the 13th century core of the manor house. Their other friends had found this amusing, but such a vestige of feudalism was never going to sit well with Jared's republican instincts.

'Must be grand to have your man back,' he says.

'Of course.'

When she doesn't elaborate, he checks his watch. 'If it's okay with you, I thought we might ride up to Foxfield and then back down through the woods.' She likes the way his Irish accent turns thought into taught, through into true.

'Sounds perfect.' Eve runs the grooming brush over Brandy's back releasing dust, fine hairs and that distinctive equine smell. By the time she gets back Nick will almost certainly be holed up in his recording studio – the Batcave as the workmen had christened it. Converted from an outhouse, strict sound-proofing requirements meant every window had to be blocked up. When he's busy, Nick turns on the neon sign above the door: *Enter at your peril.*

She's worked her way down both flanks. Keen to get going, Jared hands her the saddle pad. He says, 'Rory's planning to cook his famous venison wellington tonight. And, as you well know, the man's a stranger to moderation.'

In her head she continues the instructions. *Lay the saddle on the pad like this then slide it backwards until the pommel sits at the highest point of her withers.* 'Earth to Eve,' Jared says.

'Sorry – you were saying?'

'Only that I guarantee there'll be more than enough for four if the two of you fancy joining us.' Not waiting for an answer, he leads his snorting horse out into the yard.

'Thanks,' she calls after him. 'Sounds great.' Eve tightens the girth strap; dissatisfied, she loosens it a little. She leads Brandy out to join him. 'I'll need to check with Nick. He might be in the middle of something. You know how he won't stop until he's got it right.'

The grey in Jared's dark hair is more noticeable against the light. 'Then come alone if you like.' He holds up his hands. 'Up to you. No pressure either way.'

Domino is restless, his sliding hooves ringing out against the concrete. 'Hold still now,' Jared says mounting the horse. Eager to be off, he has to rein him in. From a superior height, 'So, how'd it go with that adoption woman?'

'Hard to tell. Okay, I think.' The sympathy on his face makes her look away. Brandy snorts her impatience. Foot in the stirrup, Eve swings her leg up and over the horse's back. 'Guess we'll find out soon enough.'

Jared leads them out of the yard. A band of low cloud is heading their way; the forecasted snow might arrive sooner than expected. Eve stretches to reach the lever on the field gate. Once they're through, their horses begin to circle each other. 'Seeing's you still look half asleep,' Jared says, 'I'll race you to the bothy.' Without waiting, he gallops away.

'Cheat!' she calls after him. Brandy needs no encouragement to set off in pursuit.

She wakes with a thick head thanks to the whisky that had followed a scandalous quantity of red wine. In a buoyant mood, Nick had taken along an old acoustic guitar. As the night wore on, the tunes he and Rory chose had become more earnest and sentimental. A good night – 'savage craic' was Jared's verdict.

Spreadeagled and on his back, Nick is now snoring quietly. She swallows, her throat sore from last night's singing. Their bed is so big he never seems aware of her leaving it. She slips on her silk dressing gown – the one he'd recently brought back from somewhere in the Far East. A peace offering. Hand embroidered blossom trees and exotic butterflies on a pale blue background. Holding it up to the light, she'd protested it was far too exquisite and delicate to be worn. His face clouding, Nick had thrown up his hands. 'Then what the hell's the point of it?' Relenting, she'd tried it on. 'Looks great on you.' His grin widened into a real smile. 'Matches your eyes.'

Back at him, she said, 'What – all the red bits?' A joke that wasn't really a joke.

Cool against her bare skin, this morning the fabric carries the faint aroma of a spice she can't identify. Wearing such a thing of beauty feels like an illicit act. On the landing, its patches of gold thread sparkle as they're discovered by the morning sun; she could be one of Klimt's pale-faced women.

She remembers them posing for photographs against the magnificent panelling on the main staircase. It's impossible not to admire the workmanship but the heaviness of so much old oak is hard to live with.

Reaching the kitchen, the light streaming down from the rooflight lifts her mood. Locating her phone on the charging pad, she discovers it's far later than she thought. Amber must have been and gone. The girl is a hard worker but she has an annoying habit of laying out their breakfast things as if this wasn't their home but a hotel. Eve's told her more than once they are perfectly capable of helping themselves to whatever they want. 'Might as well do in any case,' she'd protested, her colour rising in a way that spoke of defiance rather than embarrassment. The subtext was clear enough – it gave her something else to do in a house where no running feet ever tracked in dirt.

Eve gulps down a glass of water. Through the leaded-light windows the fields are frosted white where the sun hasn't yet melted it. The forecasted snowstorms had passed them by after all. She watches the quarrelling birds on the feeder, grins at the way one of the long-tailed tits is hanging precariously upside down.

Humming one of the ballads from last night, she puts a teabag in a mug then fills it from the boiling tap before breaking into song, *'Will you go lassie go? And we'll all go together.'* She can picture those purple patches of wild thyme on the slopes of a Scottish mountain, the cries of the golden eagle circling overhead.

While her tea stews, she fiddles with the coffee maker, measuring in the right dose and pressing the button that activates the steam and noise needed before the darkly pungent liquid can dribble out into Nick's favoured espresso cup. Dumping her teabag, she splashes in milk before carrying the two mismatched cups upstairs.

Nick's awake – sitting up in bed rubbing at his eyes. His expression is unusually serious. 'Just had a call from Kendra. Apparently, there's some crazy shit-storm brewing on social media.'

'Involving you?' He nods as she hands him the coffee. 'What sort of shit-storm?'

Hand unsteady, he takes the cup and knocks the whole thing back in one. 'Thanks. That really hit the spot.'

She puts her mug down. 'So, this shit-storm – what's it about?'

Nick rolls his head. 'A lot of made-up crap.' He's not meeting her eye. 'We all thought it wasn't going to amount to anything but now there's some fake footage they claim was taken after one of our gigs in Germany.'

He wanders off to the bathroom; she can hear him pissing. She goes over to stand at the open door. 'And?'

He says something the flush drowns out. Naked, he turns around to face her. 'Some girl is trying to earn a few quid by making up crazy allegations about us. I've told Kendra the whole thing's a complete fantasy.' He turns away to wash his hands. 'We've agreed she should issue a short statement – a denial – but it's already trending on Twitter and just about everywhere else. And now the newspapers are picking it up.' Wiping his hands, he says, 'Kendra knows some hot-shot libel lawyer.'

'A lawyer?' Eve drops into a nearby chair. 'So, these allegations – they must be pretty serious.'

He comes to kneel at her feet. 'Yeah – the worst kind.' Hand across his chest, he looks her straight in the eyes. 'I swear to you there's not a shred of truth in any of it.'

She can't remember the last time he looked so earnest. 'I believe you,' she tells him.

His shoulders droop. 'This girl's claiming she met us in a club after our last Berlin gig. That we slipped something in her drink that got her senseless and then passed her around in what they're calling – and I quote – *a drug-fuelled orgy*. Like I said, it's all nonsense; the woman must be some kind of fantasist.'

She goes cold all over. 'Oh my God!'

Nick stands up. Hands on his hips, he says, 'Evie, first off – you have to remember this never happened. Okay?'

She nods. 'Okay.'

'I've never met this girl. She's claiming this happened in Berlin in 2016 and that she was a virgin at the time and would never have voluntarily agreed to sex with any of us, never mind all three of us. No mention of Bernie for some reason. It's a few years back but, as it happens, I remember that night because we'd picked up a dodgy takeaway in Hanover the night before. They had to keep stopping the bus on the way to Berlin because everyone was throwing up. I was in really a bad way. So bad there was even talk of hiring another guitarist, although that was always going to be a non-starter. In the end, I went on and we got through our set. No encore – we were all too wiped-out.'

The complex pattern of tattoos on his torso could be hieroglyphics she hasn't fully learnt to read. 'I was totally knackered afterwards.' He rubs his eyes, only making them redder. 'Leon and me shared a taxi back to the hotel and the next morning we were straight off on the bus to Prague.' He runs his hand over the stubble on his chin. 'At least I think it was Prague. Easy enough to check that part.'

'What about Bernie and Gil? Did they go clubbing afterwards?'

'I'm not sure what they did though I'd be amazed if either of them felt up to all that.' He raises his hands then lets them fall to clap his bare thighs. 'Besides, this girl – this woman – is claiming *I* was the one who pulled her first. Which means we should be able to prove the whole thing is complete and utter bollocks.'

When Eve stands up, he hugs her, enveloping her in the familiar tang of his unwashed body. Pulling away she says, 'You mentioned footage?'

'Yeah. And some stills taken from it. The stuff I've seen is fairly gross. Things have moved on a lot from photoshopping. Kendra was going on about deepfakes – how with enough media footage, they can put any words they like into someone's mouth or graft your head onto someone else's body. You know, like when they bring dead actors back to life to finish a film. She says if we can find the right experts, we should be able to prove they're fakes.'

He thumps the wall releasing a shower of plaster dust from between the beams over their heads. 'Thing I can't understand is – why would they go to all that trouble?'

'*They*? So, you think this is some sort of conspiracy?' Before he can answer, a worse truth hits her. 'Oh my God – the adoption. They're never going to approve our application with all this hanging over us.'

He strokes her shoulders, tries to sooth her rising panic.

'It'll be okay once we prove it's all lies. This whole thing could blow over in a few days.'

As she turns, she catches her reflection in the mirror – teach her to dress up like some princess. 'You know as well as I do, if it's in the newspapers, Leanora or maybe someone on her team – they're bound to see it. Those sort of accusations – they stick. No smoke without fire and all that.' Tears are blurring her vision. 'That's it – we're finished. No one will trust us with a child.'

'Evie, listen to me – there's no need to panic.' He stumbles around pulling on boxers and then jeans. 'Leanora left us her card, didn't she? I doubt she's heard about any of this yet. Why don't I ring her right now; explain how it's all made-up nonsense?' He grabs her shoulders. 'We can still make this right.'

'I don't see how it can ever be *made right*,' she says turning away from him. She lets the stupid dressing gown fall to the floor. 'I need a shower.'

He comes after her, tries to catch her hand but she holds it up to stop him getting any closer. Shaking his head, he says, 'I'll go and make that phone call.'

Chapter Three

Eve pulls her hair back and fastens it securely; a serious style that makes her look older than 33. Her hangover from last night isn't helping. She knocks back a couple of paracetamols with the dregs of her cold tea.

When she chose dark blue-grey for their bedroom, her aim was to cocoon them in this private sanctuary away from everything else. Today the same walls crowd in on her. She needs fresh air, a good gallop across the fields, but already she can hear a growing commotion outside – vehicle doors slamming, the buzz of distant conversation.

Approaching the window at an angle, a glimpse confirms her suspicion – a small crowd has assembled outside their gates, long lenses glinting in the sun. Those must be trained on the front of the house; no doubt they've been clicking away – setting the scene for their nosy readers. How the other half lives – or lies. For all she knows the more determined ones could be down in the garden hiding behind the foliage.

'Better stay back from the windows.' Nick is on the landing some distance from her. Breathless from the stairs, his damp hair has been tamed by a comb. He's dressed for outdoors – more country gent than rock star.

'So, what did Leanora say?'

'She made all the right noises – agreed it must be a stressful situation for both of us.'

'D'you think she believes you're innocent?'

'Hard to know.' He rubs a hand over his eyes like someone who's been awake for too long. 'She heard me out then thanked me for being frank. But they're trained to be professionally detached, aren't they? I'd say she was non-comital.'

'Of course.' Eve's sigh is long and heartfelt. The hum outside is getting louder – an enraged swarm looking for its next target. 'I can't believe were being doorstepped already.'

'Bad news travels fast,' he says. 'They must be freezing their arses off out there. Kendra thinks the two of us should go out and make a statement – present a united front and all that. Once they get what they're after, they're more likely to piss off and leave us alone.'

'Tell me, would Kendra prefer us to approach them arm-in-arm or hand-in-hand?'

'The woman's only trying to help.'

'I'm sure she is. I imagine there must be some PR rulebook to cover situations like this. What's the accepted script, Nick?' She looks down at her jumper and jeans. 'Should I change into something more formal? Or maybe something skimpier? I could aim for the sexy-wife-you-wouldn't-need-to-cheat-on look. Do we invite them in, or just pose in front of our fucking great manor house and try to make their readers feel sorry for us?'

'Listen – we go out, make a statement; keep it short. Stick to the facts.' He rakes his dark curls back in place. 'I'll explain there's no truth in any of it.' He seems to be studying his boots. They could do with a shine.

'So, you're saying mine's more of a non-speaking role. I just stand there radiating good humour. Should I take them out a tray of hot drinks and chocolate Hobnobs?'

'No need to go that far.'

'But you want me to stand mute at your side and smile like the wife of some sleazy politician dragged out to show the world that she's loyally standing by her man, even though he's just been caught with his pants down shagging a sheep.'

'Fuck sake.' Nick narrows his eyes at her.

She says, 'Have you any idea how humiliating this is for me?'

Cursing not quite under his breath, he jabs a finger into the space between them. 'I doubt it's more humiliating than being accused of preying on a vulnerable young girl; deliberately plying her with drugs and who knows what, before instigating some sordid three-way gang-bang.'

He mutters something else as he turns away.

She raises her voice. 'What did you just say to me?'

His head swivels round. 'I said, I'm going to speak to them with or without you.' He hurries down the stairs.

Over the banister she shouts, 'Nick wait!' Catching up with him on the half landing, she runs a hand down the rough tweed of his jacket; he's hardly recognisable dressed like some country gent. 'I'm sorry,' she tells him. 'Of course I'll go out there with you. All this – it's just been a lot to take in.'

'How the hell d'you think I feel?'

Suddenly dizzy, she takes his arm, stares down at the hallway's flagstone floor – such a long way to fall.

On the ground floor the noise grows louder. 'I'm going to need a minute to, you know, get myself ready,' she tells him. 'Christ, I can't believe this whole thing's blown up so fast.'

'Yeah well, with luck it'll blow over just as quickly.'

Eve's pretty sure neither of them believes that for a millisecond.

Nick is pacing the hallway outside the boot room; a small card in his hand, he's rehearsing a statement he must have agreed with Kendra. In an English winter, his tanned face and unruly dark curls are at odds with his formal jacket. Beside him, she'll look so pale.

Though tempted to simply grab the nearest coat, she needs to get this right because, once the pictures are splashed across the tabloids, every detail will be pored over. This isn't her first encounter with the paparazzi – she's learnt the importance of controlling the narrative before it takes control of you. Like it or not, every part of her image will tell its own story.

She unties her hair hoping it will soften her face. Best not wear her riding boots or expensive insulated wellies – she needs to look relatable. Her grey lace-ups should be unremarkable. The navy pea jacket is smart enough to show she's taking this seriously but is ostensibly not the product of some swanky designer. That settled, on impulse she adds a scarf – the chunky hand-knitted one Tania sent her for Christmas; its imperfections will lend her outfit a homely touch.

'What d'you think?' she asks, presenting herself for Nick's approval.

His smile is an effort. 'You look lovely, but then you always do.'

Before she can question him further, he shuts his eyes, takes a quiet moment to control his breathing like he's learnt to do before any performance.

She waits.

'Okay,' he says, 'let's get this done.' Shoulders back. 'You ready?'

'As I'll ever be.'

He grabs her hand. 'Okay, let's go.'

Instead of the usual side entrance, they emerge through the front door. As soon as they step outside the noise is amped up and the commotion at the gate steps up a gear – camera motors whir, flashes go off in a volley. Their names are called out with increasing desperation.

Eve concentrates only on putting one foot in front of the other. Breath clouding the air, their footsteps crunch the gravel, side by side as they approach the gates – this is Judgement Day.

Like the showman he is, Nick leaves it until they're only a few metres away before blipping the small device that opens the gates. Taken by surprise, those pressed up against it stumble forward to avoid falling. Wrongfooted, they regroup and rush forward jostling for position.

Nick stills the disorder with a raised hand. Fluffy microphones are extended. They all wait upon his words.

For one moment, Eve is terrified he'll pull the cue-card from his pocket. Instead, he begins an impassioned statement refuting all the allegations. When they ask him about the footage, he's careful to insert the word deepfake several times into his answer without directly accusing anyone. It's an impressive performance – word perfect.

She's caught off guard when someone shouts her name. Like the limbs of some enormous hairy spider, all the microphones swivel in her direction. Nick's grip on her tightens. The faces before her blur. She only needs to get through this and then it will all be over and done with.

They grow quiet as they wait for her statement.

'I've known Nick since we were at school together.' Flashes light up the air like a storm. Despite the cold, she's sweating profusely. 'And in all the years I've known him, he's always shown the greatest respect not just to me but to all the women he knows and works with. Rock musicians have a reputation for behaving wildly – badly you might say – but Nick has always been a deeply moral man. I know he would never behave like… in the way he's being accused of.'

'You're saying it's a pack of lies?' A man's voice though she's not certain which one.

'I'm saying I believe my husband is completely innocent.'

A woman this time, 'So you're standing by your man, Eve?' Such a tired bloody cliché.

'Look, I know this man – he's my soulmate – and I know he wouldn't do…' She's not going to use the words. 'The awful things he's accused of.' She turns to Nick, forces her mouth into a smile. 'I believe in him. In us.'

The strain must show on her face; that picture will tell its own story. Softening her eyes, she leans in and kisses Nick – a chaste kiss she plants not on his mouth but on his cheek. The whirs and flashes reach a crescendo.

A man in a green beanie hat shouts, 'Have you spoken to Lina Wolff?' It's unclear who this question is aimed at.

'No, I haven't,' Nick tells him. 'But you can bet our lawyers will be in touch with her.'

A tall redhead thrusts her microphone in his face. 'So, you're planning to sue Miss Wolff for defamation?'

'Like I said, the group will be consulting our lawyers.' Had they noticed how he'd hesitated? Would they make something of that?

Nick looks each of them in the eye. 'That's all we have to say at this time, folks.' His raised hand waves. 'Have a safe journey home.'

Ignoring further entreaties, they plaster on smiles before turning their backs. On their heels, the pack scurries behind them, wanting more. Eve's careful to hold her head high as they continue to walk towards the house.

She's grateful their front door is strong enough to repel a siege – at least for a while. Like a blow, the sound of it closing echoes along the hallway. Vengeful wasps disturbed, the more persistent individuals continue to rap at the door.

Afterwards, when she tries to replay the scene, she can't remember any of the many urgent questions shouted after them as Nick led her back inside.

Chapter Four

Eve's favourite room has always been this kitchen. Built originally to accommodate the household's carriages, it's a long, single-storey extension to the main house. Despite its vaulted ceiling, the wood burner keeps it cosy. When Nick's away, she seldom ventures into the rest of the downstairs.

'All things considered, I think that went okay.' Nick rubs at his newly shaved chin. 'Thanks again for doing your bit out there.' He puts an arm around her.

She's quick to move away. In case someone is lurking outside, she pulls down the blinds on every window with the exception of the rooflight – the lantern as the architect insisted on calling it – which has never had blinds. Up to now, it's never been necessary, but this would be no place to hide if they were to send up camera drones.

Her parents' battered leather armchairs sit either side of the fire – the only furniture she'd kept after it happened. What would they make of all this?

Robbed of its outlook, the room takes on a strange, cell-like feel. Above them the cloud layer is uniformly grey. The breakfast things are still laid out on the table untouched. 'At least that's over,' Eve says. A restless energy is jangling her nerves; it's not yet midday – too early to pour herself a stiff gin, tempting though it is. And not a great idea on an empty stomach.

She sits down at the table and begins to pull apart a cold croissant. Nick carries on prowling the room until he makes her dizzy. 'I suppose we can't close the gates until we're sure they've all gone,' she says.

He doesn't answer. Instead, his eyes are welded to his phone. 'Well at least that's something.' He looks up. 'Kendra's managed to pull in a few favours. She's spoken to the lawyer she told me about. Royston Mallard-Jones – can you believe that name? Anyway, he's apparently tied up in court over the next few days, but he's sending someone called Legg – an associate she calls him. He's coming down here this afternoon.'

'So, that's good, right? This Royston Mallard-Whatsit has agreed to represent you all.'

'Not exactly. In the attachment here it says that his associate will carry out *an initial consultation*.' A huff of a laugh. 'They're certainly not taking any chances – Kendra's had to pay them for the visit upfront.'

To placate her rumbling stomach, Eve swallows a piece of the torn-off croissant. She sets about finishing the rest though it couldn't be more unappetising.

Nick finally pulls out the chair opposite and sits down. His right leg judders like he's playing a bass drum. He breaks off from monitoring his phone to pour a long glass of cranberry juice. 'Mr Legg should be here in a couple of hours,' he tells her.

As if seeing him afresh, she watches the way Nick's Adam's apple moves up and down as he gulps the juice. After draining the glass, he wipes his mouth with the back of his hand and then tops it up to the brim again; doesn't notice the juice running down the outside of the glass to form a small pool on the table. 'You know I'm actually bloody starving,' he says, shaking oatmeal followed by cereal flakes into a bowl then spooning on fresh fruit and a large dollop of yoghurt.

She's surprised he can eat with such gusto. 'Wouldn't mind another coffee,' he tells her between mouthfuls. Grown used to his every need being catered for on tour, he can forget she's not one of his many gofers.

Her mouth is dry from the croissant and so she swallows half a glass of milk. Left out too long, it's beginning to turn sour.

'I'm going for a ride.' Her chair scrapes the floor as she gets to her feet. With luck, if she leaves through the back door and keeps to the right of the tree line, no one's lens will pick her out.

Mouth half-full, Nick says, 'This Legg guy might want to talk to you – better make sure you're back in time.'

'When have *I* ever let *you* down?' She hadn't meant it to come out quite like that.

Her ride hasn't helped much. It was hard to find anything but sadness in the way the frost had blighted the hedgerows and frozen the field margins. Picking up on her mood, Brandy had been skittish and easily spooked. On reaching open ground, she'd encourage her into a gallop hoping the workout would do them both good. The freezing air stung Eve's face. Slowing down, they'd taken a winding a path through the woods on the way back, falling into a comfortable rhythm and a better understanding.

Now, approaching the side door on foot, Eve pauses at the tiny grave. *Misty – a loyal friend, sadly missed.* People might scoff at raising a memorial stone to a dead pet, but Misty had been her parents' beloved cat and, for a while, Eve's only surviving link to them.

Simon, the gardener they inherited along with the house, would have something to say about the state of the flower borders since his recent retirement.

She runs upstairs but before she can shower, she hears tyres on the gravel and the unmistakable sound of a car pulling up outside. She opens the door still dressed in her sweaty riding clothes. Out of breath, she says, 'Hi, I'm Eve. I'm guessing you must be Mr Legg.'

He makes a show of removing his hat – a grey banded trilby. 'Good day. You must be Mrs Quenington.' He smooths his short fair hair away from its side parting. She notes the well cut, sombre suit. 'Splendid house. I understand the architect was influenced by Colen Campbell.' He has the sort of posh accent that's dying out even amongst the Royal Family. Those patrician manners are at odds with his youthful appearance; his ruddy cheeks and neck are plagued by a rash of pimples. She hopes he has a sharp mind and reached his position through merit rather than family connections.

Before shutting the front door, she checks behind him. As far as she can tell, the reporters have all buggered off at last.

Eve shows him into the hallway where he glances around taking stock like an eager estate agent – or a thief. In the absence of a butler, he hands her his hat. Surprised, she puts it down on one of the hall chairs where it sits like a silent movie skit waiting to happen.

Nick finally puts in an appearance. He's changed back into jeans and a plain black t-shirt. Wearing his most affable expression, he gives the young man's hand a hearty shake before leading him through into the newly blacked-out dining room.

'The paparazzi were here earlier,' Eve explains. She's quick to pull aside the heavy drapes to let in light. Seeing how little difference it makes, she turns on several lamps but leaves the overhead chandelier unlit – the ornate patterns it casts seems too frivolous for the occasion.

Legg automatically takes the seat at the head of the table. His eye is drawn up to the room's ornate ceiling. 'A delightful room,' he concludes.

'Yeah, it is.' Nick begins to fidget. 'Glad you found the place okay, Mr um Legg.'

Eve starts to picture him as a Mr-Man drawing.

'Please – do call me Daniel.' He extracts a large pad and a Dictaphone from his briefcase. She's reminded of that other interview – the one with Leanora.

Daniel feels the need to adjust his fountain pen several times until he's satisfied it's at precisely the right angle to the legal pad. Bizarrely, he then spreads both hands out on the polished surface of the table as if testing its strength in preparation for a headstand or some other gymnastic manoeuvre.

After a long sigh, he sits back leaving two sets of damp

prints on the polished surface. 'I should begin by explaining that the purpose of my visit today is simply to gather all the relevant information, so that we may, um, fully assess your case and advise you as to the best way forward.'

'Got it,' Nick tells him.

Her nod is meant to encourage him to just get on with it.

'Your representative, Miss Harris, has advised us of the, um, salient points. I will, of course, be speaking separately to the other members of the, ahh, *group*.' He sounds the last *p* as if the word, or perhaps the concept, offends him. 'As I understand it, Mr Quenington–'

'Call me Nick, please.'

'Very good. As I was saying, you are personally accused of initiating what is alleged to have taken place and so it makes sense to start with your statement. I will be taking notes and of course will be recording this interview – assuming you have no objections.'

'No, I'm fine with that.'

'Good then let us begin with your precise recollections of what took place in Berlin on the night in question.' Before Nick can speak, Daniel holds up a hand. 'Please be as precise as possible, leave no stone unturned as it were. God – or occasionally the devil – tends to lurk in the detail.' He follows this mix of metaphors with a short laugh as if he's cracked a fine joke.

Eve shuts her eyes. How had it come down to this? Their house has always been a private retreat with one rule – only the people they chose are invited here. Under normal circumstances she would never allow a pompous little prat like this to sit at their dining table. But right now, what choice do they have? Nick is convinced Royston Mallard-Whatsit is the best in the business – 'the courtroom tiger you want on your side' according to the all-knowing Kendra. It's clear this odd young man is, in effect, the great man's gatekeeper.

She goes off to make tea – an excuse to leave the room – intending to take her time about it. To get through this, she needs to believe in Nick's innocence. She'd meant every word she said to the press earlier. How could she stay with Nick if she didn't believe he's fundamentally a good man? But he's no saint and never has been. If he's going to court to accuse this Lina Wolff of making everything up, he'd better be telling the complete and unvarnished truth.

It's a relief to see the back of Daniel Legg for the time being, to have the house to themselves once again. Nick doesn't say a lot about how the interview went and she chooses not to initiate a post-mortem. Instead, they eat supper – a pie from the freezer with a hastily assembled salad – in a silence broken only by requests to pass the pepper or the salad dressing. No stars are visible through the glass lantern above their heads; tonight the sky is shrouded by heavy clouds.

It's well past nine when Kendra arrives dripping water onto the hall floor from her umbrella. Her dark hair is plastered to her head. 'The heavens have just opened,' she tells them. This is no exaggeration; Eve had watched the Uber she arrived in drop her off at the gates.

'Sorry I couldn't get here any sooner,' is aimed at Nick exclusively. She bestows a couple of air kisses on him before squeezing his arm. 'You poor man. This must be absolute hell.' The size of her bag suggests she's planning to stay overnight.

'Hello, Eve. Didn't see you there.' Kendra's painted-on eyebrows come together like two slugs about to mate. More air is kissed. 'How are you holding up?' doesn't require an answer.

Nick gives her his lopsided grin. 'We've had better days.'

The woman's lips have been freshly stung by hypodermics. Given the amount of surgical intervention, it's near impossible to determine her age with any accuracy.

'Right,' Kendra says, 'First things first. I've had a long chat with Leon and Gil. As you know, they were more than happy to corroborate everything you told me about that night. Although I have to say Gil's recollections are a bit vague. Oh, and I finally managed to track Bernie down to his farmhouse near Lake Bolsena. Lucky him, eh?'

'You spoke to him directly?'

'Yep, on my way down here – not half an hour ago. Have to say his memory's more than a bit shot, as we all know. He does remember how sick you all were just before a gig on that tour. Sadly, he couldn't be certain which one it was.'

Kendra squeezes Nick's arm again. The woman seems rather tactile with him. 'Don't look so worried,' she says, brightening her voice. 'This thing will soon blow over. Like they say, today's news, tomorrows chip-paper.'

'Although the chippies don't use newspaper anymore,' Eve interjects. 'I expect it's a health and safety thing. All the germs they might carry from one person to the next.' She should definitely stop talking now.

'You're soaked through, come and sit by the fire.' Nick leads her towards the kitchen where she holds her hands out to the wood burner's warmth. Beneath her trench coat, Kendra's wearing beige cashmere with chunky black jewellery. She hands Eve her wet coat without a word.

Coming back from the boot room with a towel, Eve's greeted by raised voices. Kendra is on her feet. 'But you know as well as I do how these things work, Nick. The insurers are so risk averse, they wouldn't dare cross the bloody road without a lollipop lady.' She puts a finger to her lips. 'Perhaps they're lollipop *persons* these days.'

'Yeah, but to cancel our whole fucking tour just like that.' He snaps his fingers very near her face. 'Because some lying bitch fancies making a few bucks with her utter bullshit story. I mean, what about loyalty, for Christ's sake?' He shakes his head over and over. 'And what about his contractual obligations?'

'Listen Nick, the word they used was *postponed*. Gerry himself made a point of stressing they've merely put things on hold until this is all behind you. The tour hasn't been cancelled outright.'

'Makes sense,' Eve tells them coming further into the room. 'How can they run promotions with all these accusations hanging over the band?' She hands Kendra the towel.

'You're right.' Nick sits down heavily, his head in his hands. 'Fuck!' Mumbling now, 'I bet the record company will be next to bail on us. Shit – radio stations might even ban our music.'

Kendra takes care to dry only the ends of her hair – squeezing rather than rubbing. Her continued silence says everything.

'It's all coming apart like a pack of cards,' Nicks says. 'And a fucking rigged one at that.' He drops his hands, stares at nothing. 'We've already lost.'

Dropping the towel, Kendra rubs both shoulders. 'I wouldn't put it quite like that. If Mallard-Jones can get this crazy woman to back down…'

Nick's answer is incoherent. He throws up his hands. 'This cannot be happening. It's a bloody nightmare.' A sniff. He could be crying.

They both jump when his fist hits the arm of the chair. 'This woman must have set out to deliberately ruin us all – there's no other explanation.'

Kendra's about to speak when Eve shakes her head. The rain carries on hammering at the rooflight. Eve clears her throat. 'Can I get you a drink, Kendra? Are you hungry? There's some chicken pie in the fridge; I can easily warm up a slice.'

'I'm vegan. And I've already eaten, thank you.' Her face softens. 'I'd love a glass of white, if you have it.'

Nick rouses himself. 'Sod the wine – seems to me this auspicious occasion calls for something stronger.' Eve is relieved when he uncorks the vodka bottle and lines up a couple of glasses. 'Anyone care to join me?'

'I'll stick to wine thanks,' Kendra tells him.

He knocks the first shot back in one. With the second one poised, he says, 'Yeah, well my body's most definitely not any kind of temple.'

After pouring their wine, Eve finds a bag of fancy crisps and empties it into a bowl – not much but something that might help soak up the vodka. That's assuming he sticks to booze.

Kendra perches on the edge of a bar stool looking ill at ease. She's probably never seen Nick when he gets like this. Eve begins to feel sorry for the woman until she remembers she's paid a hefty salary to oversee the band's public relations. Dealing with this level of crap is what you might expect if you agree to represent a rock group.

All the same, clinking wine glasses, they share a look that acknowledges this is likely to be a long and ugly night.

Chapter Five

The room is far too bright when Eve opens her eyes; she'd been too exhausted to close the curtains. Next to her Nick is fully clothed with his boots still on. She turns away from the smell of stale booze and something sourer radiating from him.

He's pulled part of the covers over his lower half and she's careful not to disturb them as she slips out of bed. Sleeping dogs and all that. It makes her head hurt to remember what was said last night.

A shower freshens her up as much as it was ever going to. Downstairs there is no sign of their guest. Amber has cleaned up the mess they'd made of the kitchen. The girl is singing loudly and horribly out of tune somewhere. Must have her earbuds in. Someone's happy at least.

Eve plonks a teabag in a mug of hot water and leaves it to brew. She finds Amber in the dining room polishing the table. 'Thanks for clearing up all that stuff in the kitchen.' Amber keeps rubbing away as she murders a Taylor Swift song. Today her hair is a deeper shade of pink with purple tips.

When Eve taps her shoulder, she jumps. 'Sorry,' she says,

'I just wanted to thank you for cleaning up the mess we left. Nick got the munchies.'

Lifting one earbud, Amber gives her an easy smile, the stud through her upper lip catching the sun like a cartoon starburst. 'No worries,' doesn't quite work in her broad Bristolian accent.

'I'm off out in a minute,' she tells her. 'Nick's upstairs, still asleep. Best not disturb him. Oh, and we have a guest staying, though I doubt she's up yet.'

'D'you mean that tall, dark-haired woman?'

'Sounds like the one.'

'She left in a taxi a good half-hour ago. Said to thank you both for your hospitality. I asked her if she wanted summat to eat and she looks at me all snooty-like then shakes her head like I'd offered her crack for breakfast.'

'Oh. Right.'

Amber hesitates. 'The woman couldn't get away from here fast enough.' She doesn't try to hide her curiosity. Like most of the country, she must be fully aware of what's happened.

Why did Kendra rush off? Admittedly, Nick had been at his most obnoxious last night, but wasn't that understandable when not only his livelihood but everything he's achieved in his music career is under threat? Is Kendra about to quit? Christ – the headlines would write themselves.

She groans aloud remembering that drunken phone call. Shit – Gil and Leon are meant to be arriving today. She has no idea when. All those long lenses are bound to find them first.

Amber's done a good job on the table. Eve clears her throat. 'Would you mind sorting out the main guest room before you go. If you could change the sheets and towels and so on.'

'Course.' A look clouds the girl's face. 'Ent being funny like, but which room would that be? I mean, there's so many of 'em.'

'The big yellow room that faces the garden.'

'Okay, got ya.' Amber gives a thumbs-up.

At the end of her morning ride, Eve takes an impromptu detour up one of the narrower lanes. The cottage is set back from the road, its mellow stone picked out by the weak sun. She's disappointed to see Jared's car isn't in the driveway. After tying Brandy's reins to the wooden fence, she walks up the front path. Against the front porch, a winter jasmine is in flower. Here and there a few spring bulbs are poking their heads through the soil.

Rory opens up with a smile. 'Eve. Good to see you.'

'Hi.' She can't speak – has to fight to control her emotions. He steps forward to envelop her in a hug. Where Jared is tall and wiry, his partner is shorter and, as her mother would have put it, amply covered. She sinks into his chest. The smell of oil paints still clings to his shirt.

Checking his expression as he lets her go, she says, 'I'm not disturbing you, am I? If you're in the middle of something, I can, you know, bugger off again.'

Rory bats away her concern. 'Ach, I'm always in the middle of something. Come on in for pity's sake.' He leads her into their kitchen. 'Cup of tea?' Before she can answer, he lights the gas ring under the kettle.

'Great,' she says as the little flames leap and pop.

'Does that nag of yours need a bucket of water or something?' He wipes some vestiges of paint off his fingers.

Eve grins. 'No – she's just swallowed half the village stream; she'll be fine for a bit.'

'Don't stand on ceremony – sit yourself down why don't you? Can I tempt you with a slice of my lemon polenta?' He pats his stomach. 'Himself isn't keen on it so you'll be doing me a favour.'

'Okay – why not?'

'Why not indeed.' After washing his hands, he cuts two enormous slices from a delicious looking cake. He sets down a mug of tea next to her loaded plate.

To resuscitate the fire, Rory throws on some kindling followed by a couple of logs. A wisp of smoke escapes into the room. A bolt of sparks showers the hearth rug. 'Bugger and blast!' He does a little dance as he stamps out the embers. She can smell singed wool. Though familiar with the cottage, she takes note of the many postcards propped up on the bookcase, the herbs along the windowsill. In front of her the piled-high fruit bowl is a ready-to-paint still-life.

Eve takes off her jacket and hangs it on the back of her chair. 'I'm guessing you've seen all the stuff in the media about Nick and the band.'

A solemn nod. 'When I nipped out for milk, there were a couple of reporters in the shop buying fags and trying to winkle out comments from customers. Far as I could tell, they were being cold shouldered.' He sits down next to her. 'This must have knocked the two of you for six.'

'You're not wrong.' The bittersweet smell of lemons is rising from the slice of cake in front of her. Though not in the least bit hungry, she distracts herself by taking a bite. 'This is really delicious,' she tells him, tasting nothing.

Rory makes short work of his own slice. He pushes his plate aside before his blue eyes search her face. 'So how are you holding up?'

'Getting through it.' She does her best to smile. 'Don't have much of a choice, do I?' Cake sticks in her throat; a gulp of tea helps to wash it down.

'I thought Nick's statement was really good,' he says. 'Very dignified and convincing. All the same, I mean, this whole thing is one hell of a clusterfuck.' Rory stops himself. 'Sorry, that was such a terrible choice of...'

She splutters into her tea. When she starts to laugh, she can't stop because it's all so totally and utterly ridiculous. Tears spill down her cheeks.

'Eve,' he says. 'Lord almighty – is this where I'm supposed to slap your face and tell you to calm down? Eve!'

Her amusement finally dissipating, she wipes her face on her sleeve and then with a tissue from the box Rory holds under her nose. 'Sorry about the hysterics. It's just that, my life... It's turned into a fiasco just when I thought things were beginning to come right...' She blows her nose.

'You'll find a way out.'

She shakes her head. 'Even if Nick does manage to prove he's innocent, this will have tainted them all. It's spreading like poison...' With an apologetic look, she sets the cake aside half finished. 'No reputable adoption agency will take a risk with us.' Time to admit it. 'Who's going to let us have a child now?'

Rory puts his hand over hers. 'P'raps there's another way.'

She sets him straight: 'I'm not about to buy somebody else's baby because their parents are too poor to look after it.'

'That's not what I meant.' Squeezing her hand, he says, 'Nick told me himself you've ruled out IVF. Not my place to suggest it, but, once this is behind you both, might it be worth giving it a shot; or two?'

'You make it sound like some fairground game.' She snorts. 'Roll up, roll up – score a bullseye – win a baby.'

'Only a suggestion.' Looking hurt, he withdraws his hand, turns his face away.

'Look, I'm sorry. I know you're only trying to help.' Shutting her eyes, she inhales, holds her breath before letting go. 'I'm guessing Nick didn't tell you all of it. Maybe I shouldn't say anything.'

It's no good, she can't keep it to herself. 'The main issue – our problem – was to do with Nick not me. The aftereffects of what our counsellor referred to as his *unfortunate lifestyle choices.*' She puts air quotes around the words – says them in a tone that would make light of it in front of him. 'The doctors – the specialists we saw – said IVF would be a waste of time.' Trusting him, she adds, 'Nick is infertile.'

Rory nods several times like everything makes sense now. After a moment, 'I'm guessing you discussed using donated sperm.'

'We did but Nick wouldn't hear of it.'

'Whyever not?'

She hesitates, knowing Nick might consider this another betrayal. All the same, she can't stop herself. 'He said it was because the baby would be mine but not his. That he'd rather we adopt and that way neither of us would be the biological parent – we'd be equals.'

'Honest to God…'

'I know. It took him a while to be honest and admit that his real objection is that he can't stand the thought of another man's child growing inside my body.'

'You've got to be kidding me.' Rory runs a hand over his mouth. 'Sorry, it's not my place to judge.'

She looks past him to the new painting on the wall; unmistakeably one of Rory's.

'I've done my best to talk him round. The trouble is, as soon as I mention it, he shuts me down. Says it's his red line and that's that. End of discussion.'

Rory opens his mouth to speak then changes his mind.

'That Irish word – banjacked,' she says, 'isn't that when something's completely buggered and there's no way out?'

'I think snookered might be more the word you're looking for.' His sad smile drops. 'No matter how hopeless things seem, there's always a way out, Eve.' He reaches forward to rub her upper arm. 'Be sure and remember that.'

Tired after her ride and the mucking out that followed, Eve retraces her footsteps, approaching the house from across the fields. Ducking under the fence, she hears barking and, rounding the corner, is confronted by a uniformed security guard and his snarling dog.

'Here, what's your game?' The man's Doberman, hackles up, is straining at the leash.

'I could ask you the same.' She stands her ground against the dog's frenzied air-snapping. 'I happen to live here. You and your dog are standing in *my* garden.'

Narrowing the gap to a couple of metres, his face softens. 'Pardon me, Mrs Quenington. I didn't recognise you for a second there.' A mountain of a man, like a servant in a period drama, he actually tips his hat to her. His eyes are hidden in the shadow of its brim. A mishappen nose suggests it may have been broken more than once. As an after-thought, he adds, 'Sorry to have startled you like that, madam.'

She's never seen him before, but he's acting like he knows her. 'Did Nick hire you?' she demands.

He's still struggling to bring the snarling dog to heel. 'Sorry – didn't catch that. Enough, Dax. Sit!' The dog drops its rear end to the gravel, its bark subsiding into a low whine that slowly peters out. Those suspicious eyes remain fixed on her, muscles atremble in preparation for the counter command.

'I asked if my husband hired you?'

He shrugs. 'No idea. We just go where the agency sends us. Only got here about an hour ago.' He looks around. 'Nice place.'

'You said *us* – how many of you are there?'

'Three at the moment. There'll be more on the night shift.' His thumb jerks towards the front of the house. 'My mate Jermaine's round the other side there and there's a chap name of Paul outside the gate. I only just met him myself.' The smile sits awkwardly on his face. 'I'm Rafal by the way.' He bends to scratch the dog's head. 'And this here's Dax. He's all show; he's a bit of an old softy really. Aren't you, mate?'

Looking into the animal's dark eyes, Eve is far from convinced. 'Yes, well I'm going inside now,' she tells him. 'Just make sure you keep Dax under control.'

'Yes of course, madam,' is said like he's from central casting. Rafal makes a great show of speaking into his lapel. 'Number Two, come in. Owner's wife coming towards you, Jermaine. I repeat – owner's wife heading your way. Acknowledge, over.'

A series of loud crackles, and then a disembodied voice says, 'Copy that, Number One.'

'Fuck sake,' she mutters striding off towards the side door. The phrase *owner's wife* continues to niggle.

Hair a rook's nest, dressed in jeans and a creased t-shirt, Nick is waiting for her on the other side of the door. 'I'm so glad you're back,' he says like there'd been an emergency in the meantime.

'What's going on?' She steps back from his hug. Obviously wired, his hands are shaking, his jerky movements directionless. 'Has something happened? I've just had to run the gauntlet of the security guards you hired. They've got proper dogs out there – the snarly biting kind.'

'I didn't hire them – didn't even know about it until just before they turned up.'

'Couldn't you have warned me?'

'I tried to, but your phone was switched off and I had no idea where you'd gone. Didn't you get my text?' His bare feet must be cold against the stone floor.

'Haven't checked my phone for hours,' she admits. 'Seriously though – do you really think we need this kind of security? As far as I can tell, the photographers have buggered off.'

'Doug arranged it.' He rakes back the corkscrew curls obscuring his eyes.

'Doug? But surely he's your manager, not your security advisor.'

'Yeah well, I suppose he must have thought that, with Gil and Leon on their way down here, he ought to protect his meal ticket.'

His huff is followed by several shakes of his unruly head. 'Though our market value seems to be diminishing hour by hour, minute by minute. I kid you not – if things keep going like they are, we could soon be facing bankruptcy.' His eyes are serious. 'To top it all Kendra told me her EA's just resigned because of this.'

'Really?'

'Yep. Apparently, the man had the nerve to use the phrase *ethical considerations*.'

'Let's face it,' she says, 'if we can't make these accusations go away, he won't be the first to worry about guilt by association.'

Nick heads off towards the dining room then changes his mind and strides back towards her again. 'You're right. Kendra's EA might be the first, but he won't be the last – the rats will be queueing up to jump ship. Did I mention we're being cancelled on every fucking platform there is? Erased like the last fifteen years meant sod all.'

Mixed metaphors might be her pet hate, but this is probably not the time to quibble about his use of English. Using the wooden jack, she levers off her boot. 'Speaking of Kendra,' she says, 'she'd already left before I got up.' The other one is always more of a struggle. Task done, Eve straightens up. 'I bet you don't remember half of what you said to her last night.'

Nick scratches his head causing more hair to stick up. 'Not my finest hour, I'm guessing.'

'An understatement.' She hangs up her jacket. 'Anyway, you've obviously spoken to Kendra this morning.'

'Yeah – she called a couple of times with updates.'

'Did she seem okay to you? Like she's happy to carry on acting for the band?'

'Christ – was I that bad?' Reading her expression, he runs a hand over his stubble. 'She seemed, you know, business-like, as always. I suppose I should apologise though I can't remember what I said. You'll have to fill me in.' His eyes brighten with anger. 'Or maybe I should issue a general statement apologising to the world for my continued existence.' The bitter smile does nothing to mask how dejected he is.

To brighten the mood she says, 'So do we know when the boys are arriving?'

'Not sure. You know what they're like. Anyway, I asked Amber to knock up some grub. She's still here by the way – seems pretty excited at the prospect of meeting Leon, though I expect she'll be disappointed when she sees him in the flesh. Did I mention he's bringing some girl with him?'

'Is he now? Well it sounds like it's going to be quite a party.'

'More like a wake.' He scoffs. 'R I P and let's kiss goodbye to our careers.' Then, running his hand along an imagined headline, '*Double Barrels Get Stuffed.*'

'Come on, Nick.' She ventures a nudge to his ribs. 'I know things might look bleak at the moment, but you've got truth on your side. The big advantage of being famous is that people tend to notice you; they remember seeing you. They post snaps on Instagram and all that. There must be loads of potential witnesses – lots of evidence to back up your version of events.'

He looks unconvinced, defeated already. She squeezes his hand. 'We will get through this, I promise.' She wishes she could smooth out the furrows in his forehead. 'Don't know about you,' she says, 'but I could really do with a coffee.'

'That sounds great, Evie. Be with you in a sec.' He disappears into the toilet for what she hopes is only a call of nature.

Amber is in the kitchen. Bunch of parsley in hand, she's balancing sprigs on a buffet of sausage rolls, sandwiches and bowls of crisps; a bright green afterthought on food more suited to a child's birthday party. All it lacks is balloons.

Chapter Six

Amber steps back from her handiwork. 'Hope this is okay,' she says. 'Nick told me to use me initiative. You didn't have much in, so I nipped down to the village shop. They don't have a massive selection.'

'This isn't meant to be a party,' she tells her. Seeing the girl's face drop, Eve adds, 'But it looks great. Perfect for the occasion, you might even say.'

A bell interrupts them. The iPad screen shows someone's at the front door. 'I'll go,' she says blocking Amber's overenthusiasm.

Eve opens up to a different security guard. This one is tall, black and disarmingly good looking. His German Shepherd seems placid enough. 'I'm guessing you must be Jerome,' she says.

'Jermaine, actually.' Dropping the sideways grin, he nods towards the driveway. 'There's a Mr Leon Kelly at the front gate.' He says the name with no hint of recognition – clearly not a rock music fan. 'Passenger is a Miss Medora Fraser.'

'Must be a Byron fan.'

'Sorry?'

She shakes her head. 'Nothing.'

'So anyway, their IDs check out. Okay if we let them in?'

'Yes, please do. Oh, and someone should have told you we're also expecting Gil Davis.' Again, there's no flicker of recognition. The man's unbroken eye contact is disarming. 'Gil, um, has a couple of swallows on his neck – tattoos that is, not the real thing, obviously.' Eve clears her throat. 'Anyway, please go ahead and let him in when as he arrives.'

'Will do.' Jermaine enters the information onto some sort of pager. 'Gil – would that be short for Gilbert?'

'Know what – I really have no idea. He's always been just Gil. Guess you'll find out.'

The guard speaks into his lapel. 'Come in number Three.' He could be in charge of a boating lake. After a crackling response, 'We have a green light on the car. Over.'

'Copy that.'

The gates open and a silver Mercedes SL drives on through. Nick squeezes past her in his rush to greet Leon. Their bear hug is finished off with a series of backslaps that look quite painful. At 43, Leon is eight years older than Nick, though from a distance he could pass as the same age. Quite a fashionista these days, his outfit looks casual at first glance but is anything but. His trademark floppy fringe is sun-bleached with darker roots.

While the two men are chatting, a pair of long legs emerges from the passenger side. Medora is a statuesque brunette dressed for anything but an exceptionally cold English spring. After shaking Nick's hand, she pulls her inadequate jacket tight against her thin frame. Her heels sink into the gravel as she walks – sashays would be a better description. Three men and a dog watch her progress up the front steps with undisguised interest.

'You must be Eve,' she says offering no handshake or air-kiss – she's too preoccupied with rubbing her arms and stamping her feet against the cold. Her heady perfume could be rising from the outsized lilies on her dress. She's young – twenty at most. Her hair's sprinkling of golden highlights could almost pass for natural. 'Brass monkeys out here,' she says, looking past Eve to the promised warmth beyond. 'Mind if I just nip to your loo. Cold weather always makes me pee more.' Medora doesn't bother to wait for permission or directions.

All heads turn as a car pulls in, its horn playing the first bar of the group's anthem: *Shoot Me at Dawn*. 'That must be Gil,' Nick says. 'Going for a low-key entrance, as usual.'

The car spitting gravel is low-slung convertible. Mustang of some sort. It's paintwork is extraordinary – like it's been driven through one of those Festival of Colours they hold in India. It's throaty engine dies and Gil gets out looking smug. He's wearing a formal tweed waistcoat over a collarless shirt. His jeans are distressed to the point where they might disintegrate if you gave them the good wash they need. Reaching into the car, he retrieves his fedora from the passenger seat and positions it at a precise angle on his bald head. His greying beard has been neatly trimmed. Smiling broadly, he flicks a glance towards the car. 'So, what d'you reckon?'

'Subtle as a sledgehammer, mate.' Leon slaps him on the back. 'Is that thing even street-legal?'

A sheepish grin. 'Just about.' Gil runs a loving hand across the multi-coloured bonnet. 'You, my friends, are looking at a customised Mustang Bullitt. She's got a 5-litre V8 super-charged Coyote engine under there. 0 to 60 in 3 1/2 seconds.'

'How are you, you old bastard?' Nick shakes the drummer's hand then shadow punches him – the mock blows landing just short of his stomach. Playing along, Gil pretends to dou-ble-over in pain.

Leon peers inside the Mustang. 'How much did this thing set you back?'

'Including the sound system and special paint job – just under a hundred.'

'You forked out *a hundred grand* on that?' Leon shakes his head. 'And you actually chose that finish?'

''S what they call pearl bombed.' Hands on hips, Gil is ready to retaliate. 'Guessin' this is your Merc.'

Leaning against his car, Leon crosses his arms. 'As it hap-pens the SL also has a V8 bi-turbo engine. *5.5* litres. Bought it a couple of months ago with less than 6k on the clock for a shade under 85 grand.'

'Listen,' Nick says, 'as fascinating as this little dick-waving contest is, I'm standing here freezing my arse off. Why don't we go inside?'

Reaching her on the top step, Leon spreads his easy charm. 'Eve – it's been far too long.' He grips her shoulders as he plants a kiss on both her cheeks. The famous stubble is surpris-ingly soft against her skin.

'Glad you could come,' she tells him. 'Shame about the circumstances.'

Ignoring the last part, he says, 'You're looking well. Country life must suit you.' These days his Liverpool accent only tends to emerge when he's being interviewed. 'So here you both are – Lord and Lady of all you survey.'

'Not exactly,' she says. 'Our land actually stops at the river.'

'Bummer, eh?' Wiping a grin from his face, Leon gazes up at the house. 'You know, I almost forgot what an enormous great pile you have here.'

'Yeah – some gaff you got.' Gil pats her on the back.

'Come in out of the cold.' Nick is all smiles, transformed into the relaxed and genial host. 'First things first,' he says. 'Fancy a drink?'

Leon hangs an arm around each of his bandmates' shoulders. 'Do grizzly bears shit in the forest?' The three of them laugh like this is original, like they've already forgotten they're here because they're caught in the eye of an enormous and ever-growing crap storm.

Nick leads them through to the drawing room. Someone's already lit the fire and turned on the lamps. Amber brings in a tray of drinks. She then circulates with a platter of sandwiches, which turns out to be cheese and pickle. Utterly star-struck, she parks herself in front of Leon and blushes to her roots when he says, 'Ta, luv. Great butties by the way.'

Eve shakes her head when Nick holds a decanter in front of her. The three men clink their glasses and down generous measures of whisky in a few short gulps. Just when she thinks the afternoon couldn't get any more surreal, someone puts on music. She recognises the classic Bowie track.

Glass already in hand, Medora strolls over to join the men.

Introductions over, she begins a slow, sexy dance like someone auditioning for a part.

Above the noise, Eve hears the doorbell. 'I'll get it,' she says. No one else seems to have noticed.

Jermaine's at the door again. His dog raises its nose, sniffing the inside air with a generalised suspicion. 'Sorry to disturb you,' he says. 'Man at the gate claims he was invited here by Mr Davis.'

'Gil?'

'That's what he says.'

'Does this man have a name?'

'Thing is, his ID looks genuine enough.'

Handsome or not, he's trying her patience. 'So who is he?'

Running a hand across his mouth, Jermaine tries his best to stifle a smirk. 'His name's Lance Hardshaft.'

'You're kidding me.'

Jermaine is now openly laughing. 'Have to say, he don't look like no stripper.'

'And this certainly is no hen party. Wait there,' she says, 'while I go and find out what this is about.'

Someone's cranked up the music. Eve locates Gil and taps him on the shoulder. 'There's a man called Lance at the gate, he claims to be a friend of yours.'

'Sorry, darlin'.' He cups a hand around his ear. 'Say again.'

When she leans in, the smell of spent cigarettes and weed is overpowering. 'There's some bloke called Lance at the gate. Did you ask him to come here?'

'Lance – yeah, he's an old mate of my dad's.' He nudges Nick. 'That bloke – the one I told you about on the phone – he's just arrived.'

'Who are you talking about?' Leon wants to know.

'My dad's old mate,' Gil says, gesticulating with a sausage roll. 'Used to be plain old Larry Smith till he changed his name officially to Lance Hardshaft just to stick two fingers up to the law.'

Amidst the general hilarity, Gil says, 'Don't let his name fool ya – what he don't know about the law's not worth knowing.'

'But I thought you'd agreed to hire Royston Mallard-Jones.' Eve resents having to shout above the music. 'Isn't he supposed to be the best in the business?'

'Yeah – that seemed to be the general opinion when I Googled him.' Leon frowns. 'Wouldn't have thought we need two lawyers, mate, one's already likely to bleed us dry.'

'He's no lawyer,' Gil says, 'he's more what you might call a *legal advisor*. Had more than a few shaves with the law. Ended up doing a ten-stretch. Thing is, workin' in the prison library and being banged-up for that long gave him a lot of time to gen-up on the law. Trust me, Lance is a good bloke to have on your side.' Gil finally bites into the sausage roll. The rest of his opinion is lost in a mumble of pastry.

Lance Hardshaft turns out to be a shortish man with a sparse white beard; Eve guesses he's in his sixties. The thick beige cardigan, well pressed trousers and thinning white hair lend him a benign, avuncular air at odds with his prison record and outrageous name.

'I've told them you're our man.' Clapping him on the shoulder, Gil steers Lance into the centre of the room. 'First things first, what can I get you, mate? Whisky, beer – you name it.'

Lance rubs his hands together. 'Wouldn't mind a small rum and Coke. The diet stuff if you've got it. Type two diabetes is a bastard.'

While Amber goes off to fetch his drink, the others step forward to shake the man's hand. 'And this is my wife, Eve,' Nick tells him with a look that could have been a warning not to cross a line in front of her.

'Nice to meet you,' she says. 'Help yourself to anything you fancy.' Noticing how the old man's eyes have picked out Medora dancing by herself at the far end of the room, she adds, 'Any *food*, that is.'

'Good of you to come all this way,' Nick tells him.

'Yeah, well I heard you lads was in a spot of hot water. Like I told your dad, Gil, more than happy to help.' Perhaps due to nervousness, or something more serious, Lance has a habit of nodding every few seconds. His eyes are roaming the room. 'That's a big old fireplace you got there. Basket looks to be Arts and Craft – worth a fair bit, I shouldn't wonder.'

Before she can respond, Leon says, 'Thanks for offering to help but –'

'The thing is,' Nick interrupts, 'we're already talking to a leading lawyer. I'm not sure we need any more legal advice at this stage.'

'Ah, but what you have to remember, my son, is that this is what you might call the *critical stage*.' Lance lowers his voice forcing them all to lean forward. 'You're going to be asked to make a sworn affidavit – a statement in front of a solicitor or what they call a *judicial officer* and the crucial thing about that is…'

He takes his drink from Amber. 'Thanks, darlin' you're a life saver. Bottoms up.' Raising his glass, he takes a long swig while they wait. His fingers are tattooed with the letters C and L. Probably self-inflicted. 'That hit the spot,' Lance says putting down his glass. 'What was I sayin'? Ah yes – the important thing to remember is that you lads need to make sure you're all singin' from the same hymn sheet, if you get my drift?' He actually taps the side of his nose. 'The opposition will go through them statements of yours with a fine-tooth comb lookin' for discrepancies – little inconsistencies they can niggle away at until it starts to look like a pack of lies you've cooked-up between you.' He drains his drink and slams the empty glass down. 'Rule number one – you have to make sure your stories add up.'

Leon looks unconvinced. 'But the night we're talking about was years back, the four of us are bound to remember things a bit differently. Though, these days, poor old Bernie can't remember what he had for breakfast.'

'And I don't think we should over-rehearse,' Nick says. 'Won't it sound suspicious if we come up with exactly the same version of events, word for word?'

'Listen, you can agree to disagree about the irrelevant stuff but that's where it ends.' Lance points a finger at each of them in turn. 'What you say about that night – the stories you tell – have to be the same when it comes to what you might call the *salient points*.'

'You keep using the word stories,' Eve says, 'like you've assumed they're making everything up.'

'The thing is, love, I've had to learn these things the hard way.' Lance shakes his head at her as if he's disappointed. 'It's not for me to play judge. I'm only here to offer these lads the benefit of my advice; up to them whether they choose to take it or not. Like they said when Mick Jagger was up on a drugs charge in the sixties: *let he that is without sin jail the first Stone.*'

Chapter Seven

At the appointed hour and carrying their drinks with them, they move to Nick's study. Faces become sober despite the quantity of drink consumed. After a whispered conversation with Leon, Medora takes the hint and goes off to unpack. Eve wonders at him inviting her here under the circumstances.

She follows the four men inside determined to hear what Bernie might have to contribute. The three bandmates line up in front of the screen while, at Nick's insistence, Lance occupies an armchair near the back of the room. He looks like an aged parent. Eve tucks herself into the window seat hoping she'll be out of shot.

It takes a bit of fiddling around with the technology before Bernie's face looms large on the big screen. 'Ciao. Come va?' he says. 'Greetings from Bella Italia.'

In response they all speak at once confusing the system. Looking pleased with himself, Bernie steps back from the camera to show them he's dressed in a white hazmat-style suit without the helmet. 'Been learning all about bees,' he says. 'We're getting a few hives in the orchard and Lia's dad's just lent me his beekeeper's outfit.' He puts on the hat with its veil. 'What d'you reckon?'

Nick gives him a thumbs-up.

'You know, when you open a hive and look into their world, it makes you feel like a spaceman. Or that Gulliver bloke.'

Chuckling, he takes off the hat and rearranges his thatch of dyed black hair, Bernie's life-lined face has taken on a ruddy outdoors hue – quite a transformation from the last time she saw him; the picture of health at least at this distance. He could pass for Italian until he opens his mouth. 'Bees are really clever little bastards,' he tells them. 'They buzz about totally ignoring you most of the time, but, you know, the little buggers will defend the hive to the death. After a bit of smoke, they calm right down. Bit like sharing a joint I suppose.' When he laughs his damaged teeth are at odds with the rest of his face.

'Good to see you looking so well, mate.' Leon raises his hand in a gesture that's close to a salute.

'Yeah – we all miss you, you old bugger,' Gil adds.

'Have to say you're looking great,' Nick tells him. 'Sounds like you're embracing rural life out there.'

'Yeah, you could say that.' Bernie's smile drops. 'Like I already told Kendra, I can't help you boys with any of this. She told me I'm not in any of the footage. Truth is, I can't remember a bloody thing about Berlin. In fact, that whole fucking tour's a total wipe clean. Like they say about the sixties – if you remember it, you weren't there.'

Nick clears his throat. 'First off, Bern, I just wanted to – I mean I'm sure I'm speaking for all of us when I say it was hard to do what we did. It had reached a point… if you know what I'm saying. Things just couldn't have gone on like they–'

'No need to say more, man,' Bernie cuts in. 'Let's face it, if you lot hadn't kicked me out of the band when you did, I'd probably be long dead.' Bernie's right hand fills the screen like he's bestowing a blessing. 'Tough love and all that.' A wry smile. 'I'm nearly two years clean.'

'That's fantastic,' Nick tells him.

Bernie shakes his head. 'But like I said, afraid I can't help you. These days I'm all about the future. Even if I could remember, I'm done with raking over the past.'

Leon leans into the camera. 'Try to cast your mind back. We were in Germany. We were running late for the gig because the bus had to keep stopping for people to throw up. You must remember something.'

'Sorry, mate.' Bernie points two suicidal fingers to his head and pulls an imaginary trigger. 'Brain's shot to bits. My specialist says I've got some syndrome; it's got some fancy name.' He chuckles. 'Trouble is, I can't remember what that is.'

Leon opens his mouth but, before he can speak, Nick stays him with a hand forcing him to lean back. 'Fair enough,' Nick says. 'Listen, Bern, we'd all love to catch up some more, but we've got a lawyer coming here shortly so we'd better wrap things up for now. It been good to see you – so to speak. Look after yourself. Give our love to Lia. Let's have a longer chat when there's more time.'

'Yeah, sure thing. Arrivederci.' Bernie smiles into the camera. Close up, his teeth are even more shocking. Sotto voce he says, 'Won't hold my breath,' as he severs the link and disappears.

'Yeah well, we knew it was a longshot,' Nick says. When no

one speaks he puts down his glass and slaps both thighs. 'Don't know about you lot, but I need some caffeine.'

As Eve had guessed, their next visitor arrives precisely on time. She parks Daniel Legg in the dining room – far enough away to muffle the hubbub further down the hall. Refusing any refreshments, like he's talking to an assistant he says, 'Before I speak to your husband again, I need to take statements from the other two members of the group. Could you send Mr Kelly in first.'

Back in the kitchen they're on the black coffee. 'He wants to interview Leon first,' she announces.

Lance is pacing in front of the others, his fingers tucked into his striped braces. Before Leon can stand up, he pushes him back onto his seat. 'Hold up a sec – we can afford to keep this geezer waitin' for a few more minutes. What you say from this moment on is important. Your brief is the top man, right? He can pick and choose who he represents, right? We need to convince his lackey – and through him the firm – to back you lads to the hilt. So, let's take a minute or two to go over what you're plannin' to say to him.'

Frowning, Leon insists, 'There's no need. I'm going to tell him exactly what Nick's already told him.'

'Which is?'

'Well, that I felt all-in after the gig and went straight back to the hotel with Nick, to get some kip. It must have been well after midnight when we arrived and both of us went straight up to our rooms. End of. There's nothing more to add.'

'Were there other people in the lobby? Did you speak to

anyone?' Lance grabs his shoulder. 'It's them little details that make a story sound convincin'.'

'Can't remember. I'm guessing we must have spoken to the receptionist to get our room keys or keycards or whatever. To be honest, my mind was more on getting some kip.'

'Well, that's somethin' they can check with the hotel staff. Movin' on to this takeaway business the night before that had you all pukin' up – do *you* remember what you had? Did you start to feel groggy right away or did it take a few hours to come on?'

'How am I supposed to remember stuff like that? We're talking about one particular night years ago.'

'Gil told me you'd played in Hanover the previous night.' He waits. 'And..?'

Leon looks mystified. 'And what?' His hand chops the granite surface. 'We stopped off at some late-night place – I'd been dozing. I have no idea where it was. The food wasn't good but no worse than we were used to on tour. After a few hours, Nick got in a really bad way and I wasn't much better.'

'But you'd stopped throwin' up before you went on stage in Berlin. So you felt better by then?'

'Better but still not great. I wasn't as bad as Nick, but I felt pretty rough.'

'Did you hear anyone suggest goin' on to this nightclub?'

Leon shakes his head several times. 'And if I had have done, I wouldn't have been interested. Like I said, the two of us shared a taxi back to the hotel. I can't even remember the name of the place we stayed in, but that must be easy enough to check with our accountants' receipts.'

'And you went straight up to bed? You didn't stop for a quick nightcap in the bar? Hair of the dog and all that. You didn't nip out for anythin'?'

'For what? It was late. The mini bar had bottles of water and that's all I could stomach. As I recall, I was out cold until morning.'

Lance slaps him on the back. 'That should do nicely.'

'It happens to be the truth,' Leon says getting up.

Convinced by what she's just heard, Eve dares to hope. Photos can be cleverly manipulated – everyone knows that. They'll get expert witnesses to prove it. The two of them are adamant they went nowhere near that nightclub where the girl claims she met them. She lets herself believe it will all get better. She could hug Leon; instead, she takes his arm. 'I'll show you where I've put Mr Legg.'

As they leave the room, Lance says, 'Right then Gil, my son, seein's how you didn't share this taxi ride, let's go over *your* version of what happened that night.' It's clear that, for Lance, the exercise has got nothing to do with uncovering the truth.

Gil's raised voice carries along the hallway. Closer she hears him say, 'Don't you think I've been tryin'? You know what it's like, Nick – when you're on tour each day's like the next, they all blur together.' Eve lingers on the threshold. At the other end of the room Gil is on his feet and red-faced. 'I may not be as bad as Bernie, but it's not like I've got total fucking recall.'

'So, you can't be sure you didn't go on to that club?' Lance asks.

'Like I've been tellin' you, I don't bloody know. I remember we were worried Nick wouldn't be able to go on. It was a bloody relief when we got through the whole set. After that…' He shakes his head. 'I've been rackin' my brains, but it's a blank.'

He smooths his bald head like he might once have smoothed back hair. 'Some bands I could name, I mean they *really* take advantage of the girls – or p'raps the blokes – who hang around backstage. The ones that wait outside ready to ambush you when you leave.'

Nick is nodding. When they first married, she used to interrogate him about such things, but that only led to rows and the lingering misery of suspicion. In the end, they'd reached a tacit agreement not to discuss what he might or might not have got up to on tour. Never once did she imagine him capable of rape.

'Let's face it,' Gil says, 'the girls make it clear they'd be up for more or less anythin'. They ask you to autograph their tits and stuff like that.' His face grows serious. 'You know, this may sound corny but, for me tourin' is all about playin' our music live to the fans. That's how I get my rocks off. The rest I can take or leave.'

Again, he looks to Nick for support. 'When you leave that stage you're on this amazing high; you have to come down from it before you can sleep. I'd be lyin' if I said I didn't give in to temptation once in a while, but this group orgy thing – that's just not us, man.'

Lance says, 'If you so much as mention givin' in to temptation, all they'll think is that's exactly what happened on that night.'

'I'm not about to make out I'm some sort of monk.'

'No one's askin' you to. Just stick to the facts – don't go volunteerin' any more information.' Lance takes a breath. A tone lower, he says, 'When you make your statement, you tell the bloke how you were dog tired that night. You'd been ill like the others, and you don't remember going on to any club.'

Gil flings his hands up in the air. 'Yeah, but it's possible I might have done. Although, let's face it, I'd been throwin' up all day – probably couldn't have got it up if I wanted to.'

'Say stuff like that,' Lance tells him, 'and you'll straight-away be plantin' all them seeds of doubt. Them seeds are like that Japanese knotweed – you can't get rid of 'em once they're there.'

'Hold on a minute.' Nick inserts himself between the two of them. 'Someone released all these images that are meant to show this girl getting down and dirty with the three of us, but Leon and me – we were definitely not at that club, so it's immaterial whether Gil might have gone on there or not. Even if he happened to bump into this girl, if me and Leon are in them that stuff's fake. No argument.'

'And that's exactly what your brief will say.' Lance points an arthritic finger at Gil. 'I'm just sayin' whatever you do, don't go mentionin' groupies or discussin' what you may have got up to on that or any other bloody night. Stick to the facts as you remember them, mate. Somethin' you need to bear in mind: when they ask you a question, people have this general desire to please the person doing the askin'. It's some sort of psychological thing. So anyway, you get tempted to embroider your stories and that, my son, is what can trip you up.'

'He's right,' Nick says.

Gil nods. 'Yeah, okay I get it. I'll tell him I don't remember what I did after the gig and leave it at that.'

'You've got it.' An unlikely Professor Higgins, Lance raises a fist in triumph. In their closed circle, the three of them nod in unison.

As Nick turns away, he catches sight of her in the doorway. She sees the surprise on his face and then an expression that worries her. He covers it with a smile as he walks over. 'You okay, Eve?' He strokes her arm. 'All this must be hard on you.' Behind him, Gil is helping himself to more coffee. Mentoring over, Lance seems to be sizing up their artwork and its possible value.

'I'm fine.' She lifts a thumb like a hitchhiker. 'I'm just going to sort out…' She hasn't figured out what could require her urgent attention. In any case, she strides off along the hallway. Her retreat upstairs is blocked by Medora on the half-landing and heading her way. Amber is right behind her. The two of them appear to be deep in conversation.

Through the side window she sees Rafal prowling the knot garden with his evil-looking Doberman. It occurs to Eve that at this very moment, a long lens could be picking her out. She writes the headline: *Rock Star's Wife Showing Strain of Rape Claim Scandal.*

Out of options, she dives into the downstairs loo and locks the door. A few days ago, she'd been the sole occupant of the house; now she's under siege from every direction.

Chapter Eight

Checking her phone, Eve finds a text message from Jared.

Hope you're bearing up. Call me anytime. I mean it. J xxx

She's tempted to go straight over to their house and ask for sanctuary. Instead, straightening her shoulders, she heads back to the kitchen. Amber should have left hours ago but she's stacking the dishwasher. Leon and Nick are deep in conversation on the other side of the room. Medora is sitting at the central island picking at leftovers and chatting to Amber but not lifting a finger to help her.

Eve touches Amber's arm to stop her. 'Thanks for all your help,' she tells her. 'It's time you went home.'

'But I haven't finished this yet.'

'Nick and I can clear up.' She's fond of the girl but not entirely sure she can be trusted not to add to the gossip that must be circulating in the village.

It's already growing dark outside. Noticing Eve's return, Nick smiles and beckons her over. 'We're wondering how Gil's getting on.' He plants an arm around her shoulder.

'He's been in there a bloody long time,' Leon says. 'The guy doesn't need to hear all his war stories.'

'Lance advised him to stick to the facts and not elaborate too much,' Nick says. 'Just hope he hasn't gone totally off-piste.'

At the mention of Lance, she looks around and locates the man himself slumped across the sofa, head thrown back, eyes shut and out for the count. At his age, an afternoon nap is probably a regular occurrence. He gives a loud snort before rearranging his limbs and dozing off again. After the way he was knocking it back earlier, he should probably stay the night instead of driving home.

'Bye then,' Amber says with a farewell wave. 'Oops.' She narrowly avoids colliding with Gil in the doorway.

'So, how'd it go in there?' Nick asks striding towards him.

'Okay, I guess.' Gil has certainly sobered up – she's never seen him look so serious. Nodding towards the door, he says, 'Daniel wants us all in the dining room.'

'Sounds like *Daniel* fancies himself as Hercule Poirot,' she mutters to no one in particular.

'Best you sit this one out, babe.' After kissing her, Leon rubs Medora's shoulders to further placate her. 'I'm sure we can find you something to watch in the meantime.' Medora looks like she's about to protest, but in the face of his determination she acquiesces. It makes sense to exclude her but, given the circumstances, why bring her down here in the first place?

Eve certainly has no intention of babysitting the girl. 'We have a movie room downstairs.' Reluctantly, she adds, 'I'd better show you the way.'

When Eve gets back, they've gone ahead without her. She opens the dining room door feeling like a late comer to class. She stops herself apologising for disturbing everyone because, damn it, this is still her house.

The three of them are sitting opposite Daniel Legg who is on his feet as if he's about to give a presentation. The light from the chandelier casts a halo around his blond hair. He could be about to become their unlikely saviour.

She pulls out a chair and sits down next to Nick. Legg clears his throat, then leans forward to adjust his legal pad and pen. His hands appear to be trembling slightly. If he's nervous, does that mean he hasn't done this before?

They wait.

Legg clears his throat again. 'Right,' he says so suddenly she's taken by surprise. 'Thank you all for answering my questions so frankly.' The word frankly gives Eve some concern. 'I certainly have a clearer picture to present to the partners.'

More throat clearing. Should she fetch him a glass of water? Before she can offer, he says. 'I've now had a chance to examine the various images allegedly taken on the night in question. Whilst I'm certainly no expert in that field…' A self-deprecating smile. 'I thought it might be useful to go over some of the basic issues that are likely to arise with, um, this regard.'

He checks to make sure he has their full and undivided attention. 'Let's begin by assuming the images widely in circulation are what are commonly referred to as *deepfakes*.'

'They have to be,' Nick tells him. 'There's no other explanation.'

Showing no response to this interruption, Legg instead refers to his notes. 'It seems the software needed to produce such convincing facsimiles was initially developed back in 2016. A Reddit user calling him or herself *Deepfakes* created an application for people to use in the privacy of their own homes.' He coughs into his fist. 'This quickly led to its use mainly for the generation of, um, pornographic images in which faces that had been gleaned from social or more mainstream media sources – some famous, some not – could be added to what they termed *donor bodies.*'

He pauses to put air quotes around the last phrase. 'For as little as $30 or so, people could commission fake videos involving their fantasy figures to indulge in whatever activities took their fancy.'

Nick guffaws. 'I'm sure we can all hazard a guess.'

'Quite so,' Legg says. 'The term "*Facesets*",' (more air quotes) 'was used when referring to the faces borrowed in this way – a suitably dehumanising term, I think we'd all agree. Some individuals whose likenesses were being used without their knowledge or consent, began to seek legal redress, but in this matter they were hampered by the fact that in UK law this was not regarded as a criminal offence.'

Leon shakes his head. 'You've got to be kidding me.'

'However, when the sheer scale of this reprehensible practice became apparent, there were moves to include the generation and use of deepfakes in the 2019 Voyeurism Bill. This was ultimately unsuccessful because, at that time, it was argued that such images were openly acknowledged as fakes and were therefore not harmful to the complainants in the same way that other image-based sexual offences are. For example, with so-called *up-skirting* or the circulation of what is generally referred to as *revenge porn.*'

'So where exactly do we stand legally?' Nick demands.

Legg rubs a hand back and forth over his hairless chin. 'Although it's now acknowledged that these images *are* harmful to what one might term "the victim", legislation has been slow to follow; complicated by the fact that the task of distinguishing false images from genuine ones is increasingly fraught with difficulty.'

His eyes flick down to his notes again. 'In much the same way former thieves are sometimes employed as security consultants, some former developers are prepared to use their expertise to unmask the fakes. For example, at one point these poachers turned gamekeepers were able to prove that certain films had been falsified when the eyes of the borrowed faces failed to blink. After the developers solved that particular problem, the facesets still blinked at unnaturally infrequent intervals. However,' he raises a warning finger, 'I'm afraid the fakers were able to improve their software until they had them blink with a more natural regularity. Unfortunately for us, the falsifiers have proved adept at evolving their software to remain one step ahead of those trying to detect them.'

Nick gets to his feet. 'So, are you telling us there's no way we can prove these images are fake?'

'I'm certainly not saying that, Mr Quenington.' Like someone calming a dog, Legg pats down the air in front of him. 'What I'm suggesting is that – assuming Mr Mallard-Jones agrees to represent you all in this matter – for us to establish that these images and the associated footage have been falsified, it will certainly be necessary to engage the help of one of the foremost experts in this particular field. If we're lucky, the greyhound we employ will be a step or two ahead of the hare they will be pursuing, so to speak.'

'And what if we're unlucky?' Nick asks.

Holding out his hands, Legg says, 'At this stage there can be no guarantees.' He takes a moment. 'Gentlemen, I suggest there is another way of looking at this.' He seems to waver a little, even leaning on the table in front of him for support. 'Let us assume, purely for argument's sake, that these images are in fact genuine–'

'Hold on,' Gil says. 'Aren't you meant to be on our side?'

Legg raises his right hand like he's about to take an oath. 'I'm merely speaking hypothetically here, Mr Davis.'

'Let's hear the man out,' Nick says.

Gil curses under his breath.

'As I was about to explain.' A bit flustered, Legg pauses to collect himself. 'Due to the very existence of deepfake technology, we are in a position to cast doubt on apparently genuine photographic evidence which might previously have been considered conclusive proof.'

'But–'

His raised hand once again blocks Gil's interruption. 'There can be no question you gentlemen have suffered *serious harm* in the form of reputational damage, which has already been extremely costly both financially and in more personal ways.'

Eve is disconcerted when his gaze falls on her.

'In law, the burden of proof is on the other side. *They* are the ones who will need to prove their accusations are *substantially true*.'

Gil exhales. 'Okay – so you're saying the law's on *our* side.'

Legg musters a thin smile. 'To be specific – the law's *presumption of falsity* is on your side.'

After checking his watch, Legg caps his pen and slides it into the breast pocket of his suit. 'And now, I'm afraid, I really must be going. Thank you all for your time today. Assuming he's not tied up, I hope to present my findings to Mr Mallard-Jones sometime tomorrow.'

He straightens his papers before tucking them carefully into his leather attaché case. 'We will be in touch as soon as a decision has been made,' he says, already halfway out of the door. He's eager to retrieve his hat from the hall chair.

'Thanks again for coming down.' Nick shakes his hand with too much vigour. 'I guess we'll have to wait for the call-back.' Forming a line, the others follow suit with the handshakes putting Eve in mind of an award ceremony.

'Good day to you all.' Hat now firmly in place, Legg gives her a curt nod.

After the others have turned away, she stays to wave him off in the knowledge that, for the time being, their hope of a return to normal life rests with this odd young man. Besides the other cars, Legg's grey Astra is the only sensible one. What on earth must he have made of them all?

Chapter Nine

'I expect we could all do with a drink,' Nick says leading them back to the kitchen. For several minutes they all speak at once. Opening a fresh bottle of whisky, Nick pours a clutch of generous measures. Eve shakes her head. The three men grow silent, taking their glasses with a new solemnity; no one raises a toast to anything.

She'd hope it would be easier to disprove Lina Wolff's allegations. Listening to Daniel Legg – from what he'd said and what he'd left unsaid – it seems more likely this accusation will be hanging over them for months to come.

'All that deepfake stuff,' Gil says, 'a lot to get yer head round.'

'At least we can afford to pay for a top tech guy,' Nick reminds them. 'And don't forget what he said – we're the poor sods being defamed so the law begins by assuming we're innocent.'

Finishing his drink, Gil slams the glass down with some force. 'Yeah well, in theory maybe.'

'You're right,' Leon says. 'Let's not pretend a judge is going to be approaching this with an open mind. Everybody thinks they know what rock and roll bands get up to after a gig.'

'There is another option.' They all turn to hear what Gil has to say. 'Sounds like we're goin' to be forkin' out a shed load of money on this whatever. And what if the German police want to take things further eh? So, I'm thinkin' it might be cheaper and easier in the long run just to pay this bloody girl off. Like they say – everyone has their price.'

'But if we do that, we might as well be admitting we're guilty as charged.' Nick shakes his head. 'We'd never live it down.'

'I'm with Nick,' Leon says. 'That idea's a complete non-starter. Supposing we pay this Wolff woman to go away, who's to say more chancers won't decide to try it on?' He shrugs. 'What then, eh?'

'We stand firm, or we lose.' Nick slams his hand down on the table. 'Simple as that.'

The snoring rises to a crescendo waking Lance with a start. He looks around bleary-eyed.

Eve goes over to the fridge for more wine. It shocks her to find it's more or less empty of food. The party food Amber had put out earlier is long gone. *Eaten us out of house and home* – her mother's complaint when she brought friends back. The last thing Eve needs is to be reminded of her mum at this moment.

Leon comes to peer over her shoulder. 'Slim pickings,' he says. 'Let's order take-out – might cheer us all up a bit.' He's already on his phone.

'You'll be lucky,' she says. 'No one will deliver to us.' He looks alarmed. 'No – not because of what's happened,' she's quick to assure him. 'It's just we're too far off the beaten track here.'

One eyebrow shoots up. 'You've got to be kidding me.' He's sounding increasingly American these days. Not convinced, Leon continues his internet search. 'You're right,' he has to admit. Used to getting what he wants, he's not about to give up. 'There's has to be a pub around here somewhere.'

'Not sure that's such a clever idea,' Nick says coming over to join them. 'Imagine if we all descend on The Feathers – which by the way is the only place that does food out of season – there'd be pictures of us plastered all over social media before the landlord has even pulled the first pint.'

'He's right,' Eve says. 'If anyone so much as laughed, it might be interpreted as showing they don't give a damn.'

'Besides,' Nick rubs his hands together, 'I'm sure we can knock something up.'

Leon chuckles. 'Hey, d'you remember Gil's curried baked bean and spaghetti special? Man, that was bad.'

Clutching his stomach, Nick says, 'God, anything but that.'

Eve turns the kitchen extractor to max, hoping it will help suck up the smell of the joint Gil's just lit. Lance is now on his feet and heading their way. She can't wait to hear his culinary suggestions. Not about to surrender her kitchen to some horrendous drunken cook-off, she shoos them away. 'I'll throw something together.'

Nick puts a possessive arm around her. 'Along with everything else, my wife's a great cook.'

'He has a tendency to exaggerate,' she says reaching for an onion. 'I'm an okay cook – half-decent, at best.'

Leon raises one eyebrow. 'Being only half decent is an admirable trait in any woman.' A lame joke but still they chuckle at it.

The others move out of the way, but Leon lingers. It's been a while since she's seen him in the flesh. His famously handsome face has a slightly unnatural look about it these days. 'Shouldn't you go and check on Medora?' she says.

He bats away her suggestion. 'She'll be fine.' His grin reveals a new gold tooth. 'Medora and me – well, we have what you might call *an understanding.*'

'Which is?'

'Do I need to spell it out?'

'Humour me.' Her eyes sting from chopping the onions.

'So, you recognised Medora, right?'

'Not sure I've ever seen her before,' she says, cursing the chilli for finding a cut on her hand. She tries to wash away the sting.

'She's a model. And I mean a really well-known one. Come on, surely you must have seen her in Vogue? Harpers then? No?' He frowns. 'She does the runway shows and all that. That's how we met in fact. Designers absolutely love her.'

'I can see that; she's a very striking woman,' Eve says drying her hands. 'As you might have guessed, I'm not too bothered about labels and all that stuff. More interested in practical clothes these days.'

'Medora's not just a pretty face – she's real smart too. Smart enough to know that, now she's out of her teens, her modelling career can't last for ever.' He steals an olive from the jar she's just opened. 'She's keen to break into films. Being seen with me, well – I've been able to introduce her to a few of the right people.' With a smug look he adds, 'Don't get me wrong, the two of us have a lot of fun together but, you know, she's after the media exposure I can offer, and aside from the obvious, as arm-candy goes she's up there with the very best.'

'And what about now – I mean, surely everything's changed?'

Leon frowns. 'How'd you mean?'

The man's no fool but his bemusement seems genuine. 'Forget it.' She takes a couple of cans of tomatoes from the larder along with an armful of pasta.

'Hold on a minute, Eve.' He touches her shoulder. 'Why don't you say what you think?' His smile is long gone.

'Okay.' She puts everything down. 'At the moment being seen with any of you is a risk. Someone in Kendra's office just quit because they were worried about being – and I quote – *sullied by association.*' Before he can argue, she puts a hand to her breast. '*I'm* tainted by it. We both are.' It's the first time she's admitted this out loud. Her voice cracks with a sudden and overwhelming emotion. 'This thing is going to affect … and probably spoil everything Nick and I had been hoping for.'

Seeing his appalled expression, Eve swallows down her self-pity. 'I'm sorry to say this, but I would have thought being seen with you is already really bad news for Medora's career prospects.'

'I don't think it's as bad as that.'

'I'm telling you, as long as these accusations are hanging over the band, you're, in effect, social outcasts and so, by extension, are the rest of us. I'm really struggling with that. As for Medora – my guess is that either she truly believes in the principle that no publicity is bad publicity or…' She stops herself.

'Or what?'

Eve looks him in the eye. 'Or that poor girl is a lot fonder of you than you might think.'

The pasta dish she serves up is basic at best. Nonetheless they consume it with enthusiasm – with the notable exception of Medora. The whisky bottle is passed around; not an obvious culinary pairing. Earlier the atmosphere had been upbeat, now they're all subdued. The conversation goes round in circles before coming to a halt.

Once everything's cleared away, Lance calls for a pack of cards and attempts to liven things up with a few tricks he tells them he learnt from an amateur magician serving four years for fraud. Lance cocks up most of them; the old man's too drunk and too clumsy to fool anyone.

'Don't worry these are only for me,' Medora says taking snaps with her oversized mobile. A habit too ingrained to resist. Eve can't help feeling uneasy. There'd been a few automatic smiles; all the same she must have caught the worry etched into their faces. Eve looks around the table. Caught on camera, this could look a bit like The Last Supper.

Chapter Ten

Pausing on the threshold of the kitchen, Eve braces herself for what awaits her. The pungent smell of weed and stale smoke hits her first. Every surface is randomly strewn with dirty glasses and smeared plates. The butts of cigarettes and joints have been left to drown in pools of unidentifiable liquids.

Prepared for an icy blast, she opens windows then jumps at the voice from outside, 'Morning.'

Rafal and his Doberman are patrolling the garden. 'Oh hi,' she says, 'I didn't see you there.' The dog fixes her with its red-rimmed eyes; an impatient quiver runs down the animal's sinews. Doing her best to avoid further eye contact with the beast, she addresses his handler. 'Have you swapped sides since yesterday?'

'Bit of variety keeps you alert,' he tells her by way of explanation. In his Gilbert and Sullivan uniform, it's hard to take him seriously. 'Jermaine's on the gate today and Paul's over by the pond.'

'Gone to the dark side,' she mumbles. He gives her a puzzled look. 'So, is all quiet on the western front?'

He frowns. 'S'cuse me?'

'Everything okay? You haven't flushed out any photographers lurking in the undergrowth?'

This brings on a smile of sorts. 'Most action we've seen this morning is a couple of those birds with the long tails giving each other a bit of a tune up.'

'Sounds like rival cock pheasants,' she tells him. 'They stray over here from the local shoot; I suppose we offer them sanctuary. The males can get very territorial.' Eve's not sure her headache will sustain any more conversation. 'Anyway, excuse me, I must get on.'

Rafal doesn't budge. 'Looks like you've drawn the short straw.' At her confusion, he nods towards the mess in the room. 'First one up, cleans up, eh? Sounded like you had quite a session last night.' For a moment she's tempted to apologise for the noise. The man's peering at her with an interest above and beyond any professional curiosity. How hideously ironic if the guards they employ to keep out prying eyes are, at the same time, leaking information to the press. *Disgraced Rock Band Party into the Night.*

Eve's tempted to shut the window on him. 'Like I said, I need to get on.' Altering her tone, she adds, 'Don't let me distract you from your duties.' Taking the hint at last, he strolls off whistling something tuneless.

Averting her eyes from the worst of it, Eve concentrates on loading the dishwasher. Once the first load is on, her thoughts turn to breakfast. She might be a reluctant host, but she really can't send them on their way without offering something to eat. No milk or bread left – her only option is a trip to the village.

She could drive there but it's no distance. The cold weather is a perfect excuse to wrap herself up in a hat and wide scarf leaving only a small portion of her face visible. The temperature is just above freezing under a graphite sky. Sunglasses aren't an option.

Eve takes the route through the fields though it won't take her all the way. At the churchyard, she climbs over the stile and walks the final two hundred metres on the road. A couple of cars pass, slowing down out of courtesy rather than curiosity.

The village's main street has changed little since the cottages lining it were built; their sandstone walls are the colour of dried egg yolk. No faces at the windows. The pavement she's on takes her alongside a small stream contained in a stone channel with numerous little bridges to access garden gates and driveways. The water gurgles like endless gossip. Climbing plants are trained around windows and doorways ready to burst into flower as soon as the season warms up. Seldom used, the sentinel red telephone box smells of fresh paint.

When she enters the shop, a bell rings putting her in mind of a boxing match. Round one – here we go. Heads turn and quickly turn back. As always, Mr Townsend is idling behind the post office counter. Eve grabs a basket and fills it with basic provisions.

Passing the newsstand, it's a shock to see Nick's face staring out from one of the front covers. A headline announces: *THE TIP OF THE ICEBERG*. Her stomach tightens with fear. After another glance she sees the story is about climate change and the man pictured isn't Nick but some actor who, on closer inspection, doesn't even look like him.

Rounding the final aisle, she sees Mrs Townsend in her green striped tabard. A woman with silver hair beats her to the only checkout point. Eve's forced to wait. After she's served, the woman's in no hurry to finish her tirade about the roadworks on the main road.

She finally turns to leave. Eve's polite smile dies in the face of the woman's hardened expression – a look that says: *I know all about that husband of yours.*

Instead of the usual chatter, Mrs Townsend is polite and efficient. Eve waves her debit card at the scanner and, not waiting for a receipt, she heads outside.

The smell of coffee greets her at her front door. Nick can't be up already. She follows the aroma down the hallway into the kitchen which is considerably tidier than when she left. She hears the steady hum of the dishwasher. The windows have been shut but the room still has a chill to it. Lance is sitting alone at the central island, his gnarled hands cupping a mug. The surface in front of him is spotless. He nods towards a stack of clean dishes. 'Don't know where things go, so I thought I'd better not try an' guess or you'll never know where you are.'

In the light of a cold morning, he looks haggard, his skin a roadmap of endurance. Again she notices the crude tattoos on his fingers – the letters C and L. 'Thanks for doing all that,' she says dumping her shopping on the counter. 'I've just been out to get breakfast.'

'Now that's somethin' I never touch.' Lance chuckles. 'Reckon I've had more than enough porridge for one lifetime.' It takes her a moment to understand that this is a joke and then another to smile back at him. What must it be like to have wasted so much of your life in prison? He interrupts her thought with, 'Coffee should still be hot. I hope you don't mind me helpin' meself.'

'No, of course not.'

'Great little machine you got there. You know, this one time, when I was out on probation, they fixed me up with a job in a fancy coffee shop. Course they wouldn't let me near the till, but I used to enjoy tellin' people I was a fully qualified *barista*. I'd say it quick like, so's it sounded like *barrister*. Always loved seein' that shock on their faces.'

She laughs along with him. 'I'm more of a tea person,' she tells him. 'Especially first thing in the morning. Nick's the one who's serious about his coffee; I don't think he could function without his morning espresso.'

'You'd be surprised what you can learn to live without. Decent coffee is the least of it.' Under the heavy folds of his eyelids, those pale blue eyes miss nothing.

Unnerved, she busies herself with unpacking. A line from one of the band's lesser-known tracks comes to her. *Better wake up and smell the coffee, girl.* The tune repeats in her head like some sort of cosmic message.

'The C and L,' she asks, 'what do they stand for?' She throws a teabag in one of the clean mugs and fills it from the boiling tap.

'My kids,' he says. 'Grown up and long gone. I was inside when Charlie left for Australia. Our Linda followed him out there.' She fishes out the teabag. 'I've known Gil since he was a nipper. He used to be pally with our Charlie back in the day.

He's a good lad is Gil. Did he tell you his poor mum's dyin'?'

'I'm so sorry.' The usual inadequate words. 'I had no idea. I'm sure he's told Nick.'

'Always did play his cards close to his chest, that one.' He rubs a hand over his face momentarily smoothing out his wrinkles before they fall back into their folds again. 'It's probably not my place to say anythin', but I thought the other lads should know; you know, so they can make allowances and that.'

'Of course. I'll make sure they do. How long do they think…'

'They're now givin' her what they call *palliative* care.' His smile is full of sorrow. 'To look at Kath, you'd hardly know. Now they've stopped the chemo, her hair's grown back and everythin'. They don't like to say how long but, Terry – that's Gil's dad – seems to think she'll be lucky to see the summer. They got carers goin' in every day, but old Terry – he's takin' it hard.' Close to tears, he throws up his arms. 'Kath and Gil – they've always been close. Her blue-eyed boy see. She's real proud of the lad – what he's managed to achieve. Readin' all this stuff about him now – well, it can't be helpin', can it?'

'God no.' Eve shuts her eyes, shuts out the emotions threatening to overwhelm her. When she opens them again, Lance is staring into his coffee. 'I promised the two of them I'd do all I could to help him.' He tries a grin. 'But this deepfake malarkey – truth is I'm out of my depth.'

'We all are.' Tempted to hug him, instead she squeezes his hand. His skin is rough to the touch – toughened by a life lived hard. 'I know next to nothing about the law,' she says, 'but it seemed to me the advice you gave them yesterday was spot on.'

'I see you've been sweet talking my girl, you old rascal,' Nick says.

Lance chuckles. 'If I was thirty years younger, trust me, you wouldn't even get a look in, son.'

Chapter Eleven

Gone eleven and their guests are all in the kitchen knocking back copious amounts of coffee and water. The conversation is sparse. No one looks good in the unforgiving daylight falling through the rooflight. Medora is the exception – with her glossy hair and expertly applied make-up, she's Instagram-ready. Beside her, Eve feels dowdy.

Although the orange juice is opened and emptied within minutes, there are no takers for a full fry-up – not like in the old days. Leon and Nick shake their heads vigorously at the suggestion. Lance insists on rustling up his own bacon butty. Medora watches him glug oil into a frying pan with something close to horror on her face. Knowing she ought to have made more effort with the girl, Eve smiles at her. 'Are you sure I can't get you something to eat?'

'Well, maybe just a boiled egg.' The girl refuses her offer of toast or bread to go with it. 'Just the egg,' she says. 'They help to boost your metabolism.' Eve remembers reading somewhere that digesting a hard-boiled egg uses up more calories than the egg contains.

Without saying a word, Nick and Leon disappear off somewhere – probably the studio. It's a sign of optimism that they're still thinking about the next album. She's noticed before that Nick never seeks Gil's opinion on any of the music he's working on.

Seemingly unconcerned, Gil feeds a couple of slices of bread into the toaster. Without a hat, his head is showing signs of regrowth in the shape of a monk's tonsure. Little wonder he shaves it.

She decides to add a couple more eggs for herself to the boiling water. Once they're done, she takes them over to the kitchen table where the others are now seated.

It's not a pretty sight watching Lance demolish his sandwich. Medora eats her egg in slow motion. Elbows out, Gil spreads butter and then a thick layer of Marmite onto toast, leaving smears of Marmite on the butter and an edge of crumbs inside the Marmite jar.

It's not the right time to mention his mum. 'Hope you all slept okay,' Eve says to break the silence.

Pausing between messy mouthfuls, Lance tells her, 'Like a baby.'

'Don't remember much so I must have done.' Medora gives a nervous little giggle.

'It's so quiet here.' Gil shakes his head in disapproval. 'But then, when I got up for a piss, I heard this bloodcurdling scream – would have made my hair stand on end if I had any.' He runs a hand over his head to illustrate. 'After that it went quiet – dead quiet. I guessed it must have been some sort of animal. Took me a while to get back to sleep after that.'

'Sounds like a fox,' Lance tells him. 'We heard them a lot when I was in the open prison. When they're close, a vixen's call can sound like some poor gal bein' murdered.'

'Or it could have been a barn owl,' Eve says. 'They're known as screech owls around here.'

'Give me traffic noise any day.' Gil looks around the room. 'You know the downstairs of my whole flat would fit into this kitchen.'

She laughs. 'You poor thing. It must be awful only having room for a hot tub on your roof garden overlooking the Thames.'

'I suppose I manage.' Smile fading, Gil fixes her in his dark eyes. 'Don't you ever get lonely all the way out here?'

'Sometimes,' she admits, 'when Nick's away.'

'I'd definitely move out of London if it wasn't for work,' Medora says. 'My mum and dad live just outside Brighton – that's where I grew up. I'd move back there if I could.' She sighs. 'These days I spend half my life on planes.' Resting her chin on one hand, she conjures up the very picture of nostalgic longing.

'You know,' Gil says, 'when I get home after a tour, it's like – what the hell do I do now?' His toast hovers before his mouth – a flying Marmite carpet waiting to land. Instead of taking a bite, he puts it down again. 'In the old days, we had this tour bus that kept breaking down and all that. You'd eat something when you got hungry, doss down in the back when you got knackered. Simple like. These days, we got people whose job it is to organise everything. They come and remind you like – you got interviews at such and such a time, or, you know, sound check is at five. If you live alone like me, when you get back it feels weird there's no one there tellin' you when to get up and that. If there's no milk or bread, it's hard to get off your arse and go and get some.'

'You should pay someone to sort that sort of stuff out for you,' Medora tells him, her spoon poised over the last remnants of the egg. 'I use this great concierge service. Tell you, it's worth every penny. When I get home I know there'll be plenty of healthy food in the fridge, my plants will have been watered and the sheets will be clean and ironed.'

'Sounds great.' Eve taps the top of her eggshell until caves in. To Gil she says, 'I know Nick finds it hard to adjust when he comes back from touring. Most days he retreats into the studio. He can be in there a whole day without a break. For weeks on end sometimes. I used to try taking him a cup of tea and a sandwich. Later, I'd find them untouched.' A wry smile. 'I know better now.'

'Yeah – Nick's what you'd call obsessive – no offense like.' Gil chuckles. 'Me – I can spend a whole day just starin' at the bloody ceiling. Other times, I'm like climbin' the walls. I've got these electronic drums with headphones back at the flat so the bloke downstairs don't kick off. It's not the same as my regular kit, but better than nothin'. A good old bash helps me get stuff out of my system – if you know what I mean.'

After staring at his plate for a while, Gil finally takes a bite from his toast.

'Never occurred to me before,' Lance says pushing his plate away, 'but that sounds a lot like how it feels when they let you out of prison. Everythin's decided for you inside and then suddenly yer on yer tod. When I got out after that last stretch...' He shakes his head at the memory. 'Easily the hardest thing I've ever done in my life. I says to meself this had better be the last time.'

'Tourin' changes how you feel about yerself,' Gil says. 'Up there on stage – there's just nothin' like it with the whole stadium on their feet wavin' their arms about, phones glowing like so many of them fireflies you see in The States. To the audience you're like *really fucking somethin*', if you know what I'm sayin'? Some nights it's hard to come down to earth and just, you know, be a regular person again.'

'I've only witnessed it from the wings,' Eve tells him 'But all that energy – the sheer power of it is just staggering. Overwhelming. You wouldn't be human if you didn't find it hard to adjust once it's over.' Her eyes are drawn to the tattooed swallows on his neck. The artistry is exquisite; mid-flight the birds appear ready to swoop over the table and up through the lantern into the sky. This time of the year, real swallows will still be wintering in sunnier climates.

'We've played in some amazin' places,' Gil says. 'To capacity audiences of 80 k or more. And now look where we are.' Visibly choking back his emotions, 'Heroes to somethin' worse than zeros. Reckon we're in the minuses and still goin' down.'

Eve covers his hand with hers. 'You'll get through this – they'll prove you're all innocent.' She has to believe it – the alternative is unimaginable.

'You think so?'

'I honestly do.'

'And don't you go forgettin' the law's on your side,' Lance

reminds him. 'Them fancy lawyers wouldn't be gettin' the big bucks if they did know what they were doin'.'

She can hear Nick and Leon talking down the hallway. Withdrawing his hand from hers, Gil pulls himself more upright. A few minutes later the two come into the room. Like co-conspirators, they're expressions become sober.

Approaching his girlfriend from behind, Leon rubs her shoulders – a man marking his territory. He bends to her ear. 'Hi, babe.' She lights up under his touch, the poor girl. 'No pun intended,' he says, 'but I guess we should be making tracks.'

'My bag's in the hall.' Quick to get up, she's eager to leave.

Leon's announcement acts like a signal to the others and they stand up more or less together. Eve bats away various offers of help and within ten minutes they're waving the last of them goodbye. Before he disappears through the gates, Gil sounds his absurd car horn in one last defiant salute.

The thud of the front door closing echoes against the hall's hard surfaces. The two of them turn around to find themselves alone in the sudden silence of the house. Eve is caught somewhere between relief and disappointment. 'I guess that's that,' Nick says, his face dropping the act at last. Without looking at her, he says, 'Leon and me were kicking around a song. Think I'll do some more work on it while it's still fresh.' He starts to walk away.

'Wait.' She catches his arm. 'We've barely had a chance to talk since this whole thing blew up.'

'What's there to say?' He rubs a hand across his eyes. 'You know just as much as I do.'

'Why don't we go out for a walk – just the two of us? It's

finally stopped raining out there; you never know, the sun might come out if we're lucky. We'll both feel better for some fresh air and exercise.' She sounds like Mary sodding Poppins.

'*You* might,' he says. 'Remember there could still be a few paps hanging around where we can't see them.'

'So what?'

'So, if I want exercise, I'll go down to the gym. Right now, I'd rather work.'

'Nick, we need to talk about what's happened.'

'And just who's that going to help, Eve?' There's such a bitter edge to his words. 'Damned if I'm going to hang around waiting for Mallard-Jones to make up his mind. If the man's not interested, there must be plenty more who will be. Meantime, I'm going to the studio to work.'

She lets him go. Nick's not naïve – the songs he's working on are intended for the band's next album; the way things are going, it might never be released.

Eve busies herself with re-establishing the usual order to the kitchen; the rest of the house will have to wait. She remembers her desperation to make the place seem lived-in for Leanora's benefit – the woman should see it now. Shutting her eyes, she tries to banish the hopes she'd felt then. The official letter may not have arrived yet, but its contents are a foregone conclusion. She scrapes the last leftovers into the bin and then lets the lid fall on all the mess inside.

It's a shock to see Amber in the doorway. 'Hope I din make you jump,' she says. For practical reasons she has her own set of keys and knows all the codes. 'Thought I'd pop up, you know, case you need a bit of a hand, clearin' up like.'

It's the girl's day off. Eve wonders at her motives. 'They've all gone now,' she tells her.

'Yeah, I seen 'em go past in the lane. That Gil bloke really anked it round the corner in that crazy car of his. Had to jump out of his way.' She looks around the room. 'This floor could do with a good goin' over.'

'Yeah – it's really sticky. Seeing's you're here, I'm happy to pay you for the extra time if you're sure you don't mind.'

''Course I don't, else I wouldn't be here.' She takes off her coat and unwinds her scarf. The two of them work around each other though Eve gets the distinct impression Amber would rather she wasn't in her way.

'You seemed to really hit it off with Medora yesterday,' Eve says.

'Yeah – she's a right laugh, that one.' Amber rings out the old-fashioned mop she prefers to use. 'Medora's really beautiful, ent she?' She leans on the handle. 'Must be hard for her goin' out with a rock star like. I shouldn't fancy it – not with all them girls throwin' themselves at yer boyfriend every night. I mean, he's only human, ent he?' Colouring up, she's too quick to add, ''Course Leon's fair game – him bein' single and that.' Her face boiling and visibly squirming. 'I didn't mean… Just now I wasn't tryin' to suggest anythin'…'

For the girl's sake, Eve puts on a smile. 'I know you weren't,' she tells her. 'It's fine, really.' Her words have a hollow ring even to her own ears.

Chapter Twelve

Jared comes to the door. 'Eve,' he says. His surprise is replaced by a look of such sympathy it's difficult to bear. When he hugs her on the doorstep, she imagines the moment captured: *Rock Star's Wife Embraces Handsome Neighbour.*

'Come in out of the cold,' he tells her as if being warm will solve all her problems.

The tenderness of Rory's greeting finally moves her to tears. 'You poor wee thing.' She's gathered into his lumberjack shirt. It smells of washing powder and onions.

'I've made your shirt wet,' she says stepping back from their long embrace.

'Pay no mind.' His thick fingers sweep her hair back from her face – a gesture that takes her back to her father. Overcome for a moment, she shakes the memory away.

'We were planning to call round to yours,' Jared tells her. 'But when we drove past, we saw all the security guards and loads of cars in the driveway, so I thought – we thought – you know, that the last thing the two of you needed was a couple more visitors.'

'Yeah, we had quite a houseful, but they've gone now. Well, not the security guards – we're not sure how long we'll be needing them.' Glancing down at the table, she sees there's food laid out, mugs of tea only half drunk. 'I've disturbed your lunch,' she says. 'I should have called first.'

'Nonsense. You're grand.' Jared pulls out a chair giving her little choice but to sit down. Overheated now, she takes off her coat and scarf and hangs them on the back of her chair. 'Would you like something to eat?' Jared asks. 'Bought the loaf this very morning from the deli in Foxton – artisan organic sourdough no less. And you might want to try Rory's famous home-grown shallots in balsamic vinegar – I'm telling you they're a cut above ordinary pickled onions.'

'No need for the hard sell.' Rory gives him a look. 'They're not to everybody's taste.'

'I haven't long had breakfast, but I suppose I could manage a slice of bread with some of that brie.'

'Ah yes, the brie.' Jared smiles at last. 'I'm partial to it ripe but this one seems to be making a bid for freedom.' As if by sleight of hand, a plate appears in front of her, then a slice of bread that gives little space for anything else.

'You'd best help yourself to the brie,' Rory says, 'we've been spooning it on.'

'It's certainly quite pongy.' She does her best to scoop a portion from the cheese board and deposit it on her plate. 'Nice and oozy,' she says, though she prefers it a lot firmer.

After a pause she can only describe as pregnant, Jared asks, 'So how're the two of you bearing up under the strain?'

Eve takes time to consider. 'Nick is, well, I'd say he vacillates between denial and despondency. Now they've all left, he's looking pretty dejected. He's shut himself in the studio. As you might expect, he's furious that someone can make these unfounded allegations and suddenly the band's whole future is on the line. He's just trying to get through it by working on a track for the next album – which given their situation...' To finish the sentence would seem like a betrayal. Instead, she says, 'It's a nightmare for all of them.'

Looking her squarely in the eyes, Rory says, 'And yourself – how are you holding up?'

'I honestly don't know.' She looks away. 'I mean – this has landed on us like some meteorite. Or like one of those pieces of space junk that's been orbiting for years without anyone knowing it was about to go off course and plunge to earth. You hope it will pass you by. I mean you never expect it to land slap bang on top of your house, do you?'

Jared gives her hand a squeeze. 'And you'd no reason to, Eve. None of this is of your making.'

'The band are planning to sue for defamation,' she tells them. 'They're already talking to some hot-shot lawyer. He sent someone down here to take their statements.'

'Then that's a start,' Jared says.

'Yes, but that hasn't stopped the organisers cancelling their tour. No one will play their music on air. Things keep going from bad to worse.' It's a struggle to get her emotions under control. 'I'm all for people being called-out for sexual offenses, of any kind, but what's happened to the presumption of innocence?'

'Ah yes, the court of public opinion takes no prisoners,' Jared says.

'You're not wrong.' Rory points his knife like he's about to spear something. 'Social media – now there's a bloody misnomer. Mean to say, the eejits on there are anything but social. More like a fecking lynch mob, if you ask me.'

Eve stares at the little brown onions on his plate – cut in half, the concentric circles end in a darker bullseye. 'Anyway,' she says, 'it seems the band have been well and truly *cancelled*. Such a nasty, vindictive word. Like their very existence has been erased before they've even had a chance to give their side of the story.'

'They'll get their day in court.' Jared throws up his hands. 'The pity of it is, I'm guessing that could be months away.'

'Or longer.' Rory shakes his head. 'These days the wheels of justice grind slower than tectonic plates.'

She looks down at their half-finished meal. Having arrived at their home unannounced, she's only succeeded in lowering everyone's mood.

'Right, well, that's more than enough about me and Nick. What have the two of you been up to?'

Rory's knife clatters onto his plate. 'Someone needs to tell the weather gods it's fecking March. I'm desperate to get my seedlings established before I go off on my usual retreat.'

It takes her a moment to re-focus. 'Didn't you go to one of the Scilly islands last spring?'

'I did indeed. St. Martin's. Beautiful place and the weather there was positively balmy.'

'He claims these retreats are to refresh his artist's eye,' Jared says. 'Though I've often suspected the poor man needs to get away from me for a month or two.'

'Ah – sure he loves it really. Nobody here to tell him what to do.' Rory grins at his partner. 'Anyway, for better or worse, I'm booked into an old crofter's cottage on a wee island off the west coast of Scotland. No mains power just solar panels – which they warn might prove a bit hit and miss. In any case, it's got sea views and its own little sandy inlet where you can land a small boat. Or go for a swim if you're a hardy soul – which, as you know, I'm most decidedly not.'

'Sounds idyllic,' she says with some feeling. 'Right now, that's pretty much my idea of heaven.'

'Well then, as it happens, this time I've a spare room.' Rory shakes her arm. 'Nothing fancy, you understand, but if you were to find yourself needing to get away from it all, you'd be more than welcome to come and stay.'

'That's very kind of you…'

'I can hear that *but* coming,' Jared says. 'Before you dismiss the idea, let me tell you that, in all the years I've known this man, he's never extended such an invitation to anyone – not even me.'

'There's no internet,' Rory says, 'so no social media stuff can bother you. I'm told there's only a couple of spots on the island where you can get a mobile signal and one of them's halfway up a fecking mountain.' He pats his stomach. 'As you might imagine, I'm unlikely to climb to such a height.'

'I'm touched that you should ask me,' she tells him, 'but I should be on hand to help deal with anything that comes up. I wouldn't dream of abandoning Nick to face this alone.'

Rory simply nods.

She turns to Jared. 'I'll need to go up to London at some

point, so I was going to ask if you'd mind keeping an eye on Brandy – make sure she doesn't get overlooked while I'm gone.'

'Not a problem.' Jared squeezes her arm. 'Besides, she's a favourite with all the girls at the stable. Poor nag's likely to clock up more miles than Usain Bolt.'

'Hold up a minute. Yer man's a sprinter,' Rory reminds him. 'Now if you'd said Mo Farrah, that would make a lot more sense.'

'It's okay,' she tells them. 'I get the general idea.'

Rory spears an onion with his fork. 'Just remember what I said, if it all gets too much, you can come away with me. Consider it a standing invitation.'

Her phone pings. She fishes it out of her coat pocket. Nick's text is short and to the point.

She looks up to find the two of them are staring at her in anticipation. 'Good news for a change,' she tells them. 'That lawyer – his name's Royston Mallard-Jones by the way – has agreed to act for the band.' She holds the screen up as if she needed proof.

'I think I've heard of him.' Jared's all smiles. 'So the big guns are lining up on your side.'

Following the sound of his cursing, she locates Nick in the study off the main bedroom suite. Her desk is half ransacked. 'What the hell's going on?' she demands.

'We're due to see Mallard-Jones at ten tomorrow,' he says without looking up. 'I'm trying to find the stuff his office asked me to bring along. Can you believe they need me to prove I'm who I claim to be? You'd think my fucking passport would be more than enough.'

'I suppose they need to be thorough.' She opens a drawer he's missed and, after sorting through everything, hands him his birth certificate. 'I assume that'll do. You only had to ask.'

'I would have done but you had your damned phone off again. I had no idea where you were. A more suspicious man might wonder...'

'It wasn't off,' she says. A small lie. 'The signal's crap in this village in case you hadn't noticed.'

Paying no heed, he's studying the certificate in his hands. '8B Mill Road, eh. God that was such a long time ago. Another life.' Finally looking up, he says, 'Oh and they want a utility bill with this address on. Do we have any of those?'

The relevant folder is on the floor. She opens it and thrusts one at him.

'Great,' he says. 'Have you got something...'

She hands him a large envelope. She's tempted to tell him not to lose them but thinks better of it.

He pulls a holdall from the top of the wardrobe and, after the envelope throws some clothes into it – underwear, socks, a few sweatshirts and a smart jacket and shirt. He doesn't bother to fold anything – not even the jacket. Goodness knows when he last ironed anything himself. All the same, watching him, she's pleased to witness this new sense of purpose.

'So how long are we likely to be away?' she asks.

He stops what he's doing and comes over to stand before her. 'The thing is.' She finds the pale flecks in his sky-blue irises. 'As much as I'd love you to come with me, I think it might be better if you stay here.'

'But I want to be there with you.' She hadn't meant to

sound whiny. 'Surely it's important I'm there to hear what he has to say. And to give you my full support.'

'I'm not getting a medical diagnosis; this is only a preliminary meeting.' His smile has a hint of condescension about it. 'No one is on trial yet, Eve. On my own, I'm less likely to stand out amongst the London crowds.'

His expression becomes more tender. 'You're a very attractive woman – people notice you. The two of us together – we'd be way more likely to attract the wrong kind of attention. Everybody carries a phone these days. They've Instagram and Twitter accounts.' He stokes her shoulder much like Jared had – like she needs to be constantly pacified. 'You're better off keeping well out of it. There's no point in … I mean to say, I don't want you getting yourself into a state over all this.' He clears his throat. 'Believe me, I'm only thinking of what's best for you, Eve.'

He lets the weight of his words sink in. 'Besides, we're only going there to listen to the great man's advice. We should get a better idea of what his strategy is likely to be. The three of us need to talk it over – it's important we all agree.' She can see the sense in what he's saying though it doesn't prevent her feeling excluded.

Eve finally musters a smile. 'So, what time's your train?'

'I'm actually going by car. Kendra thought it would be better to avoid public transport.' Sensible advice but all the same it irritates her that Kendra should be deciding these things. The woman ought to confine herself to handling the band's PR.

'You'll need to allow for the rush hour,' Eve tells him.

'Yeah, I know. I tried to get a later appointment, but Mallard-Jones is a busy man; he couldn't fit us in any later in the day.'

Nick returns to his packing. 'I thought about taking the Lotus but it's not exactly low-profile. So anyway, an executive car is picking me up. It's all arranged; tinted windows but nothing too flash. In Central London no one gives a car like that a second glance.'

'I assume Kendra organised that too.'

'Yeah – she's very thorough.'

'Isn't she just.'

If he noticed the sarcasm in her voice, he doesn't show it. 'Thought I'd pack now. The car's arriving at the ungodly hour of six-thirty tomorrow morning.'

'Is Kendra going to be there?'

He snorts. 'I doubt she moonlights as a chauffeur.'

'You know very well I meant at this meeting with Mallard-Jones. Have you invited her? You have, haven't you?'

'Look, the woman needs to know exactly what's going on, Eve. It's part of her job for Christ's sake.' His sigh is all exasperation. 'I really don't know what your problem is with her.'

'I don't know why, but I don't trust her,' she admits. 'There's something about her – I can't put my finger on it.'

He waves his hands in the air. 'Don't tell me you're sensing her psychic energy is negative or some other bullshit theory?'

'No need to take the piss,' she tells him, pulling out the tie he'd thrown in and coiling it up before tucking it into a corner where it might not get creased. 'I can read people better than you give me credit for and I'm telling you there's something off about Kendra.'

He throws up his hands. 'Eve – you hardly know the woman. She's really putting in the hours right now; doing just about everything she can to help. I think you need to give her the benefit of the doubt.' He looks around as if he's forgotten something. 'Guess I'll need to set an alarm.'

'No point,' she tells him. 'I'll be awake long before six.'

Chapter Thirteen

'Cheers, mate.' Nick bangs on the car's roof like some cop in a film. She watches him pick up his bag as the car pulls away; the gates automatically opening to let it out. They're down to two security guards instead of three. Jermaine, who's just come on duty, is now patrolling the drive as well as operating the gates. Given their lack of visitors, the poor man must be bored rigid.

When Nick hugs her he smells different somehow. She decides not to question him too closely over why he'd stayed an extra night in London. He's all smiles – far more upbeat than when he left; she hopes his mood's not artificially induced.

'So, how did it all go?'

'Fine – quite well in fact. Royston really knows his stuff,' he tells her dropping his holdall on the hall floor.

'Ah, so it's not Mallard-Jones but *Royston* now. Next it will be all Roy this and Roy that.'

She leads the way into the kitchen where she's laid out a meal for them both. Nick seems not to notice in his impatience to tell her what's been decided. 'Royston's found us a top man over in Germany. Stefan Zimmermann. You know like Bob Zimmerman – Dylan's real name. Anyway, this Zimmermann is used to working with some woman PI–'

'By PI you mean a private investigator?'

'That's right. That footage along with the stills currently circulating – well it looks like it was filmed in the one of the private rooms above the club we're meant to have gone to. Wolff's now retained a lawyer who's claiming a former employee downloaded the security footage at the time and then hung onto it. Prompted by Wolff's claims, this unknown person felt motivated to download it to an untraceable whistle-blower style website. Royston called bullshit on that. Our investigator's trying to track down witnesses from the hotel who can back us up. Turns out the place has since gone bust, so that's going to make the search more complicated.'

He takes off his jacket and hangs it over the back of a chair.

'Can I get you a cup of tea or something?'

He waves the suggestion away. 'No, I'm fine, darling, thanks. Stopped off on the way down.'

'Oh – right, well how about a small piece of quiche? It's homemade. Won't take me a minute to warm it up.'

'Maybe later.' He finally sits down at the table. 'What was I saying?'

'That the hotel's since gone bust.'

'Yeah, but Royston says he's hopeful that the renowned German bureaucracy will work in our favour and our PI – she's called Frida Engel. Or it might have been Florence Engel. In any case, she's trying to trace former staff who were on duty when we rocked up that night.'

'Sounds like a good place to start.' Not especially hungry herself, Eve picks at the pastry crust.

'The German police aren't currently planning to charge any of us; although Royston warned us that might change if our defamation claim is unsuccessful.'

'So that's good news – sort of.'

'And Royston's also been in touch with a top expert on deepfakes. Guy doesn't even have a name. He identifies himself by a code. I say *he* – might be *she*. Anyway, *they've* already checked out the footage that's online but obviously they'll need to study it in a lot more detail. Their upfront fee is pretty eye-watering and, guess what – non-refundable.'

Eve frowns. 'So, you pay this anonymous expert even if they turn out to be no help.'

'Yep. Let's face it, we're over a barrel here.' He shakes his head. 'Twin Barrels even.' She smiles at his joke. 'Anyway, we've already transferred the money.'

'Right.' Nick hadn't mentioned this on the phone. But whatever she might think is irrelevant because it's already done and dusted.

'Don't look like that,' he says, 'it's not as bad as it sounds. Even if they can't prove the images are fake, they've assured Royston they're confident they can reproduce everything exactly. That their fakes will be indistinguishable from all the stuff that's doing the rounds.'

'I can't see how that helps.'

'Because Royston will be able to show the court that our expert can fake it all from scratch using only images that are publicly available. In which case, someone else could have done the same. Like Royston says, it will cast reasonable doubt on the authenticity of the images.'

Nick absentmindedly flips the salt grinder onto its head spilling out a pool of salt before he rights it again. He's silent for a long time. Finally, he says, 'Of course there are some big questions still to be answered. Take that surveillance footage – I mean if it was supposed to have been captured on tape years ago, why not try to blackmail us with it then?'

'And the answer is?'

'Obvious, I hope. Until now, any fakes wouldn't have been good enough to stand up to expert scrutiny.' He doodles a finger in the spilt salt to create a spiral that he goes around over and over again.

'You said questions – plural.'

'We talked about Lina Wolff and what she's hoping to gain. Why would the woman deliberately set out to ruin us?'

'The obvious answer is money,' Eve tells him. 'She must be hoping you'll pay her off.' Before he can respond, she adds, 'Although, I've been thinking about that – if you're going to blackmail someone, you'd usually threaten to reveal all if someone doesn't pay up. This way round, it comes across as more genuine.' She touches his arm. 'Not that I believe any of it.'

He gives her a critical look. 'Glad to hear it.'

'Presumably, this PI woman will also do some digging into Wolff's life?'

Nick grunts. 'Should bloody well hope so. Creating all that deepfake stuff is far from easy. What's her background? If she did it herself, she'd have to be a real expert. If it turns out she didn't, it means we need to track down the person – or people – involved.'

Brushing aside his hand, Eve sweeps the spilt salt to the edge of the table and throws it over her shoulder. 'For luck,' she tells him.

Later, Eve lies awake, her brain crowded by thoughts that keep flying in so many directions she's dizzy with it all. Nick is asleep but restless. They're lying some distance apart, but his very presence overheats her.

In the early hours, she finally gives up on sleep. The pills the doctor prescribed are still there in the bathroom cabinet, but she's determined not to go down that rabbit hole again.

Though she holds out little hope, a hot drink might help. She's careful not to make a sound as she leaves the bed. Looking out of the window at the foot of the staircase, her attention is caught by the glow shining through the tent the security guards have erected just inside the front gate. They'd asked her permission to run a cable inside to power a caged lightbulb and a small fan heater. Peering in when she took them out a mug of tea, it looked quite cosy with its camp chairs and rugs. A radio had been plugged into the overloaded adapter. Now, in the dead of night with another heavy frost whitening the grass, she wonders if they're cold out there.

She takes up the bird watching binoculars she keeps by the window and focuses in on the tent. From their silhouettes she can see they're bulked out by blankets and sitting on opposite sides of a small table. No sign of the dogs. She assumes they're sleeping at their masters' feet.

When she was little, she used to lie in bed with a torch projecting the shadow of her hand into the looming silhouette of a barking dog. She'd make the shape of a bird and a rabbit. Over the years she's learnt to recall those moments – times when she felt safe and warm and invulnerable.

Eve continues to watch the men. She deduces from their movements that the two are playing cards to pass the time. Who could blame them? In the morning she intends to tell Nick they should go – having them here is a waste of everyone's time. And money.

A mug of hot milk in hand, she glances at the tableau in the tent on her way back upstairs. She thinks she can hear the bass line of the music they're playing; very faint like the smallest of heartbeats.

She sips the drink slowly and wills her mind to relax. As she settles back on the pillows, she thinks about Rafal and Jermaine out there watching over them – the most unlikely of guardian angels.

A scream wakes her. High-pitched. A woman. Heart racing, beside her, Nick is already bolt upright. Wailing now. Amber? And then, 'Oh my God, oh my God.'

Nick is out of bed and running towards the stairs. Grabbing her dressing gown, she follows. Down the stairwell, Amber has a hand clamped to her mouth and is staring at something. Closer, the girl's visibly shaking.

Nick reaches her first. 'Shit a brick,' he says. 'Christ almighty.' He turns around, holds up a blocking hand. 'Stay exactly where you are, Eve. Stop right there.'

Naked except for boxer shorts, it seems inappropriate for him to be putting an arm around Amber, reassuring her with, 'It's okay. You're safe.' He guides the poor girl backwards towards the front door, to the hall chair where he makes her sit. For a moment his hand hovers over the phone. 'I'm calling the police,' he tells them.

Eve looks down at all the footprints. How many sets? She has a bird's-eye view of Nick's hand as he presses the same key three times. 'Police,' he says; nothing else at first.

While he's preoccupied, Eve descends one more step and then another. Grandmother's footsteps. Reaching the last but one, she's able to peer around the banister into the twilight gloom of the hallway. It takes a moment to separate what she sees from the shadows and then a few seconds for it to take on any meaningful shape.

Eve catches her breath, tries to pull her dressing gown closer, but it does no good. And now her legs have lost their strength. Afraid of pitching forward, she lowers herself down onto the hard step before daring to let go of the handrail.

Nick shouts her name but it's already too late to unsee what she's seen. Blood. Everywhere. Exactly like before.

Chapter Fourteen

Eve tries not to breathe in the sickly smell of it; she can't begin to process the words daubed on the walls obscured by drip lines. Swallowing again and again, she fights the nausea threatening to overwhelm her. Shutting her eyes, she tries to block it all out. Terrible pictures form in the dark red world beneath her eyelids forcing her to open them again.

It's beginning to get light outside. She tries to concentrate on a single flower on the sleeve of her dressing gown, on how it had been formed by all those tiny stitches – so meticulous and perfectly matched. In the dawn's half-light, she can't make out its colours.

DEATH FOR RAPE!

Head heavy, she curls up to rest its weight on her arms. What if all the thoughts trapped inside begin to spill out and never find a way back? Will they roam the darkened countryside like orphans searching for a peace that can never be theirs again?

She shakes herself, shakes her mind off that pattern of

thought. Sick; she mustn't go there. Freeze-framed on the last-but-one step, she prays the police will arrive and put an end to this bizarre vigil; for someone in authority to give her permission to escape the overwhelming stench of blood.

RAPISTS ARE ANIMALS

Tock… Tock… The hall clock hacks away at the silence as if nothing in the world is amiss. She jumps when it bongs out the half hour, and then again when it strikes to mark a full hour. One. Two… Eight o'clock; each shuddering note runs through her.

CHOP THE RAPISTS

Nick breaks first. 'How much fucking longer?' And then, 'Maybe I should go and talk to the security guys – let them know what's happened. I don't want them blundering around trampling on evidence.'

Spurred by his impatience, Amber speaks, her voice so quiet Eve has to strain to hear it. 'Jermaine gave me his number. It's, um, on my mobile.' A sharp intake. 'It's chargin' in the kitchen.'

'Sod this,' Nick says. 'I'll give the police another call.'

'They could be lost,' Eve says.

Nick stabs the button three times, his fury palpable – a wave pressing on her. 'Police. Yes, I called before but they *still* haven't arrived.' He's forced to repeat the same details. Then, 'You said the same thing more than an hour ago.' He's shouting now. 'Bloody good job we're not being held at gunpoint, or someone might have been shot by now.' The climbdown is swift. 'No. No one's life is in danger, as far as I can tell.'

Eve breathes into the naked flesh of her forearm, inhales her own skin's familiar smell. 'Oh, I see.' Nick sounds chastened. 'Okay, yes. Sorry about that. Okay Thanks.

'The first lot got diverted to a fatal car crash,' he tells them. 'She promised someone will get here soon.'

The clock ticks on regardless. 'What I want to know,' Nick says, 'is how in God's name this could happen when we're paying people to guard this bloody house.'

Bloody house – he's right about that. It must be seeping into the walls. *All the perfumes of Arabia will not sweeten this little hand.*

Where are Rafal and Jermaine? Surely, they must have heard Amber's scream. She tries not to picture the little tent awash with their blood. Is that where it came from?

No. No one would do that to two innocent men. Besides, they're way too substantial, too stubbornly alive for such a thing to happen to them. If they'd been attacked, their dogs would have gone for the attackers. And they'd have barked their heads off.

Did she hear barking? Is that really what woke her?

No – Amber's scream had torn into her dreamworld. Eve reinstates the image of the two men playing cards, their fierce dogs curled around their feet snoring. In that Sherlock Holmes story, the dog didn't bark because the person who broke in to steal the horse was someone the dog knew. Could that be what happened here?

Lots of shouting; dogs definitely going spare now. Getting louder. Someone bangs on the door three times. Not once. Or twice. 'We're in here,' Nick shouts though they probably can't hear him with the racket the dogs are making.

The front door bursts open. A blast of cold air rushes in along with more daylight. The intruder alarm shrieks but is quickly silenced by someone. Amber must have reset it after she came in. 'Police,' a male voice shouts.

Jermaine shouts over him, 'Is everyone okay in here?'

Lights go on though it's already light enough. 'We're all fine,' Nick says, speaking for himself.

'Holy shit,' Jermaine again. 'Man – that's sick. Like something out of a Stephen King film.'

'Careful!' Nick shouts. 'They might have left footprints. Try not to step on them any more than we already have.'

'Can you confirm none of you are injured in any way?' a woman wants to know.

'Like I said, we're all fine.' Nick has appointed himself their spokesman.

'What about the young lady?' she persists.

'I'm okay,' Amber tells her in an uncertain voice. 'Bit shocked and that…'

Legs shaking, Eve pulls herself upright – makes sure she's visible. 'I'm not, um, injured,' she tells her like it's the truth.

'Good to hear it.' The policeman again. He's in uniform, stab vest and everything. They both are. Not detectives then.

The newcomers – three of them – are frozen just inside the threshold like they're held back by an invisible forcefield. Outside the barking is quieter; muffled like they've been shut up somewhere.

The policewoman's torch beam scans the floor in front of her. 'Hallway appears to be clean back here,' she concludes. 'Can you all stay exactly where you are for just a bit longer. My colleague needs to get some shoe covers from the car.' Sounds like an order. She must be his superior.

The policeman nods before retreating. On his way out, he puts a hand to Jermaine's shoulder turning him around. 'If you wouldn't mind stepping outside now, sir. Thanks for your help. We'll take it from here.'

Take what exactly? Can they take away the stench? Those hateful words? Or the fact that a person or persons have broken into their home and defiled it in the most obscene way?

A sharp gust of wind blows through the house. Paintings shudder in its wake; curtains stir themselves and a piece of paper from the hall table sails off to land on the floor before anyone can grab it.

The policeman returns; taking a careful step forward, he hands over a wad of blue plastic to his colleague. 'Here we go.' She slips a cover over each of her boots. 'Ambulance ETA in five,' he says.

'Is that really necessary?' Nick asks. 'None of us are injured.'

Ignoring him, the policeman adds, 'The DS is on her way.'

'Okay, so let's start by getting you all out of here,' the policewoman says. 'We'll do this one at a time in reverse order, starting with the young lady here.'

Keeping near to the wall, she reaches Amber first. Once the girl's feet are protected, she stands up. She's told, 'Keep as close to the edges as you can.'

Once Amber is outside, she turns her attention to Nick.

'Now you, sir.' He struggles to stretch the covers over his bare feet. He could be wearing a couple of shower caps – the sort they give you free in hotels.

'Right now, try to keep to the sides, sir,' she tells him as if he might have forgotten. When he reaches the front door, someone in a green jumpsuit comes forward to drape a shiny blanket over his bare shoulders.

It requires an awkward sideways shuffle for the police-woman to reach the bottom of the staircase. Beneath her hat, her dark hair is pulled back. Up close, her face looks older than Eve had imagined. Hand at full stretch, she passes her a pair of foot covers. Shivering and all too aware of being naked beneath her thin dressing gown,' Eve says, 'Perhaps I ought to go and put some more clothes on first.'

'I'd rather you didn't.'The woman tries a smile.'Don't worry, they'll soon get you warmed up in the ambulance.'

'Ambulance?'

'They'll just need to check you're okay.' She beckons her forward like someone directing a car into a narrow parking space.

Eve looks down at her bare feet. It's hard to balance while lifting one foot. Hands shaking, she struggles to stretch the plastic cover over her toes without it slipping off the back again. 'It's my big feet,' she says. 'Size ten would you believe. This one's half a size bigger than the other. Not very balanced – that's me, I'm afraid.'

'What's your first name, dear?'

'Eve; as in Adam and Eve. Don't see her wondering around the Garden of Eden with a couple of plastic bags on her feet.'

'Take your time; you're doing really well, Eve. That's it; now just try to hook it around your heel. Great – you're done.'

'They're a bit flimsy – not much protection. You know, I think I might just go upstairs and get a proper pair of shoes.'

'Eve listen to me.' Her impatience is showing through. 'We need to get you out of here so the SOCOs – that's the Scene of Crime Officers – can do their job. Do you understand what I'm saying? I'm sure you want us catch whoever did this.'

'Why would they break in and do this?'

'Let's not worry about that right now, okay? Can you take a step toward me? That's it; you're doing great, Eve. Now all you need to do is follow me.' Her hand is surprisingly warm to the touch. 'It's okay – I won't let you go. Let's get you out of here, shall we?' It's not really a question.

She tries but it's impossible not to glance sideways to check it's still there and not something she'd imagined. A lot of blood has pooled underneath **DEATH FOR RAPE**

The words leap out at her like an attacker. Turning the other way, two white-suited and masked figures are waiting on the threshold to enter. Their home, her sanctuary reduced to the scene of a crime.

Chapter Fifteen

Lying in a strange bed in a strange room, Eve might almost fool herself they're on holiday. Almost. The room, like the rest of the cottage, is simply furnished and depersonalised – another welcome break. Only ten miles from home and located down a narrow, anonymous track, the place is far removed from all the turmoil and madness. Nick is humming downstairs. She checks her phone. Time to get up – their visitor is due in less than twenty minutes.

PC Harcombe says he's their liaison officer. Dark curly hair shaved close at the sides. In his twenties and pleasant enough; if he wasn't in uniform, he'd be difficult to pick out in a crowd. Handing her his card he says, 'Call me Ivan.' She has no idea if this is normal procedure.

Perched on the edge of an armchair, he waves away her offer of tea. After a few niceties he clears his throat. 'We're now able to confirm that the blood they used was definitely not human. It was mostly from pigs with a bit of sheep mixed in.'

'Well, that's something of a relief,' Nick says. They both

look at her like they expect her to feel better about things now. She pictures the bloodless corpses of all those animals.

'This might sound a touch gory,' Ivan says, 'but getting hold of that sort of quantity of fresh blood can't have been easy. The local abattoirs we've checked so far haven't noticed any missing.' His dark uniform is at odds with the chair's overblown florals. 'The SOCO team have finished in the house, so you're free to go home any time you like folks.'

'I've already arranged for a specialist firm to go in and give the place a deep clean,' Nick says. 'I'll give them the go ahead. We'll be staying on here for a couple more days,' he says.

'Maybe longer,' she adds.

'Though I'm sure I'll be popping back to use the studios,' Nick feels the need to tell him.

Ivan checks his notes. 'Anyway, as you know, the SOCOs found lots of footprints. They're pretty sure there were three of them. Unfortunately, all wearing mass-produced trainers. Two sets were size ten and eleven – typical men's sizes. One wore size fives. Don't ask me how they can tell but, apparently, that individual was less heavily built – so more than likely either a woman or a young lad.'

It shocks her to think a woman might be capable of dipping her brush into a bucket of animal blood to daub terrible words on someone else's walls.

Ivan rubs a finger along one eyebrow – backwards and forwards it goes. 'The forensic guys – and um, women – tried to pinpoint the origin of the mud that was mixed in with the blood. It had the exact same composition as the soil in some of the fields near yours. Land belonging to your neighbour Mr

Harrison. He didn't notice any trespassers and so far, no one's come forward to say they saw a vehicle parked in the lane by his field gate.

'Early yesterday morning, Mr Harrison drove his tractor in and out of the field abutting the lane and, what with that and heavy rain, if their vehicle left tyre marks, they've since been obliterated. We've been able to identify the route through the fields onto your land and from there into your garden.'

While letting this sink in, he picks up his hat. 'That's it so far. Any breakthroughs and I'll be in touch straight away.'

Eve shows him to the door, thanks him once again. Waving him off, she notices a touch more warmth in the air. A cobweb hung with water droplets is lit by the weak sun. The birds are singing out a promise of better days to come. Seems unlikely.

They leave early. In the taxi, they're both on edge. 'We don't have to do this,' Nick says. The twin lines etched into the bridge of his nose have become fixtures; they remind her of a pause button.

'We can tell the rental people we've changed our minds,' he says. 'Or, if you like, we can find a hotel – treat ourselves to a five-star. We could put the house on the market for that matter. Honestly Eve, we never need go back.'

'Not sure there'd be too many takers after what's happened.' She squeezes his hand. 'And anyway, we can't let them drive us out of our home.' She can only use the word *them* or *they* for the anonymous culprits.

Passing through the village, they soon reach the point where she normally feels relief to be almost home. Daffodils are nodding from front gardens – no longer held back by the unseasonal weather.

Approaching the turn off, their driver slows down. 'Looks like you've got company,' he says, nodding towards the motley collection of reporters waiting at the gates. Oh joy – a reception committee.

Nick curses as microphones are extended towards the car. A barrage of flashes. Faces stare in at them, distorted in proximity; damp breath clouds the windows. Eve jumps as hands hit glass and then the side doors as if all that slapping might persuade them to open.

It's been more than a week. These people can't have been camped out here the whole time; someone must have tipped them off they were on their way back.

Rock Star and Wife Return to Horror House.

Nick holds his mobile higher to stop the signal getting blocked. The gates dutifully respond to their approach although they shudder several times as the sensors pick up would-be obstructions.

She recognises Rafal waiting on the other side, Dax, his Doberman, eyeing up potential prey. The gap is finally wide enough to drive through. Rafal and dog sweep in behind the car but a couple of journos end up on the wrong side as the gates close again.

Another guard joins Rafal; they spread out to block the path of the intruders. Dax is straining, eager to take a snap at a resistant leg or two. She half-hopes he succeeds.

'You ready?' Nick asks.

'As I'll ever be.'

Together they sprint for the front door. Nick struggles with the new set of keys. Once inside, they close it safely behind them. A dull thud that echoes down the hallway.

Daring to look, everything appears to be exactly as before except for the new and overpowering smell of paint and cleaning fluids. They've done a remarkable clean-up job. Even so, she can't stop seeing it; her memory not so easy to erase.

Grown used to the scale of the rental cottage, the proportions of the hallway are a jolt. So much space. The potent mix of chemicals is enough to induce a migraine.

'God, it stinks in here,' Nick says, wrestling with the lock on the nearest window. Once it's opened, she gulps in fresh air half expecting a lens to pop up in front of them to capture the moment.

Cleaners Fail to Expunge Bloody Horror

Made of stern stuff, the oak panelling has survived the experience remarkably unscathed. The far wall is freshly painted and the floor, if anything, looks cleaner than before. Only the rug is absent – unsalvageable they'd been told. She was very fond of that rug.

The clock is still ticking away; someone must have wound it up. She opens the case to stop the pendulum mid-swing. 'That's enough.'

They walk past the window – the one *they* had forced open. No fingerprints found – they'd worn forensic-style gloves.

A shiny lock has been fitted to the repaired window frame. She can smell the new putty. The catch and locks are tricky to undo when all you want is a breath of fresh air.

It's comforting to learn that at least that hateful trio hadn't ventured beyond the hallway into any other rooms.

In the kitchen Eve's energy leaves her; she slumps down on the sofa revelling in its familiarity. Running a hand over the pile of the mustard velvet cushion, she remembers how she'd chosen it to introduce a pop of colour against the plain linen upholstery. Turns out blood makes a more memorable pop of colour.

Eve studies the tea stain on one of the sofa's arms – a blemish that had so annoyed her at the time. Up close, it takes on the unlikely shape of Australia.

Nick says, 'Who tipped them off that we were coming back today?' That word *them* again.

'I heard you mention it to Kendra,' she says. 'D'you think someone at her agency spilt the beans?'

'Possibly.' After spooning in tea, he fills the pot from the boiling water tap. 'Although I also told the cottage owners we were leaving today. I suppose one of them might have let it slip in the pub or something. Or maybe one of the cleaners going in this morning.'

Eve stares out into the garden. She feels a pang of guilt to see the birdfeeder empty. How long had they continued to visit it in hope? Before she can rouse herself to go and fill it up, Nick brings over the tea. 'Didn't you book a supermarket delivery for today?'

'Yes. It's due to arrive around lunchtime.'

'They're a massive company; any one of the people working for them could have leaked the information to the press. The story's been all over the newspapers; they could have recognised our address and put two and two together.'

Their lives are at the mercy of so many unknown *theys*.

Eve sips her tea though it's almost too hot to drink. 'P'raps they made a few quid out of it,' she says. 'Pretty tempting when you're not paid a fortune.' She stops short of adding *like you*. 'I suppose you can't expect them to have much sympathy when the two of us are living in a massive house like this.'

Rapist Rock Star and Wife Get What's Coming.

'The media decides the narrative and we've been found undeserving.'

'That's an oversimplification,' he says.

She doesn't argue and yet it's clear no one cares that the impoverished last owner of the house had let it fall into a terrible state of disrepair. How they'd deployed an ever-increasing array of buckets to catch the rain coming through the many holes in the roof. Water had gradually rotted the roof timbers and made the walls so damp some sections were in danger of imminent collapse. Eve had project managed the three-year struggle – at mounting and horrifying expense – to bring the house back from the edge of dereliction to its former glory.

She trails the tip of her finger around the coast of Tiny Australia surprised she'd never seen the similarity before. 'I know I said I was determined to come back but now I'm really not sure this was a good idea.' Her sigh is heartfelt. 'Maybe you were right in the car – perhaps we should just sell up and go.'

'I only said it was an option.' Nick sits down beside her, the upholstery sinks under the additional weight, throwing them closer together. He puts an arm around her shoulders and pulls her to his chest. 'Things will get better. There will be a time when we've put all this behind us.' He kisses the top of her head. 'This is a high-profile break-in that's had a lot of publicity for obvious reasons. There's a lot of pressure on the police to catch the bastards who did it.'

'Even if they do – which I'm beginning to doubt – I'm not sure it will fix things.' Pressed into the hard wall of his chest, she feels smothered instead of comforted. She pulls herself upright to face him. 'Nothing can change the fact that they defiled our home in such a vile way.'

Looking around her once favourite room, she feels no fondness for it. 'Being back here – it's worse than I thought it would be. With all those sodding paps at the gate and guards patrolling the grounds – it's like stepping back inside a prison. Or your worst bloody nightmare.' Having used the word *bloody*, she pictures the terrible words scrawled in the hallway, each and every letter dripping with blood. 'You know what – I give up.' She holds up her hands in surrender. 'They win.'

'Evie my love, coming back here was bound to be difficult.' Nick strokes her hand. 'Let's not make any hasty decisions, eh?' He picks up his phone. 'We both need a complete change of scene. Why don't I start by booking us into some swanky London hotel for a few days?'

'I'm not sure I can take off just like that. What about all the food I ordered? And then there's Brandy to think of, for a start.'

He puts his head on one side like he's seen right through these feeble excuses. 'One of the guards can stick the food in the fridge – or Amber can take it home with her. You can pay the livery yard to exercise Brandy for a few days. Come on, Eve, the day's still young; let's live a little.'

He taps at his phone. 'Place here has a massive indoor pool and full spa facilities. They have two penthouse suites with roof terraces with heated rooftop plunge pools. Says here you can sip champagne while gazing up at the stars.'

'Oh yeah – through a thick blanket of cloud?'

Nick looks up at the glass lantern above their heads. 'If I'm not mistaken, that big blue thing up there is the actual sky.' The pale sun lights up his profile. 'If it pisses with rain, we'll be far too drunk to care. What d'you say?'

'But if we're photographed indulging ourselves, won't it seem callous?'

Rock Star Lives It Up Despite Rape Charge.

His face falls. 'Mmm – Good point. Maybe I should run it past Kendra.'

'Oh so now your publicist gets to decide where we go and what we do?'

'Hang on a minute – for a start you brought it up.' The pause button reappears on his brow. 'I'm not asking her permission. I'm only thinking that, if we do get papped, she'll need to be ready to put the right spin on it. The country's been poring over the gory details of our break-in. It would be hard to criticise us for needing a bit of time out.'

'You're wrong about that – no one finds it hard to criticise these days. Everybody has a fucking opinion about everything, and their default setting is to condemn.'

He grabs both her hands and shakes them. 'Okay, so all the haters out there are going to bitch about us whatever we do. Meanwhile, we'll be up on the roof looking out over the London skyline and drinking champagne.'

With the sunlight narrowing his pale eyes, he looks exactly like he did all those years ago. Another lifetime. She smiles back. 'Put like that, how can I refuse?'

'That's my girl,' he says.

Chapter Sixteen

Leaning on the rail that surrounds their roof terrace, Eve looks down on the city. With all the bridges and every high-rise building lit up, tonight Central London is utterly seductive. The night is surprisingly mild. Despite all the light pollution when she looks up, she can pick out the Evening Star, Venus, well below the waxing moon. Or it might be waning – she can't remember which way it should face. She raises her glass to the silvery old man up there.

Not much more than a three-hour drive and yet it seems such a long way from darkest Somerset. Earlier, they'd walked through the streets hand-in-hand, Nick slouched and unrecognisable in his grey hoodie jacket. The spring sunshine had given her a valid excuse to wear sunglasses. They'd eaten street food sitting on a park bench and bought a few daft things they didn't really need just like they used to when home was a flat in one of the leafier streets in Highgate.

Her music selection randomly moves on from a Sean Paul track to Sex on Fire – still one of her favourite tracks. It's impossible not to move her body as the song builds towards the chorus. A cloud of steam is rising from the hot tub. As if to illustrate the lyrics, Nick's naked torso could be smoking as he motions her to him. When she doesn't respond, he tries to shout above the blaring siren way down below them. She can guess what he's saying.

Glass in hand, Eve dances a few steps closer to him, imagining herself a fan gravitating towards this charismatic rock star. She's on the point of striping off her heavy cardigan when a buzzer breaks into the music. It takes her a moment to register that someone is at the suite's outer door. Ignoring it, she slips the cardy down over her shoulder, mouthing the words of the chorus as she advances on his wet and steaming body.

The buzzer sounds twice more before whoever it is leans on it to show they mean business. Probably some maid offering a turn-down service. Such a silly idea. Why would anyone want chocolate or rose petals laid on their downturned sheets? Given that Nick is currently naked, she answers the door.

It's a shock to find Leon and Gil filling the doorframe. Gil raises one hand – his usual Spock-style greeting. 'Oh,' she says. 'This is a surprise.' It's hard to believe Nick could have invited them over at this hour.

Stepping inside, Leon pulls her into a hug that goes on longer than she finds comfortable. Breaking off to look into her eyes, he asks her in an earnest voice, 'How are you, Eve?'

She turns away as much as she's able to without seeming rude. 'I'm okay,' she tells him. Raising her glass of fizz – 'Feeling no pain, as they say.'

'This is pretty swanky.' Gil's attention strays towards the

roof terrace. Waving overhead like drowning men, the two of them stride out to join Nick. 'How's it going?' they ask each other though no one answers the question.

Leon picks up the champagne bottle. 'Looks like we'll be needing several more of these.'

Mouth already full of pastry, Gil adds, 'And more nibbles.'

'Your wish is my fucking command,' Eve mutters to herself as she phones down the order. Through the glass doors she watches their guests strip down to their underpants before jumping into the hot tub. A tidal wave slops over the edge. Tanned and tattooed, the three of them look in remarkably good shape – physically at least. Like toddlers in a paddling pool, they set about splashing each other.

Shielding her drink, Eve joins them, standing well back until the horseplay subsides. 'So,' she finally asks, 'how did you know we were here?'

Leon has the decency to look embarrassed. 'Kendra mentioned it. Gil and me – we were just having a few bevvies and we thought, you know, this might be a good opportunity to nip over and have a bit of a catchup.'

It's tempting to question why it couldn't have waited until morning, but, by band-time, the night hasn't even got started yet.

The buzzer goes again. Eve half expects to find a group of scantily dressed women at the door, but it's only a uniformed waiter. 'Your order, madam.' He props open the door with some ceremony before wheeling his trolley into the room. A solid man in his fifties with unnaturally black hair, he affects a superior air. 'Chef has taken the liberty of pairing a selection of savouries to go with your Dom Perignon, madam.' A wave directs her attention to the trolley. 'Here we have some mustard-mascarpone bruschetta; some individual pine nut tarts with rosemary cream and, over here, some warm pistachio crusted scallops.' Straightening up, he waits for her response.

'Thank you – this looks great.' She searches her handbag for her purse, tries to calculate the appropriate tip to give the man.

A cry goes up from the hot tub where the three of them are in the middle of a ridiculous dance routine worthy of a poor tribute band.

She holds out a banknote only for the waiter to wave it away like she's just insulted him. 'Thank you but we never accept gratuities, madam.'

Eve feels put in her place.

The man's eyes flick to the raucous behaviour going on outside. 'Would you like me to wheel the trolley out onto the terrace?'

'There's no need,' she tells him. 'I'm sure I can manage.'

A look of dissatisfaction clouds his face. 'Shall I ask housekeeping to send up more towels?'

'I'm sure that won't be necessary. There's already a huge pile of them in the bathroom.' Faced with his apparent reluctance to leave, she crosses the room to hold open the door. 'Thanks very much,' she says. 'Goodnight.'

Having closed the outer door, Eve wheels the trolley out onto the terrace where its arrival is greeted with cheers. Wet fingers extend from the tub to grab the savouries. Nick leans across to grasp a champagne bottle by the neck. With a practiced hand, he takes off its wire cage and pops the cork, spilling some of the precious wine into the foaming water.

'Don't waste it.' Aware of its price tag, Eve prises the wet bottle from his grip. She takes care to pour the wine in the proper fashion before handing it around. 'Cheers!' Leon raises his glass. A rather hollow gesture and yet they follow suit, raising and clinking their glasses in solidarity.

Gil says, 'Here's to putting all this crap behind us.'

Nick huffs. 'Fat chance.' After a long sip, he adds, 'Realistically, it looks like this thing is going to grind on and on for months and months. In fact, given the current backlog in the courts, it could be even longer before it finally comes to trial.'

Leon tips the contents of a scallop shell into his mouth. Still chewing, he says, 'You're not wrong.' It's a stretch for him to put his glass out of harm's way. 'And in the meantime, we can't work, our royalties have taken a spectacular nosedive, and the legal costs will keep escalating until we start to eat into whatever savings we have left. Let's face it – in the end this could bankrupt all of us.'

'Yep – that just about sums up the situation.' Nick knocks back his champagne and reaches for a refill.

Standing up, Leon's expression grows serious. 'Eve, Gil and me feel really bad about the way you've been dragged into this. It's hard to imagine the sick mentality of those idiots who broke in.'

'Must have a screw loose.' Gil twirls a finger next to his ear. 'Hope they catch the sick bastards; they need bangin' up.'

Leon's not finished. 'And Eve, you of all people shouldn't have to put up with shit like that.' He gives her a knowing look. 'I don't know if you're aware of what's been happening with Medora.'

She shakes her head.

'Well, as you rightly pointed out to me back at yours, fashion brands are pretty sensitive about their public image. Turns out, no one would dare book her because she was going out with me.'

'I had no idea,' she tells him. 'Whatever lies they choose to believe about you, how can anyone hold that poor girl accountable for your actions? I mean the two of you weren't even dating at the time this was supposed to have taken place.'

'Makes no difference. After we were papped coming out of a restaurant, some trolls accused her of condoning rape. As far as the brands were concerned, the optics were bad. They thought, you know, why take a risk? Her agency stopped sending her to jobs. The work dried up just like that.' He snaps his fingers. 'I wasn't going to let that happen. So, anyway…' Voice cracking, he clears his throat. 'I broke up with her. It wasn't what either of us wanted, but I was left with no choice.' Eve's never seen him look so serious – or so sad. 'Nothing else I could do in the circumstances.'

'That's just awful,' she tells him.

'Thing is,' Gil interjects, 'if this was only hurting us, it wouldn't be so bad.'

'He's right. We have to consider the repercussions.' Leon turns to Nick. 'The toll this is taking on our families, and the people we really care about.'

'You make a good point,' Nick says. 'So, what's the solution?'

Before Leon can answer, Gil takes over. 'I know it's not

what we agreed before, mate, and I know it's goin' to stick in your throat just like it sticks in mine, but me and Leon think we should consider payin' this bloody woman off – givin' her whatever it takes to shut her up and make this whole bloody thing go away for good.'

Narrowing his eyes, Nick says, 'So after she makes up those accusations and then goes all-out to ruin us, you want us… I mean seriously? Are you really proposing we should simply hand this Wolff woman a shed load of money?'

'Just being pragmatic,' Leon says. 'Simple damage limitation.'

Nick glowers at him. 'But that would make us look guilty as hell. It would seem to the world like we were admitting it – like we're all bloody rapists buying our way out of trouble. We'd never live it down.' He shakes his head. 'I'm just not prepared to do that.'

'We have everything to lose even if we eventually win,' Leon reminds him. 'Let's face it, lots of people in similar positions to us have given in to the pressure. We can all think of examples.'

Nick goes to say something, but Leon holds up a hand. 'Hear me out, okay. Our lawyers are bound to know the best way to make sure the payment is conditional on her withdrawing all allegations. They'd need to draw up some sort of NDA agreement – or whatever form of words was needed to make sure she keeps her mouth shut from now on.'

Nick hauls himself out of the tub. Still streaming water, he wraps a towel around his waist and slings another across his shoulders. 'I find it hard to believe you two are prepared to give in to blackmail.'

Rising from the waves, Gil, the defiant merman, folds his arms. 'It's the lesser of two evils, mate.'

Nick goes off to supposedly get dressed but he doesn't return. Embarrassed, Eve smiles at their guests. 'I expect he's just um—'

'It's okay,' Leon says, 'We know what he gets like.' Of course they do – they've spent far more time with her husband than she ever has.

She's tempted to go after Nick but, changing her mind, comes back only with a pile of fresh towels. Despite the champagne, the collective mood has sobered. Hair plastered to his head, Leon grabs a towel before climbing out of the tub.

Gil follows suit, his bald head glistening in the artificial light. Once he's towelled off, he wraps himself up like a sultan to pour another round of drinks. She nods enthusiastically to the refill. 'Why not?'

'This is bloody good stuff,' Gil says studying the label, 'be a shame to waste it.' She glimpses the tattoos on his bare torso – some so crude they could be self-inflicted.

Hungry now, she picks up one of the tartlets and of course it's utterly delicious. Blindfolded, she'd find it hard to work out any of the ingredients. The same is true of the topping to the bruschetta. They've chosen the perfect accompaniment to the wine.

How bizarre it is to be standing on a city rooftop drinking champagne next to two wringing wet, towel-clad men. A camera drone could fly over at any minute to capture the moment. *Rock Star's Wife Entertains his Half-Naked Bandmates.*

'For what it's worth,' she says, 'I think you're right about putting an end to it.'

Leon's damp hand squeezes her arm. 'Maybe after Nick's slept on it...' He doesn't continue; his stubbornness is legendary.

Peering into his glass, Leon gives a wry smile. 'You know the first time I tried champagne was on the day my father remarried. I was almost thirteen and someone handed me a full glass for the toasts. I remember enjoying the sensation of all those sharp bubbles in my mouth; and I have to say it took the edge off an otherwise miserable day.' He gives her that famous smile. 'Let's open another bottle, eh?'

Gil is the first to ask about the break-in. 'The cleaning people have done a brilliant job,' she tells them. 'I mean, you would hardly know anything had happened if you hadn't seen it with your own eyes.' Hand shaking, she takes a long sip of her drink. 'Except there are these new window locks everywhere you look and they've, um, installed a new video surveillance system. When we arrived home this morning, the paps were besieging the gates. We've got security guards and their sodding dogs patrolling the garden. You'd think *we* were the criminals. Although I suppose some people must think we are. To be honest, I don't know how much more...'

Towel rising from his shoulders like a cape, Leon bends his head to look deep into her eyes. 'It's no way to live, Eve.'

Chapter Seventeen

Nick is sullen the next morning, and on edge, continuously tapping at every hard surface to impose his own rhythm on the world. She stops short of pointing out how annoying his fidgeting is – how the ceaseless movement and noise is doing nothing to help her raging hangover.

She drinks copious amounts of water and tucks into the elaborate late breakfast they bring to the room, hoping the extra calories will help replenish the missing nutrients her body is protesting about. Nick knocks back an espresso then orders another. He picks at the fresh fruit selection but not much else.

Below them, London now lies overcast and grey; lights on at midday under a leaden and threatening sky. The capital might offer a thousand diversions, but none of them appeals right now. Though luxurious, their hotel suite holds few distractions on a rain-soaked afternoon in late March.

Out of boredom, they make a brief foray into the streets, dodging an army of umbrellas and sidestepping streams of head-down, determined pedestrians. Out of step, she envies their collective sense of purpose.

They pause here and there to window shop along Bond Street. Nick buys a hat – its wide brim shades his eyes. There's not a flicker of recognition in the middle-aged assistant's eyes.

Eve has never been very interested in buying impractical clothes with crazy price tags. One front window displays a pastel confection of children's clothing – some outfits so impossibly small they tug at her heart.

They move on to Piccadilly – which is predictably busy. Too busy for anyone to give them a first, never mind a second, glance. Diesel fumes catch in her throat, frustrated motorists blare out their irritation – the pent-up aggression that comes with sitting in snarled-up traffic. They pass The Wolseley. A couple of damp paps are peering in through the steamy windows hoping to snap a few celebs taking afternoon tea. It gives Eve some satisfaction to walk straight past without provoking any interest.

They make their way back to the hotel, their footsteps in sync. She decides not to mention the argument with Leon and Gil, aware of their shared need for time-out.

The hotel lobby is pleasingly deserted. Back in their suite, she cranks up the temperature gauge. There are puddles out on the roof terrace. A couple of bedraggled pigeons are strutting around occasionally tussling and fluttering over the scraps they had carelessly dropped last night. Fearless, the birds come right up to the glass door as if reasonably expecting to be let in. Descendants of the rock dove, London pigeons are far leaner and scruffier than the plump woodpigeons she's used to seeing.

Damp hair wrapped in a towel, she flicks through the complimentary magazine, her throat dried by the room's filtered air. Towards the evening, they make love in an absent-minded way; a familiar pattern of movements that ends in physical satisfaction but nothing more.

Coming back from the bathroom, she stops to survey the lit-up city. In place of yesterday's appreciation of its glamour, all she can think of is the colossal amount of electricity wasted to light up empty office buildings.

Next morning, staring up at the shadowy ceiling, she says, 'I think maybe we should go home.'

Only half awake, Nick rubs at his eyes. 'If you like,' he says, smiling at long last. After a bit he adds, 'As long as you're sure you can handle it.'

'To be honest with you, I'm not sure about anything right now. But I think I'm ready to face it again.'

'Then okay,' he says. Just that – nothing more.

Rain is lashing the countryside in successive windblown waves as if driven by a giant machine positioned just out-of-shot. Eve is relieved when the colour palette slowly shifts from grey to muted shades of green. Through a streaked window, she glimpses more signs of spring. Many of the bare branched trees are coming into bud at long last.

There are things they ought to discuss though not when a chauffeur is sitting only a metre or so away. Instead, they confine themselves to a few minor observations about the weather and then fall silent in the latter part of the journey. She wonders if Nick might have reconsidered. Once they're home, she might suggest they ask the lawyers to explore the wider options. An informed decision – that's how she'll phrase it.

The village is deserted, the only sign of life is the smoke rising from various chimneys to hang in a pall over the buildings. Eve pictures people sitting by fires, nodding off open-mouthed with a good book open on their laps. Wet, exhausted dogs asleep at their feet.

Turning into their drive, she's brought up sharp by the sight of the people besieging the gates in even larger numbers than before. 'What the hell.' Nick utters a string of curses. 'I can't understand why they haven't buggered off.' His phone fails to open the gates – the signal must be blocked by the massed bodies.

Their driver is forced to stop the car. Caught off guard, inside the gate she can see Jermaine hurrying to press the button. It seems slow to kick in. 'Sod it,' Eve says struggling with the door handle. 'I'm not putting up with any more of this crap.'

Nick grabs her forearm, but she wrests it away and climbs out of the car to confront them. They surge towards her. 'What the hell's the matter with you bloody people?' she demands.

Initially taken aback, they nonetheless brandish their furry microphones right in her face. 'Why don't you just…' Eve manages to stop herself there.

She's forced to close her eyes against a storm of flashes. Opening them, she focuses instead on individuals hoping direct eye contact might somehow appeal to their common humanity. 'Look,' she says, 'I'm sure you're all cold and miserable hanging around out here. And it's totally pointless – yesterday's news. I can assure you Nick and I have nothing else to say about the break-in or anything else. It's an ongoing police investigation. You might want to ask the investigating officers for updates.' She throws up her hands. 'And that's all I have to say, so why don't you pack up your tripods and your stupid sound equipment and go home to your families, or your cats, or whatever.'

The gates are now fully open, she turns away unsure whether to climb back into the car or stride off up the driveway.

Unsatisfied, they continue to call out her name like she might have forgotten it. Fighting tears, she raises her voice above the clamour. 'Why can't you just leave us in peace? What the hell else do you people want from us?'

Instead of the shame she'd hoped to induce, they close in. 'Eve! Eve!' A young man, thin beard refusing to grow, aftershave sharp and cloying. Like a wasp, his mic makes contact with her cheek. 'Any comment you'd like to make about your parents, Eve?'

Off-balance, she can only ask, 'My parents?'

Another voice – an older man. 'How did it feel to lose them in such a terrible way?'

Someone grabs her arm. It's Nick. 'No comment,' he spits back at their hollered questions. Warding their strident voices off with his free hand, he hauls her through the pushing and shoving and shouting and propels her towards the house. Jermaine's dog is barking – the sound fills her head. The front door seems to retreat before them. Nick battles on crunching up the drive as he repeats the same two words over and over, 'No comment', as if such a simple incantation might ward off the sleeping spirits now brutally awoken.

Chapter Eighteen

She's rooted to the floor, in the hallway, where she'd only just shed her coat and dropped her mum's car keys in the glass bowl by the door. Snowfall deadening the usual sounds from outside, she's back in time; back in that split second when looking through into the kitchen she refuses to accept what she sees; dismissing it as some elaborate joke staged to freak her out for a moment. Along with the acrid stench of burning, there's something else – an undernote that's metallic. And then the buzzing stops as a single fly lands and casually crawls across her mother's cheek heading straight for one of her half-open eyes. She wills her to stop pretending, to sit up and brush the damned thing away, for God's sake. It isn't funny anymore – nothing about this is funny.

'Eve!' He's a blur – so close she can't make him out. 'Here – drink this.' She wraps her hands around cold glass, stares down into the colourless depth of the offering.

It occurs to her she's sitting down. The grey sofa, the orange throw usually on the back of an armchair is now wrapped around her lower half. She wants to put this cold glass down somewhere, but he guides it back to her lips. For his sake, she takes a sip and lets its iciness slide down her throat.

It makes her shiver.

'You're cold,' he says. 'I'll get the fire going.' When she doesn't respond, he heads over to the massive inglenook with its cast iron backplate. In their absence, Amber has laid it ready with screwed up newspaper and kindling – it only needs a match.

Eve hears the strike, the tiny phosphorous explosion before infant flames turn into bigger ones, cracking and spitting and straining to consume the wood. The smell of escaped smoke drifts towards her before it gets sucked up the chimney with the rest.

Someone must have turned off the oven; some anonymous gloved hands must have finally removed the incinerated meal they were meant to share. The last supper that never was. While blue lights strobed their quiet neighbourhood, some-one remarked that, if she hadn't stopped for petrol and a coffee to help her concentrate, she would have been there. A stroke of luck that saved her. Eve wasn't so sure.

He throws on a couple of bigger logs, knocks them into place with the poker. She puts down the glass, finds her voice to say, 'I'll make some tea.'

'Stay right where you are.' He dusts off his hands before wrapping the throw back around her, tucking it in by her sides like she's a child.

She still believes he'd make a good dad.

'I'll go put the kettle on,' he tells her. 'You've had a shock; you need to take it easy.' At the door he turns to check she isn't disobeying orders. 'Back in a minute.'

She stares into the surging flames. Now the fire has really taken hold, casting a flickering glow across the room. It would be a struggle to put it out.

Back on that same spot in the hallway, she can't see much of her dad, only his legs bent at the knee like he might be lying on his side, playing a daft game with the still-kitteny cat they'd acquired after she left for uni – a stray rehomed. He really loves Misty; teases and tempts her with moving string like a boy might, not a middle-aged balding man. Doesn't act his age.

Misty has left tiny red footprints everywhere, pixelating the edges of this outrageous picture.

Shutting her eyes won't make it go away no matter how many times she tries.

A cowardly reversal. She picks up her house keys, puts on her coat to stand outside and make the phone call despite her shaking hands. Like something she's watching on television. Her mum's voice tells her, 'Don't look so worried, Eve, it's not real.' Every word is recorded. They play it back to her later.

Wrapped in a blanket. Checkered bands on their hats. They whisk her off in a patrol car. No blue lights this time; no urgency anymore.

Later, they escort her to a room with no windows and ask her to sit down opposite two strangers – a man and a woman. The man is red-faced, in shirtsleeves, his jacket draped over the back of his seat. The woman's younger. Dark hair pinned back, sits more upright; keeps her jacket on.

In a soft voice that doesn't suit him, Red-Face apologis-es, issues a warning before showing her photographs from different angles of what is no longer their kitchen but *the crime scene*. Like a game of spot-the-difference, they ask her to study the familiar objects in the room and tell them if anything is out of the ordinary, as if she can stop her gaze from being drawn back to her prone parents. The dark halo behind her dad's head. Caught out sprawling on the floor like that, Mum would be mortified.

'Take your time.' The trapped air is laced with his sweat.

They're patient. Or pretend to be. Someone comes in with mugs of tea and a plate of biscuits. Custard creams. The woman stares down at the papers on the table, fumbles with her pen. Red-Face cracks a grim grin. 'Anything at all, no matter how small.'

Hard to believe how long it takes to spot the takeaway pizza box. Innocent-looking for sure but a definite giveaway next to the block of knives with that empty slot. The one they'd all used many times before. 'They never order takeaways,' she tells them. 'Dad's got high cholesterol – he has to be careful.'

Eve swallows hard.

'Here we are.' The loaded tray rattles as Nick puts it down on the pouffe in front of her.

'I'm not ill,' she tells him. 'I just didn't expect...'

He's trying to keep his face expressionless, but she can tell he's seething. In the end he breaks. 'They had no right. Fucking vultures. Not an iota of conscience between them. Or compassion. They trample over people's lives and then claim it's in the public interest. And we let them get away with it.' He looks at the wall like he can see right through it to where *they* are waiting. 'Nothing and no one matters to that lot out there except the next fucking story.'

She pictures the headlines. *Rock Star's Wife's Tragic Family Secret Revealed.*

Nick keeps curling his fists like he's about to march outside and throw a few punches around. He just might. She reaches for his arm. 'I'm okay,' she tells him. Makes an effort to add, 'I suppose it was bound to happen – had to come out sooner or later.'

'They have no bloody right to drag *you* into all this. Whatever they believe me capable of, it's nothing to do with you.' He sets his jaw, fists curling again. She's startled when he punches one of the cushions like he means it. Bumph! And then bumph-bumph. Dull echoes in her ears.

He jumps up, pacing out his frustration in front of her.

'Please Nick; this isn't helping.'

'I'm sorry.' He sits down, perches on the edge. 'But there's no excuse, Eve. Those people out there – they're nothing but parasitic lowlife. Pond-scum the lot of them.' He shakes his head. 'Or whatever's worse than that.'

'Blanket weed?' she says. 'Or that blue-green algae that can kill dogs if they swim in it.'

'Don't try to humour me.'

'Just a silly joke.' She forces a smile. 'Anyway, you've made us tea so let's drink it.' Brushing her hand aside, he gives her a long look before he takes charge of the pouring.

Red Face hands her a mug, and she wraps both hands around it. 'Perhaps you'd like sugar, Miss Albright?'

'No. No thanks.'

'And you're quite sure about the pizza box? Could their habits have changed since you left home?'

'They got a cat,' she tells them. 'Misty. We'd never had a pet before. Mum said she needed something to cuddle besides Dad, but he was the one who made a fuss of the cat.'

Red-Face clears his throat. 'If we could get back to this pizza box –'

'Give her a second,' the woman tells him.

'Are you sure you're okay, Eve?' Nick wants to know.

'Yes, I'm fine, Nick. Really.' She turns her head away, stares into the roaring fury of the fire so he can't see the truth.

Chapter Nineteen

The rain that had started overnight continues unabated, hammering on the skylight above them. Yawning and sleep deprived, she sips her tea. Her laptop is right there in front of her. She can't resist opening it.

Nick throws her a look. 'Hope you're not planning to check out what they've written.' His hand is poised in front of the screen, ready to stage an intervention. '*You* know the truth about what happened; that's all that matters.' It's an attitude he'd adopted his whole career. As they've recently learnt, head-in-the-sand isn't a viable policy these days.

All the same, she shuts her laptop again.

After knocking back a couple of espressos, he reappears dressed head to toe in waterproofs like an explorer venturing outside to take stock of the situation.

Ten minutes later he's back dripping but looking pleased. 'Thanks to the rain gods they've all buggered off. No doubt gone to harass some other poor sods.'

For a change the two of them sit down to breakfast, talk of nothing much over boiled eggs and toast. Outside the rain begins to lose its ferocity; tattered clouds offer an occasional glimpse of the sun.

She pulls the blinds up, waves at Jermaine as he passes on his latest round of their soggy garden. Even his dog looks bored. Having been beaten down, plants are hanging their heads. With their new state-of-the-art security system on permanent alert, it seems ridiculous to keep the security guards on. A discussion for another time.

Nick has left the kitchen door open. Whenever her gaze strays towards the hall she sees again those blood-soaked words. In the end, she gets up and shuts the door. Had the people who daubed those slogans known about her parents? Were they deliberately preying on a known weakness?

Once Nick has gone off to his studio, she opens her laptop. The serious papers are preoccupied with a breaking story involving a cabinet minister and his young mistress's apparently clairvoyant financial investments. The pairs dodgy antics push the story about her parents down the pecking order to a few inches on the inside pages.

A quick search of the tabloids and she's confronted by her own image staring back. One of them carries the story across the bottom of the front page accompanied by an unflattering shot taken as Nick forcibly led her away. He looks like an arresting officer.

QUENINGTON'S WIFE: TRAGIC PAST REVEALED.

A banner promises *More Revelations Inside*. They've really gone to town on page four. Below the shot of her family home wrapped up in police tape, there's an older photograph – one she's never seen before. Colours faded by reproduction and the best part of twenty-five years, it's a snap of the three of them. The caption beneath reads: *The Albright family in happier times*. They're on a beach, rolling waves breaking just behind. Cornwall is her best guess. Their faces are over-exposed, almost bleached out. Her parents must have asked a stranger to help them preserve the moment. Eve's hardly in touch with her few remaining relatives. What's the going rate to open up the family photo albums to strangers? She lines up the possible culprits. It's a short list.

Peering again at the image, Eve guesses she would have been about eight at the time. She's wearing the one-piece costume she'd loved for its cavorting cartoon penguins. Sentries on either side, her parents smile for the camera. Her mum's hair is bleached and tousled by the sun; her dad is still lean and surprisingly hirsute. They're younger than she is now. And happy – mercifully oblivious to what's to come. Sometimes she imagines the good times were only ever an illusion; the photo offers proof of sorts.

The verdict of the coroner's court is there in black and white. Murder followed by Accidental Death. Neighbours attested to arguments heard through walls. A mysterious male visitor glimpsed once or twice. The rest is conjecture – an imposed narrative that has her father's accusations reaching fever pitch before he stabs her mother in a jealous rage. Losing his balance during the frenzied attack, his head slams into their new marble worktop fracturing his skull as he falls. Fatally injured, he tries to get up, knife still miraculously in his hand as he dies.

They hadn't listened to her protests that she knew her father – knew him incapable of such a violent attack against the woman he loved. No one appeared to want to take it further, their minds had been made up almost from the start. Murder – there could be no doubt about that. But the accidental death of the crazed perpetrator? How had they all bought into that unlikely conclusion? *Conclusion* was the key word here – it meant the case could be closed.

'Guess what?' Nick's voice drags her back from the past. 'I've just had a difficult conversation with Gil.' His expression is grave.

Guilty, she snaps her laptop shut. 'Is everything alright?' She's puzzled because his phone doesn't get a signal inside the studio. And, in any case, he always switches it off when he's working.

'Yeah, I couldn't settle so I decided to call the boys because I thought that, with everything that's happened, we should at least, you know, explore the possibility of paying this damned woman – getting her off our backs once and for all.'

'It makes sense to try,' she tells him. 'Might be better to cut your–'

'Gil's mum died last night.'

'Poor Gil.' Tears cloud her vision. 'The poor man. He must be heartbroken. I know they were really close. The family were expecting it, but all the same...'

Nick is rubbing at his forehead, agitated by more than this sad news. 'I told him how sorry I was and all that. He went quiet for a bit. I thought he'd rung off, except I could hear people talking in the background, so I knew he hadn't.

I guessed he was too upset to talk. Anyway, I told him I understood this was an awful time for them all and I'd ring back some other time. But Gil wasn't having it. He insisted he had something he needed to tell me right away.'

Eve waits.

'Just before she died, he had a long heart to heart with his mum and told her he was thinking it might be better to settle the case before it came to court. His mum was horrified by the idea of paying to silence Wolff. Hush money, she called it. He said she was fighting for breath when she made him promise that whatever it takes he would fight on to clear his name. She made him swear he would.'

'Wow.'

'That was almost the last thing she said to him before she finally passed away. So anyway, Gil's completely changed his mind. He's now absolutely determined to carry out his mum's last wishes.'

'Understandable.'

'Thinking of you, I tried to suggest that it wouldn't do any harm for our lawyers to explore our other options. He wasn't at all happy with that idea. Said he was sorry if it didn't suit me and Leon, but we'd all be wasting their time if we tried to go down that road. He was adamant he's intending to fight on whatever the cost. He even said he was prepared to lose everything if it comes down to it.' Nick shakes his head. 'I know Gil. I don't imagine he'll change his mind.'

Eve stares down at the table. 'I suppose you could still ask them to explore the possibility without Gil knowing about it.' She hates herself for even saying it.

'You want me to go behind the man's back?'

'Not exactly. I was only thinking that, you know, if this Wolff woman were to simply withdraw her allegations–'

'No.' The look he gives her couldn't carry more disdain. 'Eve, there's nothing more to say. I never liked the idea of buying her silence in the first place.' He throws up his arms before letting them fall to his sides. 'Like I said, I know Gil – he won't change his mind. We'll have to see this thing through to the bitter end.'

Chapter Twenty

Eve shuts her eyes and lets the outside world fall away until there is only the familiar smell of hay and oiled leather and the sounds of snorting nostrils and restless hooves striking wood. A horse whinnies, setting off an equine conversation across both sides of the livery yard.

She's tempted to climb the ladder to the hayloft to lie out on the hay bales unseen. Above her head the beams and rafters have survived unchanged for two centuries or more and will probably outlast them all – a thought that in the past had put her troubles into perspective; this time it fails.

Demanding attention, Brandy rears her head, one brown eye sizing her up. Eve strokes her muzzle with its elongated white star, revelling in the soft hairs under her fingers. 'Hello, you,' she says out loud as she reaches to smooth the rough strands at her forelock.

This has always been her sanctuary. Across the fields, Nick will be ensconced in his studio, lost in concentration, intent only on finding the right melody to accompany his latest words. He's always been good at compartmentalising, has a remarkable gift for shutting down all his other concerns and losing himself in music-making. Sometimes she wonders if it's the only thing that really matters to him.

'Penny for them?' Jared. Today he's looking rather distinguished in a smart tweed jacket and long leather boots. 'So, you're back.' For a second his eyes flick away before meeting hers. He lowers his voice. 'We heard about what happened.'

She must have appeared bemused because he adds, 'The break-in at yours. Although it was way more than that, wasn't it?' He purses his lips before deciding to go on. 'As you might expect, whole thing's been the talk of the village; all sorts of daft theories chewed over in the shop. And of course the bar at The Feathers.'

'I expect you've read all that stuff in the press about my parents. No doubt there are comments on social media. Opinions forcefully expressed by people who know sod all about it.'

Jared goes to say something but she raises her hand to stop him. 'Before you say it, I know I shouldn't have looked but I couldn't help myself.' She swallows hard. 'Once you've seen things you can never unsee them.'

Raising her fists, she makes a strangled cry. 'How can it be fair that complete strangers get to say terrible things when they don't know the first thing about what happened?'

'It's the curse of our times.' Jared shakes his head. 'I'm so sorry, Eve. You know, I called round your house a couple of times this week. The guards would only say you'd gone away; they couldn't – or wouldn't – say when you'd be back.'

'We both needed time…'

'Totally understandable. Still, we've been awful worried,

Rory and me. Hard to blame you for wanting the hell out of this place for good.' A fleeting smile. 'Anyway, it's good you're back home at last.'

Leaning forward, he seems to be about to hug her but instead, he squeezes her shoulder. 'I have to say the way the press have delighted in dragging up all that stuff about your parents – it's despicable. Reprehensible.' On her behalf, his brown eyes fill with tears. He struggles to clear his throat. 'I can't tell you how good it is to see you.' Another shoulder squeeze. 'You're obviously made of far sterner stuff than you'd think judging by the size of you.' His *think* becomes *tink* – a softer sound that takes the edge off something she's been doing far too much of lately.

Brandy nudges her hand. Eve says, 'This poor horse must have thought I'd forgotten all about her.'

'Ah, don't you go feeling sorry for that beast – she's not one iota of loyalty, this one.' He leans past her to pat Brandy's withers. 'Lost no time cosying up to the girls here as soon as your back was turned.' His colour rises. 'Not that I was suggesting anything by that. I only meant –'

'I know.' She puts a hand on his arm. 'Listen, I was thinking I might ride over to Oakhill Ridge and back. Care to join me?' Looking him up and down she adds, 'Although maybe you're off somewhere smart.'

'Ah – you mean the jacket.' His broad smile is full of relief. 'I had to call in at a client's place earlier on. Thought my smelly old wax jacket was unlikely to strike the right note.' He makes a show of adjusting his cuffs. 'Rory reckons I could pass for one of the local landed gentry in this get-up. Well, until I open my Irish gob, that is.'

She brushes a strand of hay from his sleeve. 'He's right – you look devilishly handsome in that outfit.'

His laugh is loud enough to startle the horses. 'Now don't go trying to turn a fellow's head with your flattery, Eve Quenington.' This time he pulls her into a hug, patting her back in reassurance much like he might a horse. Letting go, he says, 'How about the two of us saddle up and get going?'

'Too right. Day's already half gone.'

While tacking up, he calls across, 'On our way back, we could call in at The Feathers for a drink – that's if you've the time. Or the inclination. Said I'd meet Rory there around lunchtime.'

Checking her tack gives Eve time to consider. She finally says, 'You know, I think I can make time in my busy schedule. Might even take a chance on ham, eggs and chips.'

He whistles through his teeth. 'Steady on, girl – I'd say that's possibly a step too far.'

Popular with riders, a wooden rail to one side of the pub's car park is there specifically for tethering horses. A pile of fresh dung attests to another horse's recent departure.

Low beams and small windows mean every bulb is blazing even though it's broad daylight outside. With the vast outside creeper obscuring the light, the bar has an almost subterranean feel.

Looking around, she can't see Rory. A handful of drinkers meet her gaze and then glance away; it's hard to know if this is due to embarrassment or a genuine absence of interest. The sweet smell of woodsmoke drifts across from the open fire. At the other end of the room, she spots the Kirby twins with half-drunk pints in front of them staring separately at their phones.

The landlord is a sizeable man by the name of Tommy Woodcock, affectionately known as Wookie. 'Afternoon,' he says giving the two of them no more than his customary curt nod while continuing to change a barrel. After he's pulled a measure to check the beer is running clear, he says, 'So, what can I get you folks?' The order pad looks tiny in Wookie's dinnerplate-sized hand. They opt for half pints – adding one extra for Rory. Remembering past experiences, Eve settles on a veggie burger – possibly the safest thing on the menu. She declines the riskier side salad. Jared goes for fish and chips.

She leads the way over to the empty table by the fire. They hang their damp jackets on the backs of their chairs. The heat soon forces her to remove her jumper as well.

The front door bangs and Rory comes in with a current of chill air that creates a momentary downdraft of smoke like a ghost entering the room and then dissolving. 'Come here you,' he says approaching her with open arms, forcing her to stand up and submit to a hug so tight it's hard to breathe. His coat is cold and soggy against her cheek. For a moment the two of them become a spectacle freely stared at by one and all.

Peering into his beer, Jared mutters, 'Will you sit yourself down.' His partner does as he's told, pulling up a chair that scrapes against the worn stone floor – a grating sound to set teeth on edge.

Faces are openly turned their way, conversations paused in order to overhear what comes next. Though he usually insists people order at the bar, Wookie has left his usual domain to stand before them. He nods at Rory. 'Afternoon. Will you be wanting anything to eat?'

After scanning the chalkboard menu above the fireplace, Rory says, 'I'll take a chance on your special – the beef and ale pie.'

Checking the landlord is fully out of earshot, he leans forward. 'Seems a pretty safe bet, they'll have bought them in.'

After shedding his coat, Rory's face sobers. He reaches across the small table to cover Eve's hand with his. 'How're you holding up?'

'Oh, you know, just carrying on.' She shrugs – a gesture that won't fool either of them. 'Not much choice, is there?' she adds. 'When you're faced with a mountain, you just have to tell yourself to keep putting one foot in front of the other.'

'Aye, but it's a mountain of shite that's none of your making.' Rory shakes his head; his sandy curls shudder. 'I'm not normally a violent man but if any of them fecking vultures from the press were to thrust a microphone in front of *my* face – well I'd find it hard to physically restrain myself.'

'And you'd be playing right into their hands,' Jared tells him.

'Aye well, the alternative is to stand by and watch your friends being hounded and torn apart by vicious tongues. For the love of God – dredging up that terrible business with your parents from years back…'

Jared nudges him. 'I really don't think you're helping.'

She says, 'It's taken me a long time and an awful lot of therapy to come to terms with all that. Nick warned me not to read any of the press coverage. Like a fool, I didn't listen. And it's brought it all back…'

'Bound to have,' Jared says.

Louder than she intended, she tells them, 'I know my dad. He was a gentle man; he couldn't have done what they claimed he had.'

There's a flash. The shock of it runs through Eve's whole being. Her head flicks around as a volley goes off. The culprit is young blonde woman holding up her phone, ostensibly taking photos of her companion at the bar. Hardly precious moments to treasure.

'What the hell's that bloody woman up to?' Rory puts down his glass in readiness.

Jared grabs his arm, pinning him into his seat. 'Don't go jumping to conclusions.'

More flashes. Eve grabs his other arm just in case. 'I love that you want to fight my battles, I really do, but who's to say those two aren't innocently taking a few souvenir snaps? They probably haven't even noticed us.' Eve doesn't believe it for a second.

Jared adds, 'Even if that thing was aimed at us, they're too far away to have overheard our conversation. Who's going to give a monkey's that Eve is having lunch with a couple of friends in her local pub? Not exactly a scoop, is it?'

'Aye, you're right.' Looking only half-chastened, Rory curls his fist like he still means business.

'Excuse me, ladies.' Wookie's voice booms across the room. His wide back blocks Eve's line of sight. 'My customers come in here for a bit of peace and quiet. If you're going to carry on taking photos, you'll have to do it outside.'

'I don't believe this,' the blonde says. 'I was only taking a few shots of my friend here.'

'Up to you, darling.' Wookie jerks one of his enormous thumbs in the direction of the exit. 'Either stop that right now or drink up and leave. Choice is yours.'

'Fuck's sake.'

'And I'll have none of that sort of language in here.' At that, several drinkers snort into their pints. Wookie's colourful vocabulary is legendary.

Tucking her phone into her jeans pocket, the woman downs her drink before slapping down the glass.

Like a sheepdog, Wookie shadows the two women all the way to the exit.

Once he's seen them off, he turns to give the three of them the briefest of nods before taking up his usual station behind the bar.

Eve tries to regain her composure. It's hard to carry on a normal conversation with so many eyes slipping them sideways glances. Jared deliberately moves the conversation on, but she finds it hard to contribute to their talk of films and gardening.

When their food arrives, they lapse into silence.

'You know, Eve, I really meant what I said the other day,' Rory says, sotto voce. 'If you fancy getting away from everything for a bit – well except for me that is – you're more than welcome to join me on my island retreat. I'm leaving at the end of the week. The croft's totally isolated. Place was abandoned for years before it was renovated a few years back. By all accounts, the wildlife is something special. They tell me a family of pine martens comes to call most evenings. Eagles regularly circle overhead. I was thinking of taking a ferry over to Lunga to see the puffins at some point.'

'Sounds like my idea of paradise.' She takes a thoughtful sip of beer.

Jared laughs. 'Paradise with a gazillion midges.'

'Ignore him,' Rory says. 'Sure, the house itself isn't big, certainly by your standards, but there's a second bedroom. Place is totally off-grid. Up to you how long you stay.' He scans her face for an answer.

'Will you look at those big blue eyes,' Jared says. 'How can you bear to say no to this fellow?'

'Thanks. I really appreciate the offer.' Squeezing his hand, instead of turning him down as intended, she says, 'Give me a day or two to decide.'

Jared raises his glass. 'Sounds like a definite maybe to me.'

Chapter Twenty-One

A half-hearted dawn chorus is in progress when Rory pulls up in a smart grey car she's never seen before. Bouncing down the front steps ahead of her, Nick advances towards him. The two men shake hands with some vigour as if confirming a tacit understanding that they're both happy Eve is going on this trip. Side by side, of the two Nick is taller and leaner, his unruly hair and sunburnt skin a lot darker.

'What's this then?' Nick turns his attention to the car. 'Don't tell me you've finally bought yourself a decent motor? And a BMW no less.'

Rory grins. 'Only borrowed I'm afraid. Belongs to a friend of mine. Poor fella's gone and smashed his leg up in a motorbike accident. Seeing's it was going to be sitting idle for months, he offered to lend it to me for this trip.'

'Very generous of him,' Eve says. Instead of their usual hug, for some reason she double-kisses Rory like he was some dinner party guest. She notices the back seat and its footwell are piled high with boxes, a collection of wooden stretchers, a roll of canvas and a folded down, paint-splattered easel.

'Sorting out the insurance was a bit of a nightmare,' Rory tells them, 'all fixed up now and we're good to go.' He rubs his hands together – a sign that suggests he's eager to be off.

'We could have taken mine instead,' she tells him.

Rory wags a superior finger. 'Your Mini might be a fine motorcar, but the big difference is this little beauty's *all electric*. These days we need to think about the environment – climate change and the like.'

She frowns. 'I agree – but, and correct me if I'm wrong, aren't we heading somewhere that's completely off-grid?'

'Not a problem.' His smile is decidedly smug. 'This will do around 200 miles on a single charge.' He pats the bonnet, already smitten. 'It's a long drive, so we'd be needing to take regular breaks anyway. Plenty of places we can recharge – I've a special app on my phone here that shows you where they are.' He holds his mobile up as proof. 'They call it a ZapMap. Clever or what?'

Nick raises an eyebrow, 'Sounds like the two of you are going to have an interesting trip.'

'Aye, we're grand. Now don't you go giving me that cynical smile,' Rory tells him. 'That flash gas-guzzler of yours is a dinosaur heading for extinction. Besides, this'll cost around a third of the price in fuel.' He glances up at their house. 'Which, I grant, may not be such a big consideration for likes of you, but when you're a poor struggling artist such as myself…'

'Believe me,' Nick says, 'The way things are going, we'll soon need to count every penny.'

Eve can't stop herself from saying, 'All the more reason to try to settle things before it gets to court.'

Nick sighs. 'Eve, we've been through this…'

'I'm just reminding you that it's still an option.' She holds up both hands. 'You might at least explore the possibility. What have we got to lose?' She's used the same phrases, the same arguments so many times, they must both be sick of the script. Nick stays silent though his face is set hard.

'At least think about it.'

Rory has gone from gazing down at the gravel to kicking a pebble around ten metres away. For his sake, she changes the subject. 'I'm not insured – it's not fair for you to do all the driving.'

'Sounds like it's a bloody long way,' Nick adds.

'Aye but don't forget we're breaking the journey near Lockerbie.' Rory's hand bats away any argument. 'I was planning to make this trip alone. Now I've the major advantage of co-pilot; someone to check the satnav hasn't gone bananas and look out for the best charging spots. And leaping deer and the like.'

She looks at Nick. 'Are you sure you don't mind me buggering off like this?'

He smirks. 'Can't wait for a bit of peace around here.' Said in jest, she nonetheless gets the impression that he's grateful for the respite, relieved to be left alone to deal with matters as he chooses.

'Okay, then.' She does her best to sound upbeat, 'I'll go fetch my bag. That's if there's any room for it.'

'Don't worry, there's plenty of space for your stuff.' Rory pops the boot lid to demonstrate. 'There's even a wee cubby hole in the front that's perfect for boots and wellies.'

'Eve's a master – or should that be a mistress – at travelling light,' Nick strokes her neck. 'One of the many things I've always loved about her.' He smiles that crooked smile of his, the cold light of an English spring morning at odds with his Mediterranean colouring.

He nods towards Rory, 'This trip is exactly what Eve needs.' She could be a baton being passed from one man to the next.

After an overnight stop and a recharged battery, their route the next morning takes them along the shores of Loch Lomond. Glimpsed through breaks in the trees, the water flits from grey to blue under a broken sky. It's all a long way from the rolling hills of Somerset.

The house they'd stayed in turned out to be a Georgian rectory that had seen grander days. Rory's friend – an artist turned property developer with the splendid name of Finn O'Doherty-Bakshi – had insisted they sleep in the two bedrooms he'd already refurbished, assuring them he was more than happy slumming it in the dusty master suite he's in the process of upgrading. In the evening he'd served up a delicious array of authentic Punjabi dishes – all of them, it turned out, supplied by a local takeaway. The two men had entertained her with outrageous stories about their art school days. During the conversation, Eve had alluded to the fact that she needed a bit of time-out. When Finn didn't enquire any further, she suspected he'd already been briefed.

As they drive north, against all expectations, the temperature begins to rise. The scenery on all sides is breath-taking. Eve nervously watches the dashboard graphic showing the battery reserves gradually depleting. Should she be worried she's now empathising with a car?

They pull up next to a rapid charger in the last town of any size and, while it does its thing, they stock up with groceries at the only supermarket for miles. She's never bought so many tins. Fitting in the new supplies involves a complicated jigsaw of rearranging and cursing on Rory's part. At his insistence, they wait a further ten minutes for the battery to reach exactly 95% capacity. Eve silently calculates that each percentage increase only increases the range by 2 miles. Such dogged determination is a side of Rory she hasn't seen before.

Dwarfed by snow-topped mountains, they turn off the highway onto a winding single-track road. The passing spaces, with their diamond-shaped lollypop signs, become further and further apart. Though there's a rear camera to help, Rory complains every time he's forced to reverse.

Ancient rock faces towering above them; road signs warning of falling rocks. Should they speed up or slow down? On the distant hills she spots a scattering of sheep with their lambs. There are enormous bald patches in the conifer plantations spreading across the lower slopes of the mountains. This is only her second visit to Scotland and the sheer scale of the landscape they're passing through has a humbling effect. The all-pervading worries she'd left behind already seem petty viewed against the backdrop of mountains thrown up by shifting continents around 450 million years ago.

They stop to picnic on the sandwiches and soft drinks they'd bought at the supermarket, looking across a loch neither of them knows the name of; a handful of ruined croft houses along its shores. Stretching tired legs, Rory checks his watch. 'We're a bit behind schedule. Better get going.'

'I thought the whole point was not having a schedule.'

'I said we'd be there before dark. Navigating the waters around the island is a lot trickier at night.'

A shower blurs the windscreen but quickly passes. Late in the day in every sense, it occurs to Eve she knows little about where they're going. She says, 'Tell me more about the island.'

'Sure. What would you like to know?'

'Well, you said the boat hasn't got any lights.'

'Not exactly what I said but it won't be the size of a car ferry, that's for sure.' He grins. 'Did I mention there are no roads on the island – only a few rough tracks.'

'Why don't they build some?'

'The whole point of the place is that you're cut off from the outside world. And that includes traffic.' Seeing her expression, he says, 'Don't tell me you're getting cold feet at this stage?'

She's quick to deny it. 'No, of course not.'

'Anyway, the arrangement is we park on the mainland opposite. Which reminds me – I'm supposed to ring when we're about half an hour away so they can send a boat over to pick us up.'

'How do we get around once we're there?'

'There's a landing place just below the croft. It might take us a while to haul all our gear up to the house, but after that we're done. They've promised to lend us a boat – my guess it'll be an inflatable with an outboard. Doubt I'll be using it much, but you can potter about in it all you like.' Giving her a quick glance, he says, 'Don't go looking so worried. It'll be grand. Imagine the peace and tranquillity. It's an opportunity to cleanse your soul of everyday worries, wrapped in the bosom of nature.'

She cackles. 'The bosom of nature, is it now?'

'Seriously, was that meant to be an Irish accent?' He shakes his head.

Despite their banter, she hadn't seriously thought through the implications of life without a mobile signal. There'll be no internet to browse when she gets bored. No television. No DVDs even. She might consider herself a nature lover but will birdwatching and seal spotting fill all those gaps? She's never been at the helm of any kind of boat except a rowing boat on a lake. Even then, she'd mostly gone round in circles.

'I believe they've a couple of ponies that can be hired for the day. Right up your street, I'd imagine.' His hand leaves the wheel to chop at the air between them. 'Though I can assure you there's no way you're getting me on any kind of nag. Far as I'm concerned, they're all stubborn creatures who delight in refusing to go where you point them.'

Apropos nothing she asks, 'D'you think there'll be a radio at least?'

'Ah shite,' he says. 'Think I forgot to pack it.'

Chapter Twenty-Two

From the slipway, Eve follows the boat's progress across the sound, its bow-wave streaking the smooth surface. It has a wheelhouse and looks to be the size of a small fly-fishing boat. Behind the jetty it's just left, the land rises steeply behind a small sandy inlet. Ponies are grazing in the fenced fields above. She can make out a handful of white-painted buildings set back from the beach. The fields give way to wooded hills leading her eye up to a cluster of rocky peaks. It's hard to judge if their height officially qualifies them as mountains.

They've arrived later than planned and the daylight is beginning to fade. She phones Nick while she still has a signal, walking a short distance away and turning her back for privacy though she's sure Rory can still hear every word. While they talk, her eyes range over a haphazard pile of decaying lobster pots and a couple of rusted-through metal drums. A length of blue rope is coiled like a snake amongst a patch of weeds. A handful of bobbing boats are moored up on either side of the jetty.

It's odd she's the one describing her journey and her first

impressions of the place she's just arrived at. A case of role-re-versal. 'I wish you could see it for yourself,' she tells him. How many times had he uttered those exact same words to her? Did he mean it? Does she mean it now? It surprises her that she's not sure. 'Just sent you a couple of photos,' she tells him. 'Though they really don't do it justice. Everything here is on such a huge scale. It's hard to capture. And it makes you think about things… You know.'

'Looking at the pics right now,' he tells her. 'Scotland's as beautiful as I remember from when I was a kid. Maybe I'll pay you a surprise visit once things are more sorted this end.' They both know that's not likely to be any time soon.

The noise of the boat is growing louder – carrying across the water. Nick says something she doesn't catch. 'Sorry can you say that again – signal's a bit crap.'

'I said, everything's fine here.'

'Good. Listen, I should probably go,' she tells him despite the complete lack of urgency. 'I'll ring you again when I can get a signal. Probably won't be for a few days or so.'

'Not to worry,' he says. 'It's meant to be a retreat, after all. Besides, I know you're in safe hands,' he adds, like her hands by themselves aren't safe enough.

'Bye then,' she says. 'I love you.' He repeats the words back to her. Perhaps it's only the poor connection that makes them sound too off-pat.

She re-joins Rory. 'Just look at it all,' he says transfixed by the landscape in front of him. 'What a sight for sore eyes, eh?'

'Mine are certainly that.'

He reaches for her hand to squeeze it. Like evacuees, the

two of them wait to be collected, their sparse belongings piled up around them.

From an amorphous shape, the boat and its helmsman or helmswoman come into sharper focus. It must be a man – shoulders too broad for a woman.

The sea is gently lapping at the layers of kelp deposited along the shoreline; a pungent reminder of the life going on below the water. Limpets cling to the charcoal black rock that make up the broken shoreline. She spots a tiny crab trapped in a rockpool waiting to be liberated at high tide.

As the vessel nears, the tone of her engine alters. Finally, the boatman slams her into reverse, churning up the water before letting her come to rest against an old tyre put there to cushion first contact. Exhaust fumes catch in Eve's throat obliterating the fresh ozone smells.

Without the engine noise the sudden silence is a shock. She attunes to the distant squawk of gulls, an oystercatcher calling out as it skims the water's surface, an early bee's bumbling search for nectar.

The man throws out a rope and it lands with a slap between them. 'If you wouldn't mind doing the honours.' Rory dutifully winds it around the nearest bollard, fastening it with a knot in a way that suggests he knows what he's doing.

From his movements, the boatman would appear younger than she'd first thought. He leaps out onto the slipway. Throwing back his hood, he says, 'Glad you made it okay.' He's tall and, whilst not exactly handsome, undeniably striking. He rakes back his sun-bleached curly hair revealing its brown roots. The clothes he's wearing have been chosen for their practicality. Beneath his jacket, denim jeans are tucked into green wellies. He thrusts out his hand. 'As you've no doubt guessed, I'm Lachlan Maclintock – bit of a mouthful I know. Call me Lachlan.' She wonders if English schooling might be what's dulled his Scots' accent.

'And I'm just plain old Rory,' Rory says. 'And this is my friend, Eve.'

Lachlan shakes her hand with only slightly less vigour. 'Nice to meet you,' they both say at the same time. Grinning, his pale eyes flit down to her wedding ring and back. Eve finds herself blushing as she imagines what *he* must be imagining about what's going on here.

'Yes well, it will be dark before long, we'd better get cracking,' Lachlan says, turning his attention to their luggage. 'We can stow most of this stuff in here.' He lifts the lid of one of the wooden benches revealing a large void beneath.

On the journey over, Lachlan's boat is the only object disturbing the silent calm of the water. She glances back to the mainland and the tiny harbour they've left behind. In the fading light it's hard to pick out the various shades of the huddled cottages – officially a village, it's more the size of a hamlet. Overhead, rain-heavy clouds are prematurely darkening the sky, triggering a string of streetlights to blink on. She can just make out the roof of the BMW.

The island up ahead is showing no illumination. On reaching the shore, Lachlan jumps out to wade shin-high through the water. With the boat secured, he spreads his arms and announces, 'Welcome to Eilean Fluraichean – which is Scots Gaelic for Island of Flowers.' Like he's reciting a sales brochure, he adds, 'Through our conservation work here, we're aiming to make sure she lives up to her name.'

Back from the shore, the whitewashed buildings turn out to be a square Georgian-style farmhouse with various barns and outbuildings off to one side. This close she can see a faint glow in one of the downstairs windows. 'This is the family homestead,' he says. 'Now, if you'll just excuse me for a moment.' As an afterthought he adds, 'Stay in the boat. I just need to grab a few things before I take you on round to the Macraiths'.'

Eve frowns. 'I'm sorry, but who are the Macraiths?'

'Oh, they're the people who used to live in the croft you'll be staying in.' He grins. 'Silly really – but we still call it that even though the family are long gone.' She notes the *we* but decides not to ask him to elaborate.

He's gone for longer than she expected. Around them the landscape is darkening, the temperature dropping at an alarming rate. Checking her phone, it's a comfort to find that, this close to the mainland, she can still get 3G. She wonders if the farmhouse has all the modern services banished from their holiday cottages.

At first she thinks it's a bird, but the squawking is coming from the wheels of a barrow Lachlan is pushing towards them. 'Thought I'd better grab the outboard for your dingy while I'm here.' With some effort, he off-loads it into the boat then adds a petrol can. Next, he holds up a large tin box. 'This is some stuff you might need in case the solar panels fail. Candles, a couple of wind-up torches – that sort of thing.' He pushes the now empty wheelbarrow well away from the water's edge. 'Okay then, off we go.'

They hug the contours of the island from about fifty metres out. Here and there Eve spots a red marker buoy warning of the black rocks scattered around the steep cliffs. A slight swell rocks the boat. Waves are frothing white against every obstacle.

The engine putters along. It surprises her that the island is so heavily wooded. Once they're round the headland, the land begins to shelve more hospitably. She can pick out sheep grazing on gentler slopes and then a sandy bay which Lachlan begins to steer towards. As they near the inlet, she spots the crossed struts of a wooden jetty. She squints into blue gloom and is at last rewarded with her first glimpse of the cottage standing out stark white against the hillside. A no-nonsense sort of house with chimney stacks rising from both gables. A change of angle reveals a makeshift building tacked on to one end. To call it a conservatory would be too generous.

'So here we are then folks,' Lachlan says. 'Your home from home on Fluraichean. Much like yourselves, old Macraith was an artist. Bit of a drunkard too, by all accounts.' He chuckles. 'In its day, the island supported twenty or more households – some of them crofters, some employed to collect the kelp needed for glass making. These days ours is the only perma-nently inhabited house. We've managed to restore four of the derelict crofters' houses you'll see dotted around the island. We rent them out during the warmer months. They're popular with birdwatchers and the like. Of course, it's still early in the season, so we've no one else staying at the moment.'

He cuts the engine. 'The Macraiths' here is one of the larger ones. The old man built a decent lean-to extension on the back. Made a pretty solid job of it. As for the studio you see there – well, you didn't need any fancy permissions in those days. It's hardly a thing of beauty, but we've made sure it's sound enough. And watertight. It's still got the old Belfast sink for cleaning brushes. As you might guess, it has a fine view down to the water here.'

They all turn to gaze across the sound where, in the fast-failing light, land and water are quickly becoming indistinguishable. 'Absolutely perfect,' Rory declares with enthusiasm. He rubs his hands together in anticipation. That wouldn't be Eve's verdict. Shivering, she pulls her jacket tighter around her.

'Right, well let's get this stuff of yours offloaded,' Lachlan says. 'I'd give you a hand taking it on up to the house, but I really need to get back before it's dark.'

Chapter Twenty-Three

Alarmed by a piercing whistle, Eve's ready to leap out of bed when it subsides. That flaming kettle. Last night they'd used it to brew tea in oversized enamel mugs. She'd managed to burn baked beans on the single hotplate on top of the ungovernable wood-burning range. They'd eaten them anyway, spoiling the taste of a robust red they'd opened to celebrate what Rory referred to as *our escape*.

Though laid directly onto the floorboards, her mattress is surprisingly comfortable. At least there are proper pillows and clean white sheets. She yawns then swallows to ease her alcohol-parched throat. At this point on any normal day, she'd be checking her messages. Today her mobile is still in her rucksack, shut off to save the battery.

She lays her head back down to study the irregular lattice of ancient beams. Eyes half closed, they could be the backbone of some long-extinct dinosaur. Daylight is shining in through a dusty window set in the gable end highlighting the many spiderwebs hanging like so much lace between the rafters. No curtain across the window with no one to look in but a passing bird. In high summer it must be hard to sleep with so few hours of darkness.

Below her, Rory is clattering crockery as if on purpose. The smell of woodsmoke and bacon is rising up the stairwell. Bloody hell – not content with the kettle, Rory himself is now whistling. He pauses to warble on so many notes it takes her some time to recognise the Skye Boat Song. They're nowhere near Skye, for Christ's sake.

He bursts into song, *'Mull was astern, Rum on the port, Eigg on the starboard bow…'*

The man actually knows the words. Jared really should have warned her he was this sodding chirpy in the morning. He announces, 'Breakfast will soon be served, m'lady.'

'Thank you,' she hollers back, 'but there's no need to shout.'

'You're the one shouting. I'm speaking at a normal level. Afraid soundproofing wasn't a consideration in old Dougal Macraith's time.'

'Who told you he was called Dougal?'

'I'm guessing there had to be at least one Dougal in the family. They probably raised a dozen kids in this place. Alastair, Brodric, Craig – it's a safe bet they'd have got round to Dougal eventually.'

Eve pictures all those children lying top to toe like sardines, keeping each other warm on a cold winter's night.

He's off again with the Skye song.

Billow and breeze, islands and seas. Mountains of rain and sun.

Perhaps it had been a mistake to opt for the loft room instead of the larger back bedroom that was, after all, his by rights. Sweet of him to offer her first dibs all the same.

Needing a pee, Eve grabs her clothes and heads downstairs. She has to go through the kitchen to get to the bathroom. 'Don't be long or this'll get cold,' Rory calls after her.

Built into the bank, the bathroom walls are of rough stone but at least the fittings are new. Lachlan had explained how the water tank is heated by the kitchen range. A tiny rooflight lets in just enough light to see by. It feels like showering inside a cave. Hastily dressing, Eve heads back to the kitchen.

Breakfast is delicious and remarkably unburnt. 'Aye, I've got the measure of the beast now,' Rory tells her.

She says, 'Seeing's you cooked, I'll do the dishes.' When was the last time she washed-up by hand? At home she usually listens to the morning news; here, there's no way of discovering what might be happening in the bigger world.

Once everything is back in its place, she ventures into the lean-to studio. Rising from a short wall made up of sizable rocks, the structure is formed from a haphazard collection of window frames supported by blackened timber beams that look to have been scavenged – probably from the derelict croft houses the old man's neighbours had abandoned. Horizontal lengths of driftwood fill the spaces between. He'd stuffed odd lengths of rope into every gap to make it windproof. A couple of sawn timber beams have been recently installed to cross-brace the rest. The concrete floor looks newly laid.

Despite its unorthodox construction, the old man had obviously built it sturdy enough to withstand the storms that must regularly assault the island.

Against the gable wall of the house, there's a small potbel-lied stove, its long flue angled through the outside wall into the chimney breast it must share with the kitchen range. The room is chilly but, approaching the stove, her outstretched hand detects a small amount of heat radiating off it.

Having re-assembled his easel, Rory is scratching his head. 'I'll need to keep this stove banked up to keep everything dry in here.' He's dumped his paints and brushes on one of two wooden benches set either side of the wood-burner. Like Jackson Pollock paintings, both benches are layered with spilled paint, a telling palette of muted greys and browns with only the odd spot of blue or white.

Seen through dusty glass, herring gulls are wheeling and calling against the cliff face. She watches one swoop down to skim the water. The sun finds a gap in the clouds adding a sparkle to the water that would be seductive if you didn't know it was freezing and would stop your heart in seconds.

She pulls on Rory's arm. 'We should explore.' His reluctance makes her pull harder. 'Come on. You've lit the stove – all the rest can wait.'

Along with her jacket, she grabs binoculars and a camera and hurries down to the bay below. He's slow to follow her to the shore, lingering to inspect the inflatable housed in a corrugated tin "boathouse" that's seen better days.

Half a dozen curly-horned sheep are grazing on the foreshore. A lamb bleats for its mother and soon finds her, butting her udder before it suckles. The sheep stare at her with obvious curiosity; humans don't count for much in their world. The distinctive croak of a raven draws her attention; she watches it land on a rock shelf. Another raven is soaring above the same spot; the two might have a nest up there.

Bleached seashells litter the shoreline, so brittle they crunch and fracture beneath her feet. Amongst them she recognises the usual whelks, razor clams, mussel and oyster shells. For once there's no man-made detritus except a few fragments of sea-glass polished by the ocean. A tiny shell catches the light. Picking it up she identifies it as a whorl shell, its base mottled purple with a shiny mother-of-pearl tip. Eve slips it into her pocket for a talisman.

The smell of the sea takes her back to those seaside holidays with her family – staycations before the word had been invented. Storm tides have deposited quantities of sea wrack further along; the weather composting it to the point where it would be ready to spread on a vegetable garden – if there was one. Looking back at the cottage, for the first time she notices the remains of a tumbledown wall that must once have enclosed a garden. This far from any shops, growing your own veg would have been essential for survival.

Littering the shore are massive charcoal-coloured boulders that could have rolled down the mountainside but were probably deposited by the glacier that gouged out the sound between Fluraichean and the mainland. On a calm day like this, it's hard to imagine such dramatic forces at work. Eve perches on a rock to study the mainland from this new perspective. 'Floo-reech-en', she repeats its name, revelling in those exotic-sounding syllables.

When she turns around, the breeze catches her long hair temporarily blinding her. Holding it back, she sees Rory is some distance behind her. Hands on hips, he's scanning the seascape no doubt wondering how to capture its essence on canvas.

Having brought her camera, she's not tempted to use it. The last thing she wants to do is capture the soul of this place when the whole point here is freedom. There's a chill edge to the breeze. She shuts her eyes to concentrate on the rhythm of waves that gently exhale as they spread out over the soft white sand.

Nick would probably hate being somewhere this remote.

Hearing the crunch of footsteps, she senses Rory standing beside her. 'Glorious or what?' he says. 'Not another soul around and everything so pristine – so un-fecking-spoilt. Will you look at how clear that water is. Amazing – and only the two of us here to enjoy it all.'

She stands up to slip her arm through his. 'You were right – this is Paradise.' He starts to chuckle. 'What's so funny?'

'It just struck me the two us could almost be Adam and Eve.'

'Hmm.' She grins. 'No offence my friend, but I wouldn't give the human race much of a chance if it came down to us two to procreate.'

His laugh is unbridled. 'Point taken.' He nudges her. 'From the way he was looking at you yesterday, I'd say, if we did find ourselves facing such an existential emergency, young Lachlan Maclintock might be prepared to step up to the mark, as it were.'

Eve digs him in the ribs. 'Can't we just stand here and admire this amazing place without you having to bring sex into it?'

'Ha, but then sex is part and parcel of it.' He holds his arms aloft. 'Look around you – it's springtime. The birds and fecking bees are doing their thing wherever you look.' As if to illustrate his point, an orange tip butterfly flutters past. She watches it pause to check out a clump of dandelions and then move on.

'What did I tell you?' Rory points towards the hillside on their left. Squinting and with her hand shading her eyes, she's able to make out a horse and rider. Rory chuckles. 'Having not seen a woman his own age in years, the poor man's utterly smitten and can't keep away.'

'Stop it.'

'Well, you have to admit, Lachlan is a mighty good-looking fella. As the bard himself put it, 'Oh brave new world that has such people in't.''

'Sounds to me like you're the one that's smitten.'

'Nonsense. You're looking at an artist – an admirer of beauty in all its forms.' He laughs. 'Besides, I'd lay odds the man's as straight as they come.'

Chapter Twenty-Four

'Thought I'd stop by to check you're settling in okay,' Lachlan says, as if he'd simply pulled up in a car and not ridden a third of the way around the island. This morning he's wearing a white t-shirt under an unbuttoned red plaid shirt. He dismounts to stand gazing out to sea, making what her grandma would have called, 'a fine figure of a man'.

'I've brought you over a couple of welcome gifts from my mother.' He opens a saddlebag and extracts a small pot of honey and half a dozen eggs. 'Both homegrown, as it were.'

'That's very kind of her – of you both.' Eve pats his pony – a grey Highland stallion still shedding his thicker winter coat. His long fair mane is seductive to the touch.

'His name's Archie,' Lachlan tells her.

Like an idiot, Rory keeps trying to catch her eye. 'Thought I might have forgotten to mention that the water in the cottage comes from a spring,' Lachlan says. 'Don't be alarmed if it looks a wee bit off-putting at times. It can take on a faint brownish shade from the peat it passes through. All perfectly natural, I assure you. We have it regularly tested.'

Eve notices a dimple amongst the pale brown stubble on his chin. Taking a step back ostensibly to size up his pony, she says, 'What is he – about 14 hands?'

'A smidgin over. And ideal for this type of tricky terrain. Archie may look more suited to a child, but he'll happily bear the weight of a full-grown adult.' His eyes stray towards Rory. 'Up to about twenty stone, that is.'

'Eve is a *keen* horsewoman,' Rory says. 'Never been partial to them myself. I grew up by the sea in County Kerry. We moved from Dingle to Dublin when I was fourteen, thank the Lord. I'm more than happy pottering around on the water but overland, over rough ground like this, I'd choose a quad bike over a nag any day.'

'We're all about sustainability here so I try not to use the quad if I can help it,' Lachlan tells him. 'Horses are also more reliable.'

He points to the outline of a derelict stone cottage squatting on the hillside some distance away. Saplings have colonised the two gable ends left standing. He looks at Eve. 'According to my dad, Anndra Brothaigh, the crofter who used to live in that cottage over there, once kept a filly he claimed was one of the last pure Eriskays.' From his expression it's clear she ought to be impressed. 'Although I have to say my dad was never entirely convinced.'

'Eriskay? Can't say I've ever heard of that breed,' she tells him.

'They're native to the island of the same name.' Seeing their blank expressions, he adds, 'In the Outer Hebrides. Sadly, they're still critically endangered. Back in the day, they were the traditional workhorse of the island crofters. At one point – this was back in the early seventies – they thought there were no purebred Eriskay stallions left alive.'

'Bummer,' Rory says.

'But then, fortunately, they found one over on South Uist. And you know, from just that one stallion, they've been able to build up the numbers. Though there are still fewer than 300.' He smiles. 'Eriskay's human population is only around half that these days.'

'Funny you should mention extinct breeds,' Rory says. 'Before you arrived, Eve and I were just talking about what might be necessary to bring a population back from the brink of extinction.'

She gives Rory a warning look.

'In a nutshell, that's what were all about here,' Lachlan says. 'We might not have a machair like some of the bigger islands, but we desperately want to encourage more wildflowers in the grassland we do have. The sheep you see here have done a great job keeping it grazed over winter. You'll see the shepherds rounding them up shortly; this time of year, they get shipped off back to the mainland. We're looking to buy half a dozen whitehaired shorthorn heifers to do some conservation grazing.'

'Fascinating.' It would be hard to miss the edge Rory gives the word.

'Well, I won't keep you,' Lachlan says. 'I also came to warn you we're due for bit of a storm later tonight. According to the Met Office we should expect gusts up to force ten. Time to batten down the hatches, so to speak.'

'Thanks for the warning,' Eve says.

'I meant to pack a radio so we could get the shipping forecast,' Rory tells him.

Lachlan frowns. 'There ought to be a wind-up one in the tall cupboard next to the sink. Perhaps I should just come in and take a look...'

'Don't bother yourself.' Rory lightly touches the man's chest to stop his advance. 'I'm sure we can find it for ourselves.'

'In that case, I'll leave you to it.' Lachlan swings a leg over his pony. Adjusting the reins, he says, 'You'll find various maps of the island in the cottage. Best to stick to the main tracks – at least until you get your bearings. Hope you enjoy exploring.'

He turns his horse around. 'If you fancy a bit of pony trekking, Eve, you'll need to call round to the farm. We'll be more than happy to find you a suitable mount.' Before he rides away, he adds, 'One of us always accompanies guests just in case they or their pony were to find themselves in difficulties. You can't call for back-up out here.'

He's barely out of earshot when Rory says. 'And with that the man heroically rides off into the hills like a young Clint Eastwood.' He shakes his head. 'Although, that wee nag lends him a touch of the Sancho Panzas.'

When it hits, the strength of the storm is formidable. Like a ship tossed at sea, the cottage trembles and creaks under the force of each new gust. Dry lightning illuminates the sea in a succession of almighty flashes that leave their momentary imprint on her retinas. Unable to sleep through the uproar, the two of them watch the spectacle through a downstairs window. When the rain comes it pounds on the roof with no let up.

At home Eve barely notices storms, here it feels like she's inside an enormous drum. It moves closer until there's no discernible interval between the zigzagging flashes and the thunderclaps. Rory cries out, 'Jeez, that was close' when lightning strikes something nearby. 'One thing's for certain,' he says over the noise, 'there's no way you can ignore the elements living here.'

She shakes her head unable to hear what he says next. He leans into her ear, warming her face with his breath. 'I said I wonder what old Dougie Macraith and his mob would make of a storm like this? D'you think they'd be kneeling here offering up prayers for their salvation?'

'Possibly,' she shouts back, though it seems to her they'd simply be thankful to be under shelter and not caught out on some mountainside a long way from home.

They brew tea while the storm continues to crash and flash overhead. After an hour of bombardment the front begins to move on, though there's no let-up from the wind. The kitchen's central light swings back and forth while they find the maps Lachlan mentioned and spread them out on the planked kitchen table.

'I thought I noticed the remains of a little church when we were on the boat.' She points to it on the map. 'It's not that far. Maybe we could walk over to it in the morning?'

'Going by those contour lines, it looks like quite some hike.' Rory purses his lips. 'Don't know about you, but I'll still be catching up on my sleep in the morning. If you're champing at the bit to explore then, to contradict the late great George Michael, *don't* wake me up before you go-go.'

Leaving Rory snoring, she sets out having taken the precaution of stuffing one of the maps in her rucksack along with a bottle of water, binoculars and some fruit. The sun is shining, the sky swept-clear by the storm. Across the sapphire water of the sound, a soft mist is rolling over the high peaks as if those extinct volcanoes might still be smoking. The ground's been made soft and muddy, the track puddled to such an extent it's necessary to take a running leap over the widest. She sticks to the snaking path breathing in the heady coconut scent of gorse now in full bloom.

Pausing for breath after a steep climb, Eve studies her expanded view. The wind feels sharper now. Last night's ferocity forgotten, the sea sparkles between white-crested waves. A frothy tide breaks against the rocks. Her path is lined with mauve cuckoo flowers and a few stray bluebells. All around rose-purple heather is still in bloom. She's reminded of the evening they'd spent at Jared and Rory's. The way Nick had looked at her as he strummed his guitar. In a terrible Scottish accent, he'd burst into a song that had her giggling.

Will ye go lassie go?
And we'll all go together
To pick wild mountain thyme
All around the blooming heather

They'd been drunk and in high spirits with no inclination of what would hit them the next morning. And now here she is standing on a mountainside alone amongst the still-blooming heather.

Eve straightens her shoulders and continues along the path. Lachlan's farmhouse remains stubbornly out of sight – half a mountain is in the way. Down on the shores of the next bay, a couple of whitewashed cottages stand out against the hillside, renovated in readiness for fair-weather visitors.

Not a soul in sight; Eve can't remember the last time she was so utterly alone. It might be possible to get a signal at this height, but she'd stowed her near-useless mobile in her bedside drawer back at the cottage. In any case, what more is there to say to Nick? Up here, in this moment, the many questions hanging over their future couldn't seem more irrelevant. What's to stop them leaving it all behind and starting a new life somewhere?

A grazing ewe lumbers across the track in front of her, two sprightly lambs tagging along behind. Overhead, a cry alerts her to a bird of prey circling on the thermals. Too big for a buzzard, it looks like a golden eagle. Her binoculars confirm it – the profile of its wings, the head with that hooked beak are unmistakeable. She watches the bird adjust its wings to hover like a kestrel in mid-air before it dives as if in freefall. She can't see where it lands, what its prey might have been. A consummate, magnificent killer. How wonderfully free such a life must be.

Further up, the path narrows and becomes rockier. It takes her the best part of an hour to make it over the crest of the hill and on down to the remains of the tiny church.

Defying gravity, the empty bell tower stands out against the sky. Ferns have colonised its walls, clinging like seaweed to a wreck. The ruin remains the hub for several tracks spanning the island. Men, women and children, dressed in their best clothes, once must have made their way here every Sunday morning, come rain or shine.

The interior still holds a few straight-backed pews. She steps on threshold stones worn hollow by generations of worshippers all long gone. Further in, broken glass litters the slabs under her boots. Eve shivers. The smell of damp and decay is overpowering. Amongst its stone walls, the interwoven roots of an ash tree cling for life amongst so much collapsed masonry. The branches of the canopy look to be propping up the building's few remaining rafters. Buds swollen, it's about to come into leaf.

A flight of crumbling steps leads to a plinth where the altar must once have stood. Across it scattered shards of coloured glass catch the light – the remains of a stained-glass panel the tiny church must surely have struggled to afford. The congregation would have looked up at it in hope of deliverance.

She tries to imagine the building restored to its former solidity and full of crofter families singing God's praises, thanking the Lord for the ongoing harshness of their lives along with the incomparable, unspoilt beauty surrounding them every day. Did any of them envisage a time when their precious smallholding – the few acres of land they daily struggled to tame despite everything the weather could throw at them – would lie abandoned and forgotten along with this church?

Head bent, Eve stares down at the dark mould beneath her boots and weeps for all that is lost.

Chapter Twenty-Five

Days pass; they fall into separate routines. Around seven-thirty they share a simple breakfast at the kitchen table. Just before nine Rory normally stands up, mug of coffee in hand, and heads off into the studio with a 'See you later'. This was meant to be his annual retreat. Inviting her here was an afterthought – an experiment she hopes he's not regretting. For that reason, she never ventures into the studio unless invited and takes care to allow him as much solitude as he appears to want. Which is a lot. Though different in so many ways, Nick and Rory have that in common – the same single-minded dedication to their craft.

Her Kindle is loaded with books, her phone with worthy podcasts, but none of that seems relevant anymore. Most days she simply wanders wherever fancy takes her, no longer navigating by maps but by what she's seen in different places. A rocky outcrop turns out to be a favourite basking place for seals; a tiny kelp-lined bay where she often hears the peep-like whistles of cavorting otters, a high peak where she's most likely to spot a pair of white-tailed sea-eagles, their outstretched wings the size of barn doors.

While her days are serene, her dreams are anything but. Roused by the throb of the shower pump or the kettle's siren whistle, she often wakes with a sense of fear and foreboding. More than once, in a fading vision, a half-hidden figure had been about to step out from the shadows.

The weather settles into a pattern of intermittent sunshine interspersed with sea mists and drizzle. She can lose hours simply exploring the cove below the cottage – *her beach* as she's come to think of it. Barefoot and up to her knees and even thighs in freezing water, she studies the contents of rockpools or combs the shore for unusual shells. At first her training as a biologist leads her to photograph what she discovers; after a few days she leaves her camera behind – it gets in the way of simply observing. Increasingly, her thoughts turn only to the changing colours and moods of the sea, the way wet sand or sharp rocks or slippery weed feel underfoot.

Set back from the high-tide line, one rock becomes her favourite seat. Its smooth surface persuades her that others must have sat there looking out over the sound towards the distant forests and mountains of the mainland. Old Macraith himself? Or maybe his wife? Or a restless, adolescent child longing for excitement?

'Don't know about you, but my appetite for baked beans and tinned fecking soup is rapidly waning,' Rory declares after supper one evening.

'Now that you mention it, I'm developing a bit of a rash on this arm.' She holds the patch up for his inspection. 'Seeing's it's too early for midges, I'm beginning to suspect it could be scurvy.'

Rory chuckles. 'Joking aside,' he says, 'Lachlan did mention we can buy veg from their polytunnel. And we're almost out of eggs. I'd also like to check in with Jared. We should get a phone signal on that part of the island.' His eyes remain on her. 'And I imagine you'll be wanting to phone Nick.'

'Yes, of course.' In truth she's been so preoccupied she's hardly thought about him.

'Good. If we set off early, I can be back here by mid-morning.'

'What do you mean – *I* can be back here. Are you planning to ditch me?'

'Oh, I'm assuming you'll be wanting to borrow one of their nags and go riding off into the sunset with our handsome host.'

'You know, you can be really childish at times,' she tells him. 'Anyway, now that you mention it, I wouldn't mind a ride.' When he starts to snigger, she digs him in the ribs.

'Ouch!' He's so well-padded she knows he's play-acting. 'Right then, we're grand,' Rory says, slapping the table before he gets to his feet. 'Think I'll go and get the RIB ready for action before it gets dark.'

It's her first time in the dingy. Rory had taken it out fishing a couple of times though he'd returned empty handed and cursing his luck. The boat is big enough to take a half dozen passengers at a squeeze. Eve is reassured by the inflatable's ridged hull. In any case, the sea is dead calm. 'Smooth as a baby's arse,' Rory declares.

Viewed from the water, the island appears smaller. The thrum of their outboard motor cuts into the tranquillity. Rory steers her well away from the string of red buoys marking the many submerged rocks that might tear her apart.

A few more minutes and Lachlan's farmhouse comes into sight. Its jetty pointing towards the mainland, the farmhouse directly facing the row of cottages spread out along the opposite shore. Turning to scan the mainland, Eve picks out a red telephone box, the shining roof of a car travelling along the road that runs behind the village.

Rory nudges her. 'Good to see the BMW's still where I left it.' Two figures are line-fishing off the harbour wall. Ordinarily, she would describe such a village as remote and yet, after two weeks of near solitude, it seems a veritable hive of activity compared to Fluraichean.

They're nearing Lachlan's place. Rory cuts the engine, and they drift towards the beach. Jumping out, the two of them pull the dingy well clear of the high-water mark.

Rory takes his mobile from his pocket and holds it up to check the signal. '3G – should be good enough. You know I'm almost forgetting how to use this thing.'

'Say hello from me,' she says moving away to give him privacy. Having no doubt heard their approach, Lachlan is already walking their way. The two of them must look ridiculous, backs turned like they've had a row and are muttering grievances into their phones.

Nick greets her with his usual, 'Hi there, sweetheart. How's it all going?'

'Fine,' she says. 'Good in fact. I have to tell you I'm falling hopelessly in love with this island. Can't explain what an amazing, almost magical, place it is.'

'Sounds great, Evie. Glad to hear you're enjoying yourself.' Should she take this at face value?

'That's my news in a nutshell,' she says, 'What about you? How're things going?' His sigh is heavy – a burden he's about to pass to her. And he does. She can picture him rubbing away at the creases on his forehead as he tells her the latest developments in what he calls *the case* as if it were a valise and not a bitter dispute about the truth of what really happened one night in Berlin. 'They're still following up on a few leads. Frida – our PI over in Germany – has been in touch with some of her shadier contacts. She's hinting they might be able to link Lina Wolff with someone they describe as *significant*.'

Above her head a black-backed gull heckles her with its piercing cries. Blocking one ear she says, 'Sorry, I missed that last bit. Who are they trying to link her to?'

'She won't say until she can confirm it. Although it's crossed my mind Frida could be stringing things out to increase her fee.' She hears barking in the background. The security guards must still be there. Nick says, 'Aside from that, there's been little progress since you left.' He goes quiet and she wonders if she's lost the connection. 'I ought to warn you that some journo phoned here asking for you. He's looking into what happened to your parents. Can't imagine what he hopes to discover after all this time.'

She can feel her chest tightening. Nick gives a heavy sigh. 'And there's been more muck-raking about the band. On top of that, they're now speculating about your disappearance.'

'What are they saying?'

'I'm sure you can take a wild guess. Look, with luck some

big new story will come along, and they'll start to lose interest.'

'Should I come back?'

'God no.' His tone couldn't be more emphatic. 'You're far better off up there away from it all. Listen, I should go. Kendra's trying to call me. It might be important.'

'Okay. Well, love you lots.'

'Yeah, me too.'

'Take care.'

'Bye, sweetheart.' And he's gone.

Lachlan is all smiles as he comes to greet them. Dressed in denims and a black t-shirt, his bare forearms are surprisingly tanned. Squinting into the sun, he says, 'Good to see you both. Hope everything's okay.'

Eve struggles to adjust her focus. 'Couldn't be better except we've both had enough of canned food.' Rory's still deep in conversation. 'Can we buy some veg – that's if you've got some to spare?'

'Well, let's see now, I can offer you any amount of purple sprouting and spring cabbage. We've plenty of salad leaves and so forth in the polytunnel and so much rhubarb we're getting heartily sick of it. Oh, and eggs of course.'

'Yes please. The eggs you gave us had almost dayglow orange yolks and tasted so good.'

Rory finishes his call. 'Jared sends his love,' he tells her. 'Good to see you again, Lachlan.'

A fair-haired boy of about eight runs out from somewhere. Tousling his hair, Lachlan says, 'The lady here was just asking about eggs.' Turning to Eve, 'Let me introduce you to Breac – our poultry manager. I'm afraid you'll have to negotiate a price with him and, I warn you, he's been known to drive a hard bargain.' Faced with strangers, the boy hides his head against Lachlan's side.

'My name's Rory and I've not been known to bite,' Rory says. 'Mind you, I can't say the same about Eve here – she may look ordinary enough, but I've a growing suspicion she's actually a bit of a sea witch in disguise.' He raises both hands to wiggle his fingers monster-style.

The boy giggles. Still clinging to Lachlan's leg, he says, 'No one at my old school could say my name properly. They called me Breech or Breeches.' He shrugs. 'I got used to it.'

Eve squats down to even up their heights. 'Bre-ACH. Is that right?'

'Not bad,' Lachlan tells her.

'Well, Breac, your dad says you're the official poultry manager. Would it be okay by you if we bought some of your eggs?'

The boy laughs. 'Uncle Lachlan's not my dad. My proper dad buggered off when I was a ween.'

'Hey – watch your language, tich,' Lachlan tells him. Turning to them, 'Breac's my sister Aileen's boy.'

'But Mum's in a clinic so she can't look after me.'

'Oh right.' To relieve the awkwardness, Eve says, 'Anyway, I'd love to take a look at those chickens of yours.'

'I've got twelve hens and two cocks,' the boy explains. Eve shoots Rory a look for sniggering.

'They're mostly Scots Dumpies,' Lachlan says, 'a very old breed sometimes known as creepies or crawlers due to their remarkably short legs.'

The boy sighs. 'The cockerels are being very stupid just now.

They keep fighting each other.' He shakes his head. 'Grandma says one will be for the pot if they don't stop.'

'As you'll no doubt learn when you're a wee bit older,' Rory says, 'the males of any species find it hard to tolerate love rivals.'

At the mention of love, the boy pulls a face. Rory asks, 'D'you mind if we take a look at these wee creepie-crawly hens of yours?'

Breac sniggers then nods. He points a grimy finger at them. 'Now, if the cockerels go for your heels, you just have to turn round and shout at them.'

'They're all show,' Lachlan adds. 'Big cowards, really.'

'Okay, got it,' Eve tells the boy. Finally detaching himself from his uncle's leg, he leads them across the beach towards a small wooden shack to one side of the main house. A hen is making one hell of a racket to let the rest know she's laying an egg. As ever, it sounds painful.

Dropping back a couple of steps, Eve whispers to Rory, 'Don't you go making any inappropriate jokes.'

'What, about the wee boy's two cocks?' He chuckles. 'Perish the thought.'

With the veg and eggs on board, they wave Rory off. 'See you shortly,' Eve tells him.

'No need to rush on my account,' he shouts back. 'Enjoy your ride. It's a fine day for it.'

At the sound of his name being called, the boy runs into the farmhouse. The voice of an unseen woman.

Lachlan goes off to the stables then reappears leading two ponies. Suddenly self-conscious, Eve watches Rory's boat round the next promontory and disappear.

'Meet Flora,' Lachlan says. She pats the pony – a docile chestnut filly roughly half a hand shorter than Archie. Both ponies have long silver manes that hang like curtains over their eyes. Their untrimmed tails reach almost to the ground – handy for shooing away the clouds of midges and flies likely to plague them later in the year.

Lachlan mounts his pony in one athletic movement. 'I thought we might have a bit of a gallop along the shore before we head up through the trees over there.'

'Sounds good to me.' From the saddle, Eve adds, 'I'm in your hands.' She wishes she could re-phrase that last statement.

It's exhilarating to be splashing through the waves. The sky has cleared to unbroken china blue and with it the temperature is rising fast. When they finally plunge into the woodland, it's a relief to be under its relative shade. Sure-footed, her pony has a steady-as-you-go gait, happy to follow Archie's lead with no encouragement needed.

The trail they're on winds uphill until, at last, they reach a treeless peak – a clearing with breath-taking 180-degree views. Along with the wooded slopes of the mainland, several smaller islands are now visible. The sea shimmers beneath them; navy at the horizon it fades to pure turquoise nearer the shore. The sweet smell of gorse is everywhere. They could be on some faraway exotic island. 'Wow,' she says, dismounting. 'What an astounding view.'

'I expect you've noticed the way it changes all the time – hour by hour, day by day. There's always something different you've never spotted before.' He jumps down from his horse to stand beside her. 'Living here, you might think you'd grow tired of it, but I never do. Other people – well that's a different matter.'

She's moved to ask, 'Have you lived here all your life?'

'Good Lord no. I grew up on the mainland near Inverness. Boarded at Gordonstoun until the money rather dramatically ran out. Got lots of stick when I moved to the local comp.' He rakes back his hair – a gesture that reminds her of Nick. 'Took the usual gap year after school, which I extended for another year and then another after that. I spent time in Thailand – bit of a cliché I know. Then Japan and then China briefly. I came into some money courtesy of my great aunt Jeanie. Dad inherited the lion's share and, solvent again, he bought this island. Meanwhile, I flew to Singapore then on to Sydney. Got a job in a bar for a bit.' He clutches his chest. 'Got my heart broken yet again and so I tagged along with some people who were off to Paris. It was a bit tricky getting work until I learnt some French – enough to get by that is.' His expression grows more serious. 'Then out of the blue my dad had a stroke. And so, I rushed back here to help Mum out. Only intended to stay until he was up and about again. But then I got heavily involved with all the conservation work he'd started and, well, it pulled me right in.'

He turns to face her. 'I've been accused of settling for what's easy. But the thing is, this island and what we're trying to achieve here – it's so much more than that. And none of it's easy, I can assure you.' Dipping his head, he says, 'Sorry. I get carried away at times – a touch too evangelical for most people's liking.'

'I'm not most people,' she tells him.

He gives her a slow smile. 'I can see that.' She's first to break eye contact. Lachlan clears his throat. 'You know I don't usually bore our guests with my life story. Comes with having so few people to talk to.'

'There's no need to do that,' she says.

'Do what?'

'Make light of things.'

'Maybe it's preferable to letting things get serious.' He holds her gaze, questions in his eyes. 'Anyway, we'd best move on,' he says, 'or Rory will be wondering where we've got to.'

'He's not my lover,' she says too quickly. 'I mean – just in case you'd got that impression. He has a loving husband at home.' It's the perfect moment to add something about her own loving husband but she doesn't want to talk about Nick or any of the subjects it might lead on to.

Looking around she notices Flora has wandered off to graze some distance away. When Lachlan gives a soft whistle, the pony's head goes up and she trots back to stand at his side. 'You've trained her well,' she says.

Lachlan beams. 'Thank you. I do my best. My dad was the real horse whisperer. Broke his heart when he had to give it up.' Shaking his head, he says, 'You've heard more than enough about me for one day.'

He turns his horse to face the trail. 'Time I showed you some more of Fluraichean's hidden gems.' He nudges his pony's sides, and they begin the descent.

Chapter Twenty-Six

Dismounting, Eve elects to walk the last mile or so. 'I'm sure you've got lots of things you need to be getting on with,' she tells Lachlan.

'A never-ending list,' he admits. 'But I have to say this made a pleasant change. Would you like to fix up another session? I'd be happy to bring Flora to you next time. We could head further round the coast. There's a freshwater loch where the sea eagles like to fish. It's quite a sight.'

She strokes Flora's muzzle before patting her side. 'I'd really like that.'

'Also, you should be able to get a 4G signal from the top of the ridge that overlooks the loch.'

'I'm afraid that's hardly an incentive.'

'I see. Well, your call.' He laughs. 'Or not.'

'You know I'd rather not fix a time right now.' Even to her own ears this sounds absurd; it's not like she can claim some prior engagement.

'Okay – well you know where we are. This was fun. See you soon, I hope.' His fair hair catches the light as he rides away.

She takes off her shoes and socks, glad of the feel of damp sand under her feet as she follows the beach around. Getting to the tricky bits, she rolls up her trousers and lets the cooling water of the incoming tide creep up to her ankles. Weed drifts over her feet brushing her skin like a passing eel. A line of cormorants flies past, skimming the surface of the water. Yesterday she would have eagerly followed their flight but today she finds it impossible to banish thoughts of Nick and what he's going through. Although he'd effectively told her to not to come back, is it fair to be enjoying herself like this when she ought to be at home?

The sand runs out leaving her to hop from rock to rock until she reaches *her* beach. Balancing on one foot, she spots Rory standing at his easel outside the cottage. Coming closer, she notices a couple of his half-finished paintings have been propped up to dry against the wall of the house.

She dawdles along the shore picking up shells and then a piece of sea glass; polished to an aquamarine colour, today it matches the sea. Smooth to the touch, she turns it in her fingers like a worry bead.

Once she's in earshot, Rory calls out. 'Lost your horse?'

'So let me guess, you couldn't get a bite,' she shouts back.

Closer she can see his palette knife is poised ready for action. Squinting, he gives her an appraising glance. 'That ride has certainly brought some colour to those cheeks of yours.'

'Entirely down to exercise – and the sun.' Along the garden wall, a series of watercolour sketches have been weighed down by pebbles.

'Ever heard of Joan Eardley?' Rory asks.

She wrinkles her nose. 'Don't think so.'

'She was a wonderful painter; died tragically young back in the sixties. I'm not especially keen on her portraits, but I've been a big fan of her Scottish landscapes since art school. Eardley famously worked outside whatever the weather threw at her. As you know, I'm not nearly as hardly myself, but on a day like this…'

Eve frowns at the lumpy red paint balanced on his palette knife. He could be about to do some plastering. 'Seems like a strange colour choice. Have you mixed something in with that?'

'I have indeed. Eardley liked to incorporate elements of the landscape, sand and grit and that sort of thing, into the paint itself. I'm doing much the same. Don't worry about the colour, this is only the base layer. I'll be painting over it all once it's dry.'

She walks around behind him to view the canvas. He could be smearing entrails over the whole thing. 'Oh God.' She clutches her chest unable to breathe.

'Eve, darling…'

She avoids the mix of horror and sympathy in his eyes. 'It's fine,' she says. 'Really. I'm okay.' She shrinks from his outstretched gory fingers. 'You know I think I'll head inside. Probably had more than enough of this sun for one day.'

Eve steps into the relative gloom of the cottage and hurries up the steep stairs to the seclusion of her bedroom. The sun is streaming through the high window casting a golden parallelogram across her bed. She takes out her phone glad to be rid of its weight in her pocket. About to stuff it back into the drawer, she notices a whole load of messages and emails the spinning wheel must have picked up before it lost signal. Tempted to ignore the lot, she nonetheless scrolls through them in case anything jumps out as urgent.

Someone named Chetwin Lange is asking her to get in touch. The name seems familiar. In the first paragraph he tells her he's an investigative journalist. She doesn't read the rest. How the hell had he got hold of her email address? Like it's red hot, she drops the phone onto the bed. 'Bugger off and leave me alone.'

Rory's head is level with the floor. 'I was only going to ask if you fancied a glass of lemonade.'

'That wasn't aimed at you.'

His eyes swivel back and forth. 'Hate to break it to you, but I'm the only other person here.'

She smiles down at him. 'You know what, I'd love some lemonade. Might even help stave off the scurvy.'

'Afraid it's the bottled kind. Sad to say, I doubt it's been anywhere near a real lemon.'

In the late afternoon the sound of an approaching engine cuts into her thoughts. Has to be a boat; the noise so alien she imagines a landing party about to bang on the door. Could be a passing fishing boat over from the mainland. It grows louder before it fades away and then stops abruptly. It must have dropped anchor somewhere further round the island.

Eve wakes with a start, heart thumping; her vision mottled with a darkness that's slow to clear. She tries to orientate herself. Through the high window clouds are racing past. The drone of the shower pump cuts out. Rory is singing.

She takes deep breaths. All that therapy and now, when she's at her most relaxed for years, the dreams are back with a vengeance. The details are already lost leaving only impressions and one image – the classic shadowy face pressed up against a window looking in. Try as she might, she can't see his features. All the same she's certain he's no stranger.

Downstairs Rory embarks on a loud and characteristically unique interpretation of "Get the Party Started". If she'd known, she would have brought some noise cancelling headphones with her. As it is, she can only stuff a pillow over her head.

Chapter Twenty-Seven

It's almost a week since they stocked up with veg. After breakfast Rory says, 'Thought I might take the boat out tomorrow, call in at the farm for supplies and then maybe stop off to do a spot of fishing. How d'you fancy a nice fat trout for supper? Third time lucky and all that.' He gives her a curious look. 'You're coming with me, right?'

'Maybe.'

'Come on. Our friend Lachlan must be champing at the bit to see you.'

Seeing her expression, he says, 'Ah, don't mind me – just a bit of craic. Granted, the man's dashing enough to turn anyone's head, and no one could accuse him of not being passionate about his work, but I'm sure his intentions are entirely honourable.'

'What, and mine aren't?'

'Like I said, I'm just joshing with you. Got to make your own entertainment around here.'

'Then might I suggest you concentrate on catching a bloody fish.'

After advising Rory about the most likely spots to bag a trout, Lachlan suggests they explore the far side of the island and the sea loch he mentioned. His description of their route sounds arduous and challenging and for the first time he insists she wear a riding hat.

Today his shirt is pale blue. Did he choose it to match his eyes or did someone else? While they're tacking up, he shoots her a look she can't fathom. Examining the dull sky above them, he says, 'Rain's forecast for later but I think we should be okay.'

She needn't have worried, where Brandy might have slipped, the sure-footed ponies take everything in their stride. With Lachlan up ahead leading the way, for the first hour or so there's little need or opportunity to talk.

They come to a narrow wooden bridge over a fast-flowing river. Despite her encouragement, Flora straightens her legs and refuses to cross. Already over, Lachlan comes back on foot to help. 'She spooked here the last time. I think it's something about the sound of rushing water.'

Eve dismounts. He takes a firm hold of the pony's bridle and, with a lot of encouragement, persuades her across. When Eve goes to take the reins back, their hands touch – a momentary graze nothing more, and yet the sensation of his skin against hers lingers on.

Back in the saddle, he doesn't move off straight away. 'You know I'm really glad you decided to call round,' he says. 'The other day – I felt we'd made a connection. But then I thought perhaps I might have put you off. People come here for peace and solitude, not to hear me jabbering on.'

She grins. 'I can handle a bit of jabbering now and again.'

'Well, in any case, just because I pretty much told you my *entire* life story, I don't want you to feel obliged to open up about yourself. I mean, I'd be more than happy to listen if you did. What I'm trying to say is, whatever brought you here – it's frankly none of my business.'

'You're right,' she says, 'it isn't.' She hadn't meant to be quite so blunt. Without a word in response, he leads her on the winding climb towards the summit.

When they finally break out of the tree cover, she sees they've reached the vantage point he'd mentioned with its astounding view of the freshwater loch and beyond. Through binoculars she scans the sky for the promised sea-eagles but with no luck. In any case, the vista is sublime – well worth the climb by itself. 'This island just keeps on giving,' she says. 'It's going to be hard to leave.'

'That's what we like to hear.' His smile drops. 'I'm afraid you won't have the place totally to yourselves from now on. Four more guests arrived yesterday. You might have seen me ferrying them over.'

'Ah yes. I did hear a boat.'

'They're a small group of middle-aged men. Don't worry – we vet everybody in advance, make sure there are no criminals and that sort of thing.' He chuckles. 'They're here for a bit of nature watching. Keen hikers too, apparently. I put them in the two cottages around the next bay from yours.' He points to the far left. 'The ones with the red tin roofs down there.'

'I see.' She tries to smile as if she doesn't mind.

The horses hear it first, ears pricked both are spooked and

need reining in. A quiet motor getting louder. And closer. Something glints in the sky above their heads. A low-flying drone. While they watch, it circles back around.

'Oh shit,' she says, 'it's photographing us.'

Lachlan gives it an unconcerned wave. 'That'll be Gordon Henderson's drone. He promised to take some ariel footage for our website a few weeks back. I was planning to phone him about it, but he's beaten me to it.'

'You have a website. The internet?'

'Of course. How else would people book a holiday here?' A sheepish grin. 'Slight confession – we also have a television although that's mainly because we're home schooling Breac at the moment. At least that's our excuse.'

Seeing her expression, he frowns. 'No need to look so worried. From above, all they'll see is the top of your riding hat. You could be anyone, Eve.'

'How d'you know that thing up there belongs to this Gordon bloke?'

He purses his lips. 'Well strictly speaking I don't, not for sure. But honestly I can't think of anyone else who'd want to take footage of the island.'

The drone comes back around – makes a lower pass this time. Eyes wild, the ponies twist and turn under their control. Lachlan gestures for it to back off. 'I expect he wants to illustrate how you can go riding. Listen, if you're bothered, I'd be happy to show you his footage before we put it online. I'll make sure no one recognises you if that's what you're worried about.'

She stares down at him. 'So, you know who I am?'

He looks away. 'Rory passed on your details when he contacted me to let me know you'd be staying with him.'

'I see.'

He shakes his head. 'We offer a retreat here. Our guests appreciate the fact that they're cut off from the media and so on. It's a bit different when you live here all year round. I confess I also read newspapers and magazines on my iPad.'

The drone moves on at last – its wasp-like buzz slow to fade. While the horses have regained their composure, Lachlan certainly hasn't. His head drops. 'Like I said before, I totally respect your desire for privacy.' He hesitates. 'Forgive me for speaking out of turn but you're a strikingly attractive woman, Eve. You have the sort of face people remember. I swear I didn't recognise you when you first arrived. Unfortunately, this last week it would be hard to miss seeing your photo.'

'Why only this last week?'

A look of horror crosses his face. 'Shit! Me and my sodding big mouth.' He jumps down from his horse and comes over to take hold of her reins. Looking up at her, he says, 'Listen, I can see this place has been working its magic on you. Forget I said anything.'

'Too late.'

She takes her mobile out of her pocket and checks for a signal. 4G and loads of bars. The next second, a crazy number of emails and messages hit her inbox. 'I have Google,' she tells him.

He reaches to cover the screen with his hand. 'Trust me, you're better off not knowing.'

'Let me be the judge.' All the same she hesitates. Fear grips her gut, making her want to throw up. 'Why don't you give me the edited version?'

'Are you sure?'

She nods.

'Okay, well, in essence. Shit this is really hard.' He checks her eyes. 'Are you certain you want—'

'Just tell me for Christ's sake.'

'Okay. Well, this last week a lot of me-too type stuff has come out about your husband and his bandmates. Several more women have come forward with, um, allegations.'

'What type of allegations?'

'Sexual assault, harassment and so on – some of it going back years. There's been talk of some sort of class action. And –'

'Go on.'

'And speculation that you've left your husband because of it.'

She takes off her hat. Shuts her eyes. Nick must have known this was about to break. That's why he was so insistent she stay where she is. Hear no evil, see no evil – hadn't that always been her way? Their way.

Lachlan holds his hands up. 'I hesitate to suggest it, but it's possible these women could be mistaken or exaggerating.' He looks unconvinced. 'Of course, if they're not, well...'

She can't suppress a sob that turns into a scream of outrage. Beneath her Flora rears before Lachlan pulls her back. Eve drops from the saddle onto her feet.

Blocking out the sun, he lifts her head until she's looking straight into those blue eyes of his. 'It could be nonsense.' When she begins to weep, he pulls her into his chest.

It's not long before she breaks away, strokes his shirt as if that might dry it. Though she can't hear it, that sodding drone could still be filming them. What he says next is drowned out by Archie lifting his head to whinny his impatience.

Lachlan leads the horses over to a small stream to drink. 'This morning you looked utterly carefree. If only I'd kept my flaming mouth shut...'

She notices the curled shoots of the emerging bracken. 'I suppose I wanted to believe Nick. I thought, you know, it was plausible this Lina Wolff woman might have some sort of grievance against the band.'

Eve sniffs back tears, wiping her nose with the back of her hand. 'A fan scorned and all that. He told me he could prove it was lies; that he never even went to the club where it was supposed to have happened.

'I've known him since school. We got together when I'd just turned twenty. He's been there through some awful times. For me, it's only ever been him. I was sure I knew him well enough to know if he was lying to me. He swore it was all made up...'

She takes the crumpled tissue Lachlan offers and blows her nose. A sudden weariness makes her sit down on a mossy bank. Everywhere she looks the landscape is awe-inspiring. Unspoilt. Eve's head swims with its blues and greens. 'I don't know what to believe anymore.'

'Remember some people are opportunist. The band must have made a great deal of money and that makes them a target. These women – of course they could all be telling the truth. But, on the other hand, they might sniff a massive pay-out in the offing.'

'No.' She pinches the bridge of her nose, tries out a weak smile. 'I can't defend him any longer.'

'I'm so sorry.'

'Don't be.' She covers his hand with hers. 'Being here, well, it's brought me back to myself – to what's important and what you can let go; taught me about the things you can learn to live without.'

They ride back in silence. On the way round the bay, they pass the now occupied cottage. No car outside for obvious reasons. No sign of the recent arrivals. She resents them more than she can say.

'I ought to call in and check everything's okay,' Lachlan says. Then, 'No. I can do it some other time.'

'Go ahead.' She dismounts, hands him back the hat and reins. 'I'd rather walk from here anyway.'

Minutes later she hears the thud of hooves behind. Eve spins round. 'They're all out,' he says. 'Besides, I ought to see you safely to your door.'

'What in case I go all Victorian lady and have some sort of fainting fit?'

He jumps down. 'I'd feel happier knowing you'd got home safely.'

'I'm not some bloody baton you men need to pass on to the next male protector. Besides, it's not my *home*, is it? My *so-called* home is more than 500 miles south of here.' She looks past him half expecting the four hikers to be lined up to witness their conversation. 'Sorry,' she says. 'I'm sure you're trying to help but I really need to be alone right now.'

'Of course.' He looks away. 'You know where to find me.'

Eve dawdles along the beach not wanting to go back to the cottage. The mist is gathering force. Within minutes it turns heavier and then raindrops begin to dimple the grey surface of the sea. She scrambles over rocky outcrops made more slippery with shoes on.

It's a relief to reach *her beach*. She seeks out her favourite rock to watch the ever-busy seabirds. Water is dripping into her eyes. How marvellous to be a bird going about your daily life unconcerned by the follies of man. Way up amongst the clouds, a golden eagle turns against the wind and then disappears again.

So presumptuous to think she could regard this beach as hers when it so clearly belongs to no one; not even Lachlan and his family. How quick she's been to employ the possessive pronoun. *Her* beach. *Her* home. *Her* husband. As if those things could ever truly be hers alone.

Nearing the cottage, she sees a light on in the studio. Rory must have spoken to Jared; it's a fair bet he knows about the new charges being levelled at the band.

She's always been mindful that Nick could be getting up to all kinds of things while on tour. Gil is fond of saying, 'What happens in Paris, or Rome, or New York…' Never finishing the sentence though his meaning was always clear enough. She'd never quizzed Nick too closely on his return reasoning that, if he'd succumbed to temptation, she'd prefer not to know. And, in any case, he always returned to her, to their home. She'd seen for herself the way rock stars are like catnip to some women. But never once did she imagine Nick might be some kind of sexual predator. A truly sickening thought.

She knows the cottage will be unlocked. It's never had a lock or key. Lachlan had told them of his determination to uphold the island tradition of never locking any doors. 'It's all about trusting people' he'd told them.

Stepping in out of the rain, she hears whistling coming from the studio. At least somebody's happy. The kitchen range is lit; she automatically moves the half-full kettle over onto the hotplate. In search of milk, she opens the tiny fridge to find two dead trout lying on a white china plate. Rory's triumph. Poor things must have been swimming in the open sea an hour or so ago never expecting that, out of the blue, a tempting bait would lead to their undoing.

Chapter Twenty-Eight

Though they've cleared the table and dunked the dirty pan in suds, the smell of fried trout lingers on, turning her stomach. She hadn't been able to eat her fish; much easier to feign an upset stomach than explain.

It doesn't fool him. 'You're very quiet this evening.' He's doing his best to look relaxed, but his eyes say something else – he must be wondering what she might have found out. 'By the way, Jared said to say hi. Sends his love, of course.' Pulling out his chair, Rory sits down heavily. 'So did you manage to get through to Nick?'

'No, I didn't.' It's the truth after all. Holed up in his studio, Nick would in any case have turned off his phone. His way of escaping. Hers had been to come here; cut herself off as much as anyone can from the modern world. She'd chosen almost literally, to bury her head in the sand. Eve Quenington – ostrich woman. She'd be none the wiser if it hadn't been for Lachlan's slip.

Eve remembers a student debate – the whole tree falling in the forest thing. If they hadn't been sitting right here when that nearby tree got struck by lightning, would it have made a sound?

'Oh, okay,' Rory says, his reply mis-timed like a poor connection. He doesn't ask if she'd even tried. Instead, he rubs at his chin, checks her face a couple more times. 'Right, well.' He slaps the table. 'Why don't I make us a coffee. Decaf alright?'

Without waiting for an answer, he gets up to move the kettle back onto the cooling hotplate. It will take longer to come to the boil but better to save the dry wood for tomorrow. He lines up the mugs along with the sugar he adds to his when there's no one to raise a disapproving eyebrow.

It's tempting to put him out of his misery. Closing her eyes, she longs for a return to yesterday morning and all the other days before that.

The isle is full of noises,

Sounds, and sweet airs, that give delight and hurt not

If only she could remain in this bubble and not have to face the real world. She'll miss these evenings with the two of them reading in companiable silence sitting on either side of the wood burner. Balanced.

She gets up. Goes to sit not in her usual chair but in his for a change. Hot mugs in hand, he only notices at the last minute. 'You're in my chair.'

'Don't go all Daddy Bear on me. I thought I might like to look at the room from a different angle.'

He shrugs. 'I like that chair best. Besides, it's the same room whichever way you choose to look at it.'

'But my perception of it might have altered.'

'And has it?'

'No.' She gets up – leaves it to him. 'You're right. It's the same whatever angle I look at it from.'

She picks up her Kindle. Though she's about a third of the way through, she can't remember a thing about the story she's been reading. When she tries to pick it up, the words don't add up to anything that makes sense. In the end she shuts it off, throwing the room into a softer, kinder light.

Looking up from his paperback, Rory asks, 'Are you sure you're okay?'

'Why wouldn't I be?'

His mouth opens, the temptation, the struggle right there on his lips but he can't bring himself to say anything.

'I'm thinking of leaving.' She'd deliberately avoided the words *going home*. 'Since they have the internet at the farmhouse, would you mind taking me round there tomorrow? If I can't get a good enough signal on my phone, I'm sure they'll let me use their wi-fi to book a train ticket and arrange a taxi to the station.'

Rory snaps his book shut. 'It's a long way. Why pay a fortune when I've a car sitting in the car park next to the harbour? I can't pretend I'm not disappointed you're leaving but I'd be happy to drive you to the station. Selfishly, I'd rather see you off properly.'

It's obvious he's upset. She gives him a moment to come clean but he's not going to.

'I wouldn't want to drag you away from here,' she tells him. 'Your work's going so well. It's brilliant – you're really on a roll. Better not break the spell.'

'Sure, I'm not some sort of fey artist trying to summon

up – I don't know – some mercurial fecking muse that might disappear into the ether at any moment. The two of us have been rubbing along famously here. Least ways that's what I thought.'

She smiles. 'You're right. I didn't know what to expect when I arrived but being here in this place – well, it's been life changing.'

'I'm going to miss having you around. The least I can do is see you safely onto the train.'

'I can see myself onto it,' she tells him. 'I admit it's going to be a difficult adjustment. Not sure I'm fully ready for re-entry.'

More earnest than she's seen him in a long while, he says, 'Then why not stay a bit longer?'

'Because it's time I went back,' she tells him.

He doesn't argue. After a while she gets up, goes off to the loft and her little platform bedroom. She opens the bedside drawer and retrieves her mobile. Turning the damned thing on, she hopes the battery is dead. It lights up at her touch. Power still at 22%. All the little red boxes contain absurdly high numbers. For now, she ignores the voice messages along with texts that must be about something. Tomorrow will be soon enough.

She skims through her emails. There's one from a decorator, two from a boiler maintenance firm. A wine shop tries to excite her about their latest offers. On and on they go. The mundanity of her everyday concerns is obvious when the evidence is before her in black and white.

And another email from that Chetwin bloke. As if she didn't have enough to worry about. Damn the man for his persistence. Invading her privacy doesn't come close to what he's doing. The man's a professional parasite hoping to make money piggybacking on other people's tragedies.

Her eyes skip over the usual courtesies.

Bla-bla-bla. I'm sure you must have struggled to put this terrible event behind you.

How the hell can he assume anything about what she went through?

Forgive me if I get straight to the point. Reviewing the facts, it seems to me Kenneth Digby – the DI leading the investigation – was unreasonably single-minded from the outset, determined to impose his own interpretation on the evidence. He was far too quick to point the finger at your father. The coroner's verdict sealed the case as far as the police were concerned. As a consequence of their collective myopia, a number of potential clues were either totally overlooked or never fully investigated.

I remain determined to uncover the truth of what happened. To that end, since you are a vital witness, it would be of great assistance if you would consider meeting me to discuss your recollection of events however painful that process may be.

Painful – like she might have simply twisted an ankle instead of walking into a scene from a nightmare she'll never be free of.

Shakespeare had it about right: *Hell is empty and all the devils are here.*

Chapter Twenty-Nine

Eve's up early, first in the shower for once. As soon as she's dressed, she starts packing. She can hear Rory pottering around in the kitchen. 'I'm making porridge,' he shouts up the stairway. 'A good breakfast to set you up for the journey.' He sounds like her mother. Eve smiles. She'd forgotten how her mum would make porridge on cold mornings, sprinkling the top with brown sugar that would melt into a delicious caramel liquid.

Suitcase in hand, she goes downstairs, drops it by the front door – a loud slap against the flagstones. Rory's bent over the stove with a cookbook propped up next to him. 'I'm making it Scottish style. More water than milk and a good pinch of salt. It's meant to be good for an upset stomach.' Viewed from the back, there's an appealing solidness about him. Whatever he's doing, such surety about his movements. Over his shoulder he says, 'The Scots are a superstitious lot. Did you know you're only supposed to stir porridge clockwise? Stir it the wrong way and the devil himself will come for you.'

'Wow – that seems a bit harsh.' The resulting grey-brown

gruel looks unappetising. He starts ladling it out with enthusiasm. 'That's plenty,' she says, hand over her bowl.

Turns out the savoury version is quite pleasant. Not that she has much of an appetite. They eat in silence. When they're finished, Rory leans back in his chair and clears his throat. 'I didn't want to say anything yesterday in case you changed your mind. But seeing's you're all packed up and determined to be off, I think I ought to warn you.' He rubs his chin. 'The thing is, since we left there's been a few developments—'

'I already know.'

'But—'

She touches his forearm. 'I assume you were going to tell me about the other women who say they were abused by the band.'

'Aye, I was.' He pulls his mouth sideways. 'Not sure I believe it though. Your Nick's never struck me as the sort of fellow who'd do something like that.'

'Though you've only known him since he's been clean. A while back — well he just wasn't himself. Not that that's any excuse.' Looking away she says, 'When there's enough smoke, in the end you're forced to admit something must be on fire.'

He chooses not to contradict her. Instead, he starts to clear away and then stops, the spoons clattering against the bowls. 'I thought you said you'd not spoken to him.'

'To Nick — no, I haven't. Not since last week anyway. It was Lachlan who told me.'

He holds his head on one side. 'Did he now?' Suspicion clouds his eyes.

'It wasn't like that — he didn't mean to. We were chatting and he let it slip by accident.'

'Hmm.' He transfers the bowls to the sink before returning with his judgement. 'Seems to me that would be a hell of a thing to let slip *by accident*.' He puts air quotes around the words.

'You're missing the point,' she says. 'These poor women have finally found the courage to come forward. How d'you think that makes me feel?'

'I can't imagine.'

'I've always known Nick was no angel. I mean the man's a rock star for Christ's sake. It was easier to close my eyes, close my mind to whatever might have gone on while he was away. For the sake of my own sanity.'

'To suspect the man of being unfaithful is hardly the same as imagining him capable of the sort of behaviour they're describing.'

'You're right. And yet all the same, I feel I'm to blame. Perhaps if I hadn't chosen to turn a blind eye...'

He rubs her shoulder. 'Come off it, Eve. Even if it turns out they're guilty as charged – and that's a massive fecking if – none of it was your doing. Nick's his own man.'

'You know I'm really going to miss you. Miss us.' She looks around the room. 'And this funny little cottage.'

'You don't get rid of me that easily. I'll be back and in your hair before you know it.'

Though she's standing more or less in the same spot as before, the signal keeps failing at the critical point in her search. 'It's no good.' She nods towards the farmhouse. 'I'm going to have to ask for their help.'

Rory sits down on the beach next to the dingy. 'Go ahead. I'll keep an eye on the luggage.' As if a passing gull might carry away her case.

She takes a breath before knocking. If Lachlan's surprised to see her back so soon, he does his best not to show it. 'I'm trying to book train tickets and can't get a decent signal. I was wondering if I could use your internet.'

'Oh, I see. Yeah, sure.' He steps to one side. 'Come on in. You'll need the password, which must be somewhere on the router. Which is, umm, in the office.' He sets off along a narrow corridor which opens out into a wider hallway with several doors leading off. She can hear a woman's voice scolding someone. A boy's voice answers back, his words muffled. Must be Breac.

Lachlan leads her through into an office which is small but with all the usual equipment. 'I think there's a sticker underneath.' He holds up the router. 'Yep. D'you want me to read it out for you?'

'Please.' She's already in settings. The code connects her without a hitch. Her relief is short-lived. 'Bloody hell! It says it's going to take 12 ½ hours.'

'You have to add in the time it takes to get over to the mainland. With the single-track roads and all, I normally allow 3 hours from here to the station.'

'That's if I can get a taxi to take me at such short notice.' She adjusts the start time. 'Great it's now just shot up to 17 hours. The connections are terrible.'

'You could stay in Glasgow overnight.'

'What if people recognise me? The train's risky enough.

The last thing I want is to check into some hotel and then find I'm all over Twitter and Instagram.'

Wife of Shamed Rock Star books into Glasgow Hotel

'Listen,' he says, 'I've got a sick kid–'

'Oh God. I'm so sorry for bothering you like this.'

She starts to retreat. Laughing, he grabs her arm to stop her. 'A real kid. As in a baby goat? We recently acquired a couple of pregnant bagots – horrible name for a terrific little goat. Mabel and Martha – not my choice. Mabel gave birth to twins a couple of weeks back, which is unusual for the breed. Long story short, one of the kids has something wrong with its eye. I've been trying to treat it, but it hasn't worked so she's going to need a small operation. The vet is more or less opposite the train station.'

'You're 3 hours from the nearest vet?'

''Fraid so. Anyway, the point I'm making is that if you can wait a day, I'd be happy to drive you there tomorrow morning. Kill two birds with one stone.'

'Are you sure?' She adjusts the train times. 'If I catch an earlier train – say around 9.30, I'd be home by about 10. But that means we'd need to leave around 6.30 in the morning.'

He grins. 'A bit earlier in fact. It's a long journey so we'll need to stop for a bit to give the kid a bottle and so on. It gets light by around 5.30 these days. I warn you, little Bounty – what can I say, she's chocolate and white – is unlikely to be happy about being separated from her mum. Breac will want to come. He'll help settle her down. All the same, you might have to put up with a bit of bleating to begin with.'

'I've got earbuds,' she says.

A thin, grey-haired woman bursts through the door opposite. Seeing Eve, she clutches her chest in surprise. 'Mum this is Eve,' Lachlan says.

'You're staying at Macraiths'.' As an afterthought, 'Nice to meet you.'

'The same.' Eve can feel herself blushing under the woman's sharp scrutiny. 'I only popped in to use your internet,' she tells her. Those piercing blue eyes fix on her wedding ring like an accusation: eyes the same shade as her son's, though his have never been as judgemental.

'I'd better go and ask Rory if he's okay with getting up that early,' she tells Lachlan.

He follows her out. While she explains the new arrangements, Rory studies Lachlan with undisguised suspicion. 'Fine by me,' he finally says though he looks less than happy. 'I'll drop Eve off at six tomorrow.' She could be a parcel.

She loops her arm through Rory's, 'And on the plus side, I get to spend another day with you.' She smiles up at him though the change of plan is disconcerting. Discombobulating is the word her gran would have used.

Once they're clear of the shore, Rory turns the little craft around and they head back. Having said her farewells to the place, it's strange to be returning so soon. The cottage hoves into view, the glass in the makeshift studio is catching the sun, shining out like a beacon.

Her city shoes crunch on the latest shell deposits as she helps him drag the dingy clear of the water. Rory hands her the suitcase and she walks up to the house with its lockless door, leaving it wide open for him. When he doesn't appear, she sees he's busying himself with various chores – topping up the outboard and so on. She senses he's avoiding her – avoiding any discussion about her accepting a lift from Lachlan and not him.

She makes a pot of tea and carries both mugs down to the boat. A peace offering he accepts. After a few sips, he says, 'Far be it from me to give a grown woman advice –'

'But you're about to anyway.'

'I wouldn't want someone taking advantage of you when you're in a vulnerable–'

'For God's sake it's just a lift, Rory. Nothing more. Did I mention Breac's coming with us? So, we'll have a chaperone – not that one is needed.'

He gives a slight nod – an acknowledgement of sorts. 'I'm touched that you're trying to protect me,' she says, 'but, like you said, I'm a grown woman. And I'm no fool.'

'Point taken.' He sips at his tea.

'If we wrap up well, tonight we could have a whisky or two looking up at the stars. They're so spectacular here.'

'Aye and before that why not come out with me and try a spot of fishing?'

'What if I catch more than you?'

He chuckles into his mug. 'Expect my ego will survive.'

'Okay you're on, although I reserve the right to throw mine back. I'd rather see them swimming free than floundering in the bottom of a net.'

Chapter Thirty

Smothering a yawn, Eve shivers. Light is barely penetrating the low mist shrouding the little harbour. She pulls her jacket closer. Lachlan is coming towards them carrying a pet cage with Breac running alongside looking anxious. The kid is hysterically crying out for its mum as he lowers it in the bottom of boat.

Though some distance away, the nanny goat's answering cries are frantic and pitiful; the distress of their sudden separation heart-wrenching to witness.

'The poor wee thing.' Rory looks like he might be about to burst into sympathetic tears. He pulls Eve into a hug, rubbing her back with both hands. 'I'm really going to miss you, you know.'

'Me too.' She breathes in his familiar smell. 'Thank you for everything. This has all been – I can't put it into words.'

'That bad, eh?'

She chuckles. As he lets her go, she looks him in the eye. 'I've loved being here with you. And I've loved everything about this place.'

'And you're quite sure you're ready for re-entry?'

She throws both hands in the air. 'I honestly don't know. I mean, it's going to be a bit of a culture shock being in the real world again. You know, maybe this is the *real* world. In any case I have absolutely no idea what I'm going to say to Nick or what comes next. But I have to face the music sometime.' A tight grin. 'No pun intended.' She turns away so he can't witness how upset she is.

'All aboard that's coming aboard,' Lachlan announces. As soon as she steps into the boat it rocks and the bleating intensifies. 'You and me both,' Eve mutters. She sits down on the bench next to Breac and extends a finger through the mesh of the cage. The tiny kid shrinks back from her touch. 'I have a way with animals,' she tells the boy.

This doesn't begin to raise a smile. Serious-faced, he's suffering the animal's distress. His voice wobbles while he utters a stream of reassurances, poking his little fingers through the spaces in the wire to stroke her head. 'It's okay, Bounty. The vet's going to make your eye all better.' The kid bleats back a series of accusations. It's a gorgeous little creature – dark brown head and neck with a small white patch between its ears. Tufts of hair surround the buds of its horns. That one open eye is full of fear and trepidation.

'See you, mate,' Lachlan shouts to Rory as he turns the boat around and points her towards the mainland.

Eve waves in an exaggerated fashion until her friend's outline recedes to be swallowed by the mist. 'It's okay, Bounty,' the boy keeps repeating, sounding less sure each time he says it. The kid's cries compete with the chugging engine. Growing more frantic, the poor animal begins to wildly butt at the cage. Eve puts her arm around Breac. 'She's certainly a strong little thing,' she tells him. 'This is hard for her but it's going to be worth it when the vet makes her eye better.'

'I didn't think she'd be this frightened.' The boy's head drops onto his hands. 'I've been trying to get her used to drinking from a bottle and everything.' He grins. 'Mabel really hated Uncle Lachlan milking her. He said a really rude word when she kicked him in his you-know-whats.'

Too soon a cluster of brightly painted cottages emerges from the sea mist. Through the murk she sees a downstairs light shining out from one house. Someone else up early. Movement in the kelp near the harbour draws Eve's attention to what could be an otter. From a change of angle it's hard to be sure it's not simply weed flowing over the wet rocks.

The kid's cries grow louder now that they're too far away to hear the nanny goat's replies. 'This is all new to Bounty. She's never been away from her family before.' Eve nudges the boy. 'You don't see many goats in boats.'

He cracks a smile at last. 'Goats in boats – that rhymes.'

'It does.' The jetty becomes clearer and they begin their approach. No going back now.

'I expect she'll calm down once we're off the boat,' she tells him. To distract the boy she adds, 'Someone once told me that they paint the houses all different colours like this so that when a seafarer comes back after a long voyage, he can pick out his own home from way out across the water.'

'Is that really true?'

'I think so. It seems to make sense. You see, however far

they've travelled, home is always more precious to them than anywhere else they might have been.'

The BMW is still there though it looks like the roof has acquired a few bird droppings. Once Lachlan has secured the boat, he leads them up through the village to a piece of wasteland where a dusty Forester hatchback is parked. It's seen better days. He loads the complaining kid into the rear while Breac jumps in the back seat ready to lean over to comfort her.

Lachlan takes Eve's suitcase from her and stows it in the footwell behind the driver's seat. She climbs into the passenger seat as he starts the engine. It sounds lumpy, thrumming a little off-beat though Lachlan appears unconcerned. 'Everybody belted up?' He's forced to shout above all the bleating. 'Okay then, let's go.'

It takes only moments to leave the tiny fishing village behind. The scenery they're travelling through opens out almost immediately and is nothing short of spectacular. The early mist begins to clear to reveal a cloudless sky and a never-ending series of peaks descending into azure lochs with only the odd isolated cottage. Eve tries to capture the majesty of it with her camera, but her efforts are poor compared with what she sees with her naked eye. The cries and bleats from the back begin to dwindle as Bounty exhausts herself.

Halfway into the journey they pull off onto a rough side road in search of a quiet spot. Despite the open windows, the smell coming from the back of the Forester has become increasingly agricultural. As soon as the engine stops the kid wakes up and begins to bleat piteously.

Breac jumps out of the car to pee only metres from the bonnet. Thankfully, Lachlan's a lot more discrete. Eve strides off in the opposite direction towards a clump of flowering hawthorns; their heady scent fills the air as she relieves herself.

When she gets back to the car, Lachlan already has the kid pressed up against his chest, her legs restrained under one arm. Breac is holding a feeding bottle and, smelling the milk, Bounty is eager to suck on the teat, her good eye closing with pleasure as she latches on to its comfort. As the bottle begins to empty, Lachlan tells the boy to hold it higher. The kid is soon sucking only on air; even so, Breac struggles to get her clamped-fast jaw to finally let it go.

'She's peed on you.' While Lachlan looks in dismay at the dark streak on his jeans, Breac dissolves into uncontrolled laughter. The kid bleats in unison.

'And that's all the thanks I get.' Lachlan merely grins where someone else might be horrified or angry. One-handed, he lays clean newspapers over the soiled layers before lowering Bounty back into the cage. He strokes her head. 'I'd love to let you stretch your legs, sweetheart, but I don't fancy trying to catch you again out here.' Eve looks around at the vast empty landscape.

The kid is a lot calmer with its stomach full. It's all peace in the car as they head back down the potholed track to re-join the road. 'She's gone to sleep,' Breac whispers. Another child might play on some electronic device, but he pulls a book from his backpack and starts to read, mouthing the words to himself.

They rattle along on their seemingly endless journey in

blessed silence. While Lachlan is concentrating on the pitted, twisting road, she studies his profile – the way his skin has been tanned to a ruddy brown, his hair bleached by constant exposure to the island's mercurial elements. Her imagination substitutes Nick's dark head of hair; skin that over the years has acquired the globetrotter's perma-tan. On a journey like this his stereo would be blasting out music – imposing the twenty-first century onto this timeless terrain.

'It's so quiet,' she says. 'We've hardly passed another car.'

'The roads get busier in the summer, though it's mostly holiday traffic,' Lachlan tells her.

'I just can't get over how empty it is. How few houses there are. And yet so many ruined cottages it's almost post-apocalyptic. Where's everybody gone?'

'You know, the population of this whole peninsular used to be about 2,500 before the Highland clearances. Now it's only around 300 or so. And that's in an area around the size of an English county.'

She fights to supress her sudden amusement.

Lachlan glances at her. 'What?' Another quick glance. 'Come on, Eve, what's so funny?'

'Just this whole thing. We're driving through a breath-taking wilderness in a car that frankly stinks of goat. And I'm sorry but, you're calmly sitting there reeking of goat pee and reeling off facts and figures like this is all completely normal.'

'It is normal – well for us anyway.' He sounds defensive. 'The way I see it, everyone else is out-of-step.'

'Don't think for a minute I was criticising.' She turns to

include Breac though he's lost in his book. 'In fact, I can't begin to tell you how lucky you are.'

Flustered, Eve tries to settle back in her seat as the train pulls out of Reading station. No more changes to negotiate thank God. The train's packed-out, stuffy and laden with so many competing sounds and smells – none of them pleasant. Odd to be squashed in amongst so many strangers. And impossible not to eavesdrop on those one-way phone conversations voiced so loud everyone can overhear.

In their brief call Nick had offered to pick her up from Castle Cary station. She'd argued it would be better if their reunion wasn't witnessed by prying eyes, later to be plastered over social media. He started to disagree before she cut him off with, 'I've already booked a taxi.' And then the lie, 'Sorry, I have to go. See you later.' He must have noticed the absence of endearments.

A baby cries out in distress sounding not unlike Bounty. Thankfully it's more easily mollified. The panicked vigour of the goat's protests had made their goodbyes outside the station more perfunctory than she would have liked. Seeing the boy's anxiety, she'd hugged Breac, though his bony limbs resisted the gesture. 'She'll be fine' she'd told him as if she had any right to make such a prediction. Lachlan she'd been careful to keep at arm's length; a swift wave wishing them luck and that was it. Had she properly thanked the man for his kindness? She'd certainly meant to, but with only minutes before her train would leave, her focus had already shifted by then.

Eve tries to clear her mind of everything except the swaying train rushing through the flat landscape of southern England. Studying the skyline, she conjures the outline of mountains from the clouds along the horizon. An illusion impossible to sustain.

While waiting around in Glasgow she'd replied to the reporter's emails and agreed, in principle, to meet him. No hint at a date. Had he really uncovered new evidence? He'd implied that possibility, though he could simply be raking over old ground before suggesting some sensational but ultimately baseless theory to explain her parents' deaths.

An announcement breaks into her thoughts. Castle Cary in less than an hour. The taxi will get her back in around twenty minutes making eighty minutes in all. The strangest of homecomings. Where were those signalling faults when you needed them?

Despite the time and effort she'd expended on the renovations, the manor house had never bent to her will; never truly been home. In her fantasies they'd filled it with rampaging children – a proper family at last – but it was only ever a showcase. And one forever tainted by the break-in and the terrifying threats in those bloody words.

During her ten-year marriage there'd been many periods of separation to endure. She'd always keenly looked forward to their reunions; now the prospect of facing Nick fills her with something close to dread.

Chapter Thirty-One

She arrives in darkness, a soft rain misting the taxi's windows and doing its best to soften the edges of the house as it looms up in front of her. The sheer scale of the place shocks her. It could be a hotel or a care home. What the hell were they thinking?

No paparazzi thronging the driveway. Jermaine opens the gates, gives a mock salute as he waves the taxi on through. She can't see any other security staff. Possibly they're down to one man and his dog. The tent has gone.

Eve steps out of the car; a wave of exhaustion overwhelms her. She's not ready for this. Not by a long way. Lights blaze out from all directions, the house lit up like some party might be in progress. Such a profligate waste of energy. After the dark peace of the island, the intensity of so many lights hurts her eyes. If only she could flick a switch.

Too late. Nick is hurrying down the steps, arms out-stretched. 'I'm so glad you're back, Evie.' His hug is too tight and too presumptuous. 'You smell great.' He pulls back still holding on to her. 'You look great too.' The same can't be said for him. He hugs her again. 'Can't tell you how much I've missed you.'

'I probably smell of goat.' She leans back until he lets go. 'I've had quite a journey to get here. Didn't sleep well last night, and I was up before five this morning. Had to change trains four times. Right now, all I really want to do is collapse into bed.'

He narrows his eyes. 'Not straight away surely.' He checks his watch then gives a huff. 'Only just gone ten. Come and have a drink with me at least. Amber made an enormous shepherd's pie for lunch; there's loads left. It won't take long to heat some up.'

She shakes her head. 'No thanks. I had a sandwich and some crisps on the train. And I'm swimming in coffee – had to stay awake somehow.'

They've reached the front door. Looking into the hallway, she half expects those bloody slogans to have re-appeared in her absence.

Had they told the truth?

On the surface nothing is amiss as he closes the heavy door. She hears various deadlocks snap into place. His hand comes from behind, takes her suitcase from her grasp and puts it down at the bottom of the staircase.

'Let's have a nightcap at least,' he says. 'Come on, Eve. I haven't seen you in weeks. Things haven't been exactly easy of late.' He puts his arm around her waist, sweeping her past the stairway. 'Just one drink, eh? Come on, I'm not taking no for an answer.'

She stands her ground. 'Sometimes no really does means no, Nick.' The words are out before she can filter them.

He jumps back, stung. 'What did you just say to me?' The expression on his face mutates. In an escalating voice, 'I can't believe you, of all people, could stand there and say such a thing to me. I'm your husband, for God's sake. Don't I deserve the benefit of the doubt?'

She shakes her head wishing she could rewind the last few minutes. 'Look, I'm sorry but I'm so dog tired right now...'

'I don't believe this.' He cradles the top of his head like he's been hit. 'I think we both know exactly what you meant by that last remark. And now you're what – planning to trot off to bed without another word? I'd say you owe me a lot more than that.'

'You're right, I do.' She looks around with a total absence of affection for anything she sees. 'All this and more.'

He waits.

'We clearly need to talk things through properly.' She rubs her eyes like a bad actor trying to illustrate the point. 'But like I said, right now I'm far too exhausted for anything but sleep.'

She retreats towards the stairs, picks up her suitcase and has a hand on the banister when he scoffs. 'And with that you're simply going to walk away from me.'

'For the time being.' She takes a couple of steps then pauses to add, 'I'll sleep in the guest room.'

He comes towards her. 'You bitch.' He spits the last word in her face before turning his back.

It's a shock not to be staring up at the beams and rafters of the little cottage with the kettle whistling on the kitchen range below. Eve traces the patterns in the ornate ceiling above her head remembering how she'd had it painstakingly restored at outrageous expense. It reminds her of the icing on a wedding cake. Such pristine perfection. Perhaps they should have left it alone instead of plastering over those cracks and blemishes. Was it right to erase the scars the years and a leaky roof had left on this building?

Despite her fatigue, she'd slept only in fits and starts, endlessly replayed their horrible row; trying to work out how things had come to such a head within minutes of her arrival. He'd called her that dreadful word – spat it out with such venom it scared her half to death. Even now, her eyes dart to the door to check it's locked. By rights she should have given him a chance to put his side of the story; after so many years together, she'd owed him that at least.

Out of bed, she opens her suitcase. She'd taken her old towelling dressing gown to the island instead of the ornate one Nick had given her. She slips it on; finds it still smells of woodsmoke. Nine o'clock. Rory will have been up for a couple of hours by now. Probably gone off to work in his studio. Lachlan and Breac will be back at home probably tending the animals. And little Bounty – had the vet managed to save her eye?

She opens the heavy curtains on a fine spring day. At last the fruit trees are in blossom – frothy pink and white confections wherever she looks. With the gardener no longer riding around on his mower, the grass has grown longer, the whole orchard pleasingly natural.

Below her window Jermaine's dog is straining on his leash, barking at a squirrel. High in a tree, the squirrel stares back unconcerned.

Time she got up.

Eve can hear the coffee machine from along the hallway. The noise blends with the drone of the vacuum cleaner; Amber must be hoovering in the sitting room – getting on with her morning routine. Showing up every day; demonstrating more loyalty than she has.

When she walks into the kitchen Nick has his back to her. Eve is stunned by the sheer size of the room. Sunlight is shining through the ceiling's glass lantern to highlight an empty cereal bowl and a half-drunk glass of orange juice. The smell of the grinding coffee drifts seductively towards her.

The machine falls silent. Sensing her presence, he says, 'I'm sorry. I shouldn't have called you that last night.' Nick turns round, gives her a look she can't fathom. His skin looks sallow, that traveller's tan finally beginning to fade. The circles beneath his eyes make him look nearer forty than thirty-five.

He carries his espresso over to his usual place and sits down heavily. 'We should talk.'

'Okay.' Eve sits not in her usual spot but with the width of the table between them. No point in sugar-coating things. 'Tell me this,' she says, 'when we spoke on the phone why didn't you mention these other women and what they're accusing you of?'

'I would have told you about it if you hadn't been miles away. I suppose I thought – why upset you when you were so obviously happy and relaxed.' He pulls his mouth to one side. 'You'll hate me for saying this, but we both know your mental health is somewhat fragile, Eve.'

Letting that one go, she says, 'So these allegations – are they true?'

'First off, bear in mind it's not just me they're pointing the finger at. I can't vouch for Gil and Leon, but in my case it's nonsense.' His huff suggests a degree of amusement.

A long look. 'Besides, the whole thing's ridiculous. Am I really expected to remember whether I might have briefly placed a hand on some dancer's butt in the course of a conversation that took place years ago?' He holds up a hand. 'Before you say it, I concede we maybe should have kept our distance a bit more, but what you have to remember is that on tour everybody's thrown together twenty-four seven. It may sound corny but you're like a big family. At the time, not one of those women made any kind of complaint verbally or otherwise.'

He stirs his coffee. 'Shall I tell you why?' Throws in a sugar lump. 'Since this Wolff woman made those accusations, we're seen as low-hanging fruit. Better grab your share before it's all gone.'

'But you're not denying their claims?'

'Denying what?' The spoon clatters onto the table. 'Do you expect me to apologise for being a heterosexual man who likes having pretty women around?' He waves his cup at her. 'Come on, Eve, let's not pretend I'm a saint.'

'There's a whole lot of difference between not being a saint and behaving like some sleazy sexual predator exploiting women who aren't in a position to object.'

'Is that your honest opinion of me?'

'It wasn't. Remember what I said to those reporters out there about you treating women with respect?' She waves a hand in the general direction of the gates. 'At the time I meant every word.' When she looks him in the eye, she sees the way those dark blue circles have narrowed. She says, 'If we're being honest with each other, the truth is I don't know what to believe about you anymore.'

'I see.' He gives a heavy sigh. 'Well let me tell you something else you don't know – something I only just found out myself. Like I told you on the phone, that investigator we've had snooping around has managed to dig up a very telling connection.' He shakes his head. 'You're not going to believe this. It seems Lina Wolff lived in Italy a short time ago. While she was there, she moved around taking casual jobs here and there. At one point she worked as a masseuse in an upmarket spa in a fancy hotel near Lake Bolsena. The spa was popular with non-residents and was frequented by none other than Bernie's wife Lia.'

'We're talking about Bernie Davidson – the guitarist who used to be in your band?'

'The very same. Luckily for us, the hotel once fell foul of the tax authorities so now they keep meticulous records of everything. I wouldn't have believed it if I hadn't seen the proof for myself in black and white. We can prove Lia was one of Lina's regular clients. One of the other masseuses remembers the two of them being very friendly for a while. Amici stretti was the exact phrase she used. Roughly translated it means they were as thick as thieves.'

'So, hold on – you're seriously suggesting Bernie is the mastermind behind everything?'

The door opens and Amber pushes the hoover into the room. 'Not now,' they shout in unison.

'Well excuse me for breathing,' the girl says backing out.

Eve catches up with her in the hallway. 'Sorry about that. It's just Nick and I are in the middle of something important.'

'You're back then.' Looking Eve up and down, she seems to find her wanting. The ends of the girl's hair are currently lurid green as if pond weed is clinging to it. 'Have a good time, did ya?'

'I did, thanks.' Eve meets her gaze, sees the challenge lurking there. It's clear the girl's loyalties have shifted. 'Tell you what, why don't I finish the hoovering and let you get off home.' It's not really a question.

'Fair enough.' There's a clatter as the girl dumps the vacuum cleaner close to Eve's feet. 'I'll bugger off then.'

Eve watches her go. She waits for the front door to close – which it does with a slam – before heading back to the kitchen.

Nick is sitting exactly where he was before, gently tapping the side of the empty cereal bowl with his spoon. Ding. Ding. Ding. When she moves the bowl away, he looks up. 'What you just told me puts everything in a new light,' she says. 'Although I have to say I'm having a problem getting my head around it.'

'You're not the only one.' He drops the spoon. 'There's more. Get this, the expert we hired to look into that fake footage couldn't pinpoint its source at first. Now he's got a lead – thinks he might be able to trace it back to Bernie through some dodgy tech guy who was in rehab with him.'

She frowns. 'I'm finding it hard to see Bernie as some kind of Mr Big super-villain. I mean I was there when you all talked to him on zoom. Remember how he was wearing that daft outfit and going on about bees. He seemed to me more than happy with his new life. In fact, didn't he tell you he understood why you forced him to leave the band and get clean? That you'd, in effect, staged an intervention for his own good.' She shakes her head. 'Now you're saying he's been plotting to ruin you.'

'He's been clever about it, but he made one big mistake,' Nick says. 'Lina Wolff lived in Berlin before she moved to Italy, which meant he had to link the accusations to the one night the band played there. Bernie was off with the pixies at the time and must have forgotten about that food poisoning nightmare.'

'Wait a minute – are you saying if you hadn't been ill that night you might have believed the footage was genuine?'

'No, I'm certainly not saying that. Eve, you must know I would never force a woman to do anything she wasn't completely happy with.'

A loaded silence. Another time she might have asked him about the willing participants. Not now.

She shuts her eyes, conjures up the benign almost comical image of Bernie in his bee-keeping outfit. 'On zoom, I remember him saying the past was all water under the bridge – or words to that effect.'

'I guess he was lying through his rotten teeth.' Nick looks her square in the eyes. 'People do, I'm afraid.'

Chapter Thirty-Two

The heat is a surprise after the coolness of Scotland. Dressed in jeans and a thin shirt, she strides off to meet Jared at the stables. Birdsong everywhere, the fields she crosses are a mass of golden buttercups.

Jared comes out to greet her. 'Great to see you,' she tells him. Grooming brush still in hand, she can smell the citronella as they hug.

His brown eyes are full of concern. 'How's things?' When she hesitates, 'So – glad to be back?'

'Not especially. Bit of a culture shock after the island. You know I can't tell you how beautiful it is up there. Rory and I were both in our element. I suppose he still is.' The thought of him there without her makes her envious. 'I can't remember the last time I felt so at peace.' She decides not to mention her nightmares.

'And Rory seems equally besotted,' he says. 'In fact, I may need to go up there and drag him back home. At the risk of sounding shallow, I have to say that degree of isolation sounds more than a wee bit boring to me.'

'It's not always idyllic. I mean you're totally at the mercy of the weather up there. This time of year, you experience only its best side. The crofters abandoned the island years ago; presumably they found it soul destroying trying to scrape a living there. The current owners live there alone all through the winter – which must be challenging at times.'

'Winters can be hard here too.'

'Not to the same degree.' Domino whinnies to remind Jared he's being neglected. 'I may not be an artist,' she says, 'but all the same, I found the place inspiring. And thought provoking. To be honest, I'm still trying to convince myself coming back was a good idea.'

She looks past him. Aside from Domino, there are no other horses. 'Where the hell's Brandy?'

'Hey – no need to panic.' He squeezes her shoulder. 'Jenny's just taken her for a hack with a group of youngsters. She can't have known you were back. I passed them in the lane. Didn't think I could ask her to turn everybody round again at that stage in the proceedings.'

'It's fine.' She studies her riding boots feeling displaced, surplus to requirements. 'No big deal,' she says to convince herself. 'I can come back later. Or tomorrow. Anyway, it's good to know she's being well cared for.'

'Aye. Like I told you before, that nag of yours is disgracefully disloyal.' His tone is jocular and yet it hits a nerve.

To avoid further questions, Eve walks out into the centre of the yard, turns her head away when he comes after her. 'Are you alright?'

'Not really.' She turns to face him. 'You know, you're a really lucky man. Goes without saying Rory is too. What the two of you have is special.'

'I like to think so.'

She swallows hard. 'Nick and me – well…' Impossible to stifle a heartfelt sigh.

'I may be speaking out of turn,' he says, 'but I consider myself a good judge of character and fundamentally your Nick's a decent man. Maybe the two of you just need to take some time out.'

She shakes her head with conviction. 'We've had a good run. A *great* run even. He's helped me through so much. Stood by me when a lot of other people melted away. I'll always be grateful to him. But well, I think we've probably reached the end of the road.' Before he tries to dissuade her, she says, 'I need your help with something.'

'Anything for you.' He squeezes her shoulder in the same spot. 'Well, short of robbing a bank or morris dancing.'

'I'm thinking of renting a cottage. Something small and in the village would be perfect. If you could put out a few feelers. A six-month lease, at least initially, would be ideal. I'd do it myself but…'

'But you'd only set every tongue wagging.' He nods. 'I'll get onto it right away, that's if you're sure it's what you want.'

'Not sure of anything except I like living around here. At least for now.' She threads her arm through his. 'I'm lucky enough to have a few good friends in these parts. And my habitually disloyal horse is happy here.'

'And Nick? The man may have his faults, but I'm pretty sure he loves you.'

She smiles. 'And I love him. Always will, I expect. But sometimes that's just not enough.'

When Eve gets back, she heads straight for the studio. That no-go neon light is on, damn it. She bangs on the soundproof door. Predictably there's no response. She tries his mobile, but it's switched off.

She goes to find Jermaine. He's all easy charm. 'Good to have you back, Mrs Q.'

The Mrs Q tag makes her shiver. 'You seem to be the only one left,' she says.

'Yep. Them paps cleared off after a bit. Since Nick was always holed up in his studio, they soon figured there was nothing doing. Been nobody about except the postman since.'

His German Shepherd is wagging its tail in a way guard dogs really shouldn't. She can't resist stroking its head. 'This dog of yours is anything but mean. Intruders would have to dress up like squirrels to make her really bark.'

He laughs, his perfect teeth catching the sun as he tilts his head skywards. 'Mind you, it'd be a whole different story if someone was to come at me, like. Or, if they was threatening anyone under my protection.' Sounds like Jermaine might fancy himself as a superhero.

'Did Nick give you the spare key to his studio?'

'Yeah.' He sorts through the collection of keys on the large ring attached to his belt, warden style. 'Got it right here some-where.' Muttering to himself, he looks through them again. 'Has to be one of these two.'

She holds out her hand. 'Okay, give me both.' She notices

the suspicion in his eyes, the two-second delay before he complies. Does he think she's going to burst in and trash the place – the wronged wife wreaking her revenge?

'What the hell…' Nick is sitting at the mixing desk, a pair of headphones clamped to his ears.

'I need to talk to you,' she tells him.

He pulls the headphones down. 'Didn't catch that.' He rolls a chair over to her. 'Take a seat.'

'Not here.' She looks around at the massed microphones and top of the range musical instruments. 'Somewhere with daylight and fresh air.'

'Okay.' Though he looks uncertain, he lays the headphones on the mixer desk, turns off various switches and knobs before raising his empty hands. 'Since you're the one calling the shots, lead the way.'

She's forced to wait for him to set the security system before he follows her out into the orchard. Off Jermaine's usual patrol circuit, it seems as good a place as any.

Eve remembers getting two men to position a Lutyens-style wooden bench to face the sun equidistant from a pair of cherry trees. She's never actually sat on it before. She doubts Nick has either.

They sit at either end leaving a space in the middle. She checks none of the security cameras are directed their way. 'I've been thinking about Bernie,' she says. 'Tell me what's going to happen next.'

He gives a half smile. 'Well, a lot depends on whether the tech guys can trace that footage back to the bloke he met in rehab. My guess is the link might be a bit tenuous. I mean, I doubt Bernie'd be daft enough to use the guy himself; more likely an associate or someone he recommended.'

'But if they could establish a clear connection…'

Nick makes a fist, hammers it into his other hand. 'Then we've got the bastard.'

'Then what?'

He frowns. 'I just said – we'll have him by the short and curlies. Gil and Leon have already said they'll push for a criminal prosecution.'

'And what if you *can't* trace the origin of the footage or prove it's fake? Wolff might simply claim Lia became one of her clients long *after* the abuse took place. That the two of them meeting in Italy was merely a coincidence.'

'I suppose that's a possibility.'

A gust of wind dislodges a shower of blossom onto them. It looks like Nick has confetti in his hair. Dragging her mind back to the present, she says, 'Even with the evidence you need, the whole thing is bound to get really bitter and horribly personal. All kinds of other stuff might come out.' She decides not to elaborate. 'This thing could drag on for years. Is that really what you want?'

He holds his head to the side. 'Your point is?'

'Why not go over to Italy and have it out with Bernie face to face? You could lay it on thick, tell him you already have the evidence and that the only way he's going to avoid jail is to persuade Lina Wolff to retract her accusations. She's not likely to want to risk a prison sentence either.'

He shakes his head. 'What's to stop him calling my bluff?

In any case, Gil and Leon would never agree. They're fired up and after blood.'

'Then don't tell them. Think about it – once Wolff withdraws her accusations, the band are simply the innocent victims of a malicious or deluded fan. In which case, the other women might easily get cold feet and withdraw their claims.'

Seeming not to have heard her, Nick says, 'You know I never would have taken Bernie for such a treacherous bastard.' He stands up. Pacing back and forth, he rubs at his chin before stopping dead in front of her. 'Sorry, Eve, but on balance I think I'd rather punch Bernie's fucking lights out than make peace with him.'

'Then supposing I go instead. I might be able to get him to see reason.'

He sits down next to her. 'No way. Thanks for the offer but if anyone's going to talk to him, it's going to be me; this is *our* fight not yours.'

'Then you'll do it?'

'I see what you did there, Evie.' He grins. 'Okay, I have to admit you make a compelling case. I'll give it some thought. *If* I decide to go, it's on one condition.'

She narrows her eyes. 'Which is?'

'You agree to come with me.' He gives her that crooked smile, the one that would melt her heart if she let it.

Chapter Thirty-Three

She hadn't expected to be chaperoned through the airport. Camera flashes momentarily blind her before they're ushered outside and up the steps onto a private plane. Eve's taken aback by the opulence inside, the luxurious seats, the wide smile of the pretty flight attendant so eager to cater for their every need. She can smell the leather along with a masculine scent that might be sandalwood.

It's been years since she's flown in a private jet; in the early days Nick had gone full out to impress her. At the time she hadn't thought twice about the outrageous privilege and waste of world resources it represented.

The pilot and first officer come out to welcome them aboard; their conversation remains formal with no mention of the band, no hint that they might have recognised Nick. Would they have been as reserved before recent events? Eve doubts it.

With no other passengers, they take off sooner than she'd expected. It's a short flight, just over two hours. They're served champagne with eggs Benedict made with smoked salmon

– her favourite breakfast. A long way from a bleating goat on a bumpy road.

Below them the English Channel is choppy and grey. Over France the terrain gradually mutates from spring greens to fading lime; roofs turn from slate grey to bleached terracotta. They change course to cut across the sparkling Mediterranean into Northern Italy.

The plane begins its descent. Florence appears off to their left; the Arno River glinting in the sun as it bisects the city. She picks out the dome of the cathedral, Giotto's bell tower, the famous piazza where they stopped for lunch the day after Nick proposed. The photograph taken by a passer-by – glasses raised, their younger faces glowing red from the light filtering through the parasol above their heads. A silver-framed print sits on the table by the fireplace.

Ahead of them Perugia rises out of the surrounding Umbrian plain, an escalating concoction in peach-coloured stone punctuated by the spikes of dark green cypress trees. Magical. How could such improbable beauty have survived seemingly unchanged into the twenty-first century?

Their limousine drops them off at the hotel – a converted medieval castle surrounded by unnaturally verdant lawns and flower borders dotted with classical sculptures. It's a fortress, no doubt with a bloody history. The absurdly thick outer walls could repel a zombie horde.

The midday heat is a shock after the car's air-conditioned interior. Carved, ornate fountains offer only the illusion of coolness. The grounds seem deserted. Surrounded by empty sun-loungers, the turquoise surface of the pool dances an open invitation to take a dip.

A uniformed maid emerges from one of the ground floor rooms carrying a linen sack which she deposits in a trolley piled high with similar ones. 'Buongiorno signore. Signora,' she sings out as they pass.

'Buongiorno,' they reply not quite in unison.

Predictably, Nick has booked them into the best suite. The main bedroom's bare stone walls are softened by the thick drapes that surround the enormous bed. The smaller bedroom is twin-bedded and far less opulent – designed for staff. Or children. From every window there are stunning views over the valley towards Perugia.

A maid opens Eve's suitcase and begins to unpack her things before she can stop her. 'No. Grazie.' She mimes a ridiculous blocking move for good measure.

The girl frowns, 'Lei è sicura, Signora?'

'Sì, lei cela fa,' Nick tells her. 'Grazie, signorina, ecco tutto.' He presses money into the maid's hand as she leaves. When did he learn to speak Italian so well? What else about him might have passed her by?

'Thought I might go for a quick dip,' he says stripping off, throwing his clothes onto the bed in a way she resents. 'Pool looked great. Fancy joining me? We could order a poolside cocktail. Or two.'

'Not for me.' She rubs her forehead. 'Champagne with breakfast was more than enough in this heat.'

He stands naked before her, hands on hips. 'All the more reason for a top-up. Hair of the dog and all that.' The tattoos on his torso have accumulated over the years – memorabilia collected on his travels. They form a lace-like covering; en masse the scrolls and foreign characters are impossible to decipher. She picks out a scorpion – his star sign – poised on his shoulder as if about to crawl up his neck. It makes her shiver.

His face softens. When he tries to kiss her, she turns her head. He steps back, looks her in the eyes. 'You were the one who persuaded me to come here. So why did you bother? What's in this for you?'

'The last thing I want is for you to have all these dreadful accusations hanging over you.' A thin smile. 'I care about you.'

The suspicion in his eyes is still there. 'You've got a funny way of showing it.'

'P'raps I'll join you for a dip a bit later,' she says playing for time.

Nick shrugs. 'Okay. Suit yourself.'

He roots around in his case, takes out his swimming shorts and pulls them on before heading for the door. Halfway out he turns. 'I'll order lunch for around two-ish.' He pats his muscle-tight stomach. 'Something light. We can eat by the pool.'

Before she has a chance to respond, he's gone. She hears him whistling, the sound bouncing off the bare stone wall. Mambo Italiano – a classic. When she was younger, people often used to whistle a tune as they walked along. A dying art these days. Until they shared a house, she hadn't realised Rory was a habitual whistler. A passion for music is another thing he and Nick share.

The table has been laid in the shade of a sail-style awning – white tablecloth, fresh flowers, glinting glass and cutlery. A waiter appears to pull out her chair and lay a large napkin across her lap as if the effort might be too much for her to manage. White wine is cooling in an ice bucket next to a small selection of hors d'oeuvres.

Opposite her, Nick is glistening, a blue towel draped around his shoulders. Beads of water still cling to his dark curls. He leans across to pour her a fizzing glass of aqua minerale. 'I can't think why we don't do this more often,' he says. 'All that back-to-nature stuff must have been hard work. What you need is a bit of luxury. Nothing wrong with self-indulgence.'

He raises the wine bottle in a silent invitation. She shakes her head. Not wishing to initiate any further discussion, she sips her water. Nick pops a bite-sized tart into his mouth and, still chewing, holds the platter out in front of her. Mini bruschetta topped with chopped tomatoes and mint.

Not to appear too churlish, she takes one and pops it in her mouth. Simple and yet utterly delicious.

'We haven't talked about Bernie,' she says swallowing. 'When are we going to go and see him?'

Nick pulls the towel from his shoulders. Bare-chested, he sits back in his chair. That air of confidence was one of the things that first attracted her to him. 'It's only a couple of hours' drive from here,' he says. 'I've arranged for someone to bring a hire car here tomorrow. Bernie's got visitors at the moment – couple of London friends who are catching a return flight to Heathrow tomorrow afternoon. A local taxi's already booked to drive them to the airport; which means that, barring accidents, Bernie and Lia will be home alone tomorrow afternoon.'

'You've actually got people watching their house?'

'Only one – a local man. Our PI's on the case, so to speak.'

'But they must have been digging into their friends' private lives… Isn't that a bit much?'

He chuckles. 'Only minor stuff. Don't look so shocked. It's nothing by comparison with what the bastard's put all of us through these last few months. Besides, there'd be no point in us rocking up and finding the place empty. Or full.'

He pours himself a large glass of wine. 'You know, after that swim, I've really worked up an appetite.' He selects another of the hors d'oeuvres – a small green tartlet. Once he's swallowed it, he says, 'No need to look so uptight, sweetheart. It's all sorted.'

'Sounds like you thought of everything.' She'd said it with an edge.

He reaches for her hand, his touch warm, his skin dark where hers is habitually pale. Lowering his voice he says, 'This place costs an arm and a leg, but I reckoned we both deserve it after all the shit we've had to put up with lately.'

'Have you thought about what you're going to say to Bernie tomorrow?'

'Oh, I've thought about it alright.' He puts his glass down. 'Thought about little else since I found out what a duplicitous snake he really is.'

'Tomorrow you'll need to keep your temper, act superior.' She gives his hand a hard squeeze. 'You'll need to convince him you hold all the cards but you're giving him this one chance to back out because of your loyalty to the past. Your old friendship still means a lot.'

Nick shakes his head. 'If I put it like that, he'll immediately smell a rat. Trust me, I know the guy. We were like brothers once.'

Out of nowhere, a waiter approaches the table. Do they have underground tunnels in this place? Perhaps they lurk unseen behind the columns of the romantically ruined colonnade. Like assassins.

Hands clasped behind his back, the man asks, 'Would you like us to serve your main course now, sir?' Doesn't once look at Eve.

'Give us a minute.' Nick shoos him away like a fly. He goes back to his hidey-hole. Nick leans forward. 'There's nothing else we can do right now. For the next 24 hours it's just you and me. We've come all this way together, Eve. I've ordered their speciality Puntarelle – the Italian wedding soup for lunch. Let's enjoy it, eh?'

Chapter Thirty-Four

The hire car turns out to be a brand-new black Range Rover with the side and back windows blacked out – the type of vehicle favoured by visiting presidents and cartel overlords. She turns to Nick. 'You don't think something more low-key would appear less threatening?'

'If we rocked up in some cheap piece of crap, he'd be a lot more suspicious, believe me. Their farm is a long way off the beaten track. This thing will easily cope with the Strade Bianche – the rough white roads that lead up to it.'

'Sounds like you've been there before.'

'I haven't. But, like I told you, we've got an informant.'

'An informant!' Eve laughs in his face. 'You'll be calling him your snitch next.' In a deep voice she says, 'Our man on the inside.'

He shrugs. 'Like they say, know your enemy. You wouldn't want us going in blind.'

'Wow, the clichés keep on coming, don't they? Remember, this is real, Nick.'

'I'm well aware of that.' Unsmiling, he holds the car door open for her. It's quite a step up.

The interior is soon icy while all around the vast Umbrian plain shimmers under a heat haze. Nick's wearing jeans; the cuffs of his rather formal blue shirt rolled up. His pilot-style sunglasses make him appear a bit sinister. A villain from the eighties. Ahead of them puddles ripple on the tarmac only to disappear as they approach. More mirage puddles appear further on; like the end of a rainbow, they're always unreachable.

Without asking, Nick selects a Spotify playlist and Rag'n'Bone Man's *All You Ever Wanted* blasts out of the speakers. A favourite track of hers, as he must know. She's forced to raise her voice above the music. 'Tell me, Nick, why did you want me to come here? Was it all about the optics?' Headline: *Disgraced Rock Star's Wife supports her Man.*

'First off, this trip was your idea remember. Besides that, I felt the two of us needed a chance to reconnect. And you've always loved Italy.'

He's right about that. Following a family holiday in Tuscany, for a while her adolescent fantasies involved a tall, charming Italian who would whisk her away to raise a large brood of children in a farmhouse just outside Florence where they would own a vineyard, tending the vines together and teaching their tanned, bi-lingual children about art and culture.

Eve smiles at her own naivety.

Sticking to the sat-nav's instructions they pull off the main highway to follow a decrepit Fiat 500 as it heads up into the hills. Nick hangs back to escape the dust trail it kicks up. They pass through grassland studded with holm oaks, skirt around small settlements where each house seems to be surrounded by a high, chain-linked fence.

She's a bit chilly in her strappy t-shirt. 'I'm cold,' she tells him. 'Can't we wind down the windows?'

Without a word, he retracts them and the car begins to heat up. She can smell the baked earth, taste the dust in the air along with the Fiat's exhaust fumes. Each time they pass a settlement, dogs bark – the sound echoing across the landscape to set off other packs of dogs.

She says, 'Do you remember San Gimignano?'

'That place with all the medieval towers?' He frowns. 'I can't remember why they built so many.'

'Because it was literally built on conflict,' she tells him. 'Family disputes and political rivalries drove them to keep building higher and higher. Mine's bigger than yours and all that.'

'Have to say after recent events I have a fair amount of sympathy with that idea.'

'D'you think Bernie has his own watchtower?'

He shakes his head. 'Not according to the photos.'

'I know I just asked you to open the windows, but now I'm really hot...' He raises them again and, sinking into the comfort of cold air, she turns the music down. 'What's our cover story?'

'Now who sounds like they're in a movie?'

'All the same I think we need to go over the script, so to speak. Do we make out we're on holiday and just happened to be passing?'

'I've been thinking about that. Seems to me, we shouldn't start with a lie if we want him to swallow a much bigger one. I should tell him straight out we've come all this way to have a chat eye to eye, man to man.'

'D'you want me to make myself scarce at that point?'

'Let's play it by ear. If Lia wants to show you around, you could leave us to it.' He breathes in then exhales with a loud sigh. 'I can't believe it's come to this. We used to be great mates.'

'We're not there yet; there's still time to turn around.' Her own nerves are kicking in. 'You could get old Royston Double-Barrell to threaten Bernie with a criminal prosecution; keep the whole thing at arm's length.'

'No. We're here now. If this is going to work, I need to look him straight in the eye and not blink first.' He glances at her. 'Don't say it.'

'Say what? Oh, you mean the whole not-blinking-first thing. Actually, I wasn't going to take the piss. Though I should point out that people who fail to blink regularly are often psychopaths. They call it the predator's gaze.'

'I'll try to bear that in mind,' he says.

Ahead of them the Fiat turns off. The sat nav shows the chequered flag is close and a quarter of a mile further on she glimpses the farm amongst trees. They pass a row of beehives on the edge of an olive grove, the gnarled trees awash with creamy flowers. The track winds down towards a pair of rusty iron gates. 'If you put your foot down, this thing would probably flatten those,' she says.

Nick grins. 'I thought we might try a more subtle approach.' He opens the window to push the button on the entry pad. It takes a while for a male voice to answer. 'Sì?'

'Hiya, mate. It's me, Nick. Nick Quenington.'

'Nick. I don't believe it. What in fuck's name are you doing here?'

'I've got Eve with me. We thought we'd stop by and say hello, see how you're doing, you old bastard.'

There's a pause before the gates begin to slowly and noisily open, as if they're being operated by some invisible arthritic underling. The driveway in front of them is in better condition and lined with mature box hedging. A gardener in tan overalls is bent over clipping away at it. His narrowed eyes follow the car as they pass. 'Don't tell me he's your inside man,' Eve says.

Nick grins as they pull up next to a dusty jeep and a 4x4 Fiat Panda. They get out of the car and side by side they walk through the wide stone arch into a central courtyard.

Classically symmetrical, the main house has a stucco façade painted a faded orange – a pleasing contrast to all its pale green shutters. To their right, an adjoining stone building is set at a right angle. Wide steps lead up to its second floor. The left wing is longer and single storey with a colonnaded front. Gathered around a raised fishpond there are huge terracotta pots planted with clipped evergreens. It's hard to believe someone could live in a beautiful place like this and still be eaten up by their need for vengeance.

'Quite some place you've got here,' Nick says taking off his sunglasses and hanging them on the neck of his shirt.

Bernie advances to give him a backslapping hug. Thinner than she'd remembered, his face is now deeply tanned, his unnaturally black hair a little wispy on top. The over-sized shirt he's wearing hasn't been near an iron; his beige trousers are loose and hacked off at the ankles like some shipwreck survivor.

'Eve, great to see you.' This time Bernie's hug is more restrained.

Lia emerges from a side gate, her face shaded by a straw hat. She stares at them. 'Nick. Eve. Well, this is quite a surprise.' Her Italian accent is more pronounced than it was in London. She takes off her gardening gloves to air-kiss them. Though she can't be more than mid-forties, smoker's lines gather like spider legs around the edges of her mouth. Her ink-blue dress is loose and flowing, set off by a series of heavy, ethnic-style necklaces that must weigh her down.

A grey wolfhound trots up to drop a slimy ball at Eve's feet. It's hard to resist the invitation in the dog's eyes. 'Yapper's hoping you're a soft touch,' Bernie says with a smile.

'Unfortunately for him, neither of us are,' Eve says.

There's a beat before Bernie says, 'Come on in.' Red-faced and affable, he waves them towards a side entrance that opens into a large book-lined room. An acoustic guitar rests against the bookshelves alongside a black Gibson with a lot of battle scars. Eve casts a critical eye over the spines of the books; classics – mostly the Italian editions.

Without her hat, the visible white roots to Lia's red hair put Eve in mind of a radish. 'Sit down. Can I get you a drink?' she asks. The dog groans to itself before settling on the Persian rug in front of a cavernous unlit fireplace.

'No thanks, we're fine,' Nick says. Eve was about to sit but seeing everyone is still standing she remains on her feet. After a pause, Nick says, 'I won't pretend this is a social call.'

Their hosts respond by frowning as if mystified.

'We're here because I wanted to speak to you both in person rather than through official legal channels.'

'Not following you, mate.' Bernie shakes his head. 'Like

I already told that lawyer of yours, I was totally out of it in Berlin. I weren't even on them tapes, so, like I said, can't help ya.'

'Oh, I think you can,' Nick tells him. 'You see, we know what you've done. It's taken a while, but we have all the proof we need to link everything back to the two of you.'

Bernie holds up his hands. 'The sun must be playing tricks with your 'ead…'

Nick takes a step towards him. 'Don't insult me by denying it. You know, Gil and Leon didn't want me to come here. They're pretty adamant about wanting to press charges – criminal charges – against both of you. I managed to persuade them to hold off so I could come here and offer you a chance to stay out of jail.'

'You're talking like a crazy man,' Lia tells him.

'Am I?' Nick turns to her. 'We can prove beyond doubt that you know Lina Wolfe. Lia and Lina, eh? Like a pair of evil twins. Tell me, was it you or Bernie who persuaded her to make the allegations?'

The jovial mask long gone, Bernie's face boils. 'This is total bollocks–'

'Either way,' Nick says, 'you needed some state-of-the-art know-how to fake that footage. Hats off, they did a bloody good job. The level of expertise involved certainly narrowed down the field of possible candidates. Unfortunately for you, our investigators were able to sniff out a trail that led them right back to you, Bernie, my old mate.'

'You think you can come here, throwing around some wild allegations and expect me to just roll over like our Yapper over there.'

'What if I did know Lina?' Lia tells him. 'She was my masseuse. How are you going to prove I put her up to making those charges?'

Eve says, 'I don't know about you, but like Lina, after a few too many drinks, I have a tendency to be *very* indiscreet. When you're wasted it's too easy to let things slip. The next morning you might not even remember what you said or even who you said it to.'

Nick takes a step closer to Bernie. 'We now have all the proof we need to link you to the deepfakes you commissioned. Like I told you, I'm here to offer you a take it or leave it deal. You tell Lina Wolff to withdraw her allegations and admit the images are fake and the band won't pursue charges against either of you. It's in all our interests for the whole thing to fade away. This is a one-time offer. You need to decide right now. Once I walk out that door, the offer disappears with me.'

After a quick look at his wife, Bernie says, 'How do we know you won't change your mind once we get Lina to withdraw the allegations? What guarantees can you offer?'

'Listen, I've managed to persuade Leon and Gil that it's in our best interest not to have any more of our dirty linen aired in public. We just want this to go away so we can get back to how things were. We just want to get on with making music.'

'How things were. Well how marvellous that would be for you – you fucking traitors.' The extent of Bernie's hatred is there in his face. 'I don't give a flying shit about the band or your precious reputations.' The two men are eye to eye. 'Yeah, I set you up. So what? It's not like you bastards didn't deserve it.'

Nick jabs a finger close to his face. 'Don't expect me to

apologise for kicking you out. You were a total liability. In fact, if it had been up to me, we'd have done it much sooner.'

'I'm glad I've made you fuckers suffer. I want you to go through what I went through.' He rams a finger into his own chest. 'The band was my life, and you took all that from me.' Close to tears, Bernie points to the door. 'Now get out of my fucking house right now or I'll throw you out.'

They have no choice. 'See you in court,' Nick shouts over his shoulder. Neither of them speaks as they crunch down the drive towards the car. With his sunglasses on she can't read Nick's expression as he starts the engine. After her earlier suggestion about crashing through them, it's just as well the gates are standing wide open.

Further down the track she cracks a window. 'Well, that didn't exactly go to plan. You shouldn't have lost your temper. What the hell are we going to do now?'

Nick doesn't answer just carries on driving stony-faced. A mile further on, he pulls over onto a rough piece of ground, the dust swirling around them. 'I'm not so sure about not going to plan.' He takes off his sunglasses and then extracts his phone from his shirt pocket. Holding both in his outstretched hand he says, 'One way or another I think we've got more than enough on him.'

Chapter Thirty-Five

Nick's on a high – the natural kind, as far as she can tell. While speaking on the phone, he punches the air and laughs out loud. It's good to see him happy again.

He hadn't let her so much as touch the sunglasses or the fake mobile in case she accidentally erased something. 'None of this stuff belongs to me,' he'd told her on the journey back. 'I have no idea how any of it works. They set it up just before we left. All I had to do was point and shoot.'

As soon as they'd arrived back at the hotel, he'd disappeared. Walking into their suite a moment ago he was beaming like an idiot. Didn't say much before he retrieved his real mobile from the safe and started making calls, pacing the sitting room with his back turned.

At last he hangs up, goes over to the window and stretches his arms wide above his head like a someone waking up. Hands clasped behind his neck, he turns around, his elbows thrust out like horns as he comes into the bedroom. 'Sorry I abandoned you. I needed to get all that out of the way.'

He lets his arms drop to his side. 'From now on, I'm all yours.'

She stands up, does her best to frown. 'So that whole secret recording ploy – that was your plan all along. You never intended to offer Bernie a deal?'

'Don't be angry, Evie. I would have told you, but we figured it would be better if you didn't suspect anything.'

'Who's this *we*?'

'Our team on the ground here.' He snorts. 'Which includes our man on the inside – not the gardener by the way.' Nick crosses the room brushing against her in his haste to pour himself a large whisky. He turns to wave the decanter at her. She declines with a look, nothing more.

'You know, I could get quite used to this spying caper,' he says. 'Felt a bit like I was Bond back there.' Glass in hand, he comes over, puts his free arm around her waist and slowly pulls her towards him. 'I'm hoping I get to seduce the beautiful girl at the end.'

She sidesteps him. 'How long had you been planning to record that conversation?'

'Only after you suggested this trip. If you remember, I only promised you I'd think about it. And I did. Bernie's always had a hell of a short fuse. He's a canny bastard all the same. I guessed he'd smell bullshit, though I hoped he wouldn't be able to resist the opportunity to gloat; to watch my face as he stuck it to me.'

A gulp of whisky. 'We've got him on audio and visuals. Since they freely invited us into their home – no deception on our part – Roland's confident the recordings will be admissible in court. That's if it ever comes to court.'

'Does that mean you might still settle?'

'I'd say it's a possibility. Way more likely now, of course. I was telling the truth back there when I told him it was in the band's interest to make it all go away ASAP. It's possible Gil and Leon could still insist on their pound of flesh.' He chuckles. 'See what I did then? You're not the only one who can throw a Shakespeare quote into the conversation.'

'Call me a cynic, but I very much doubt you've ever read The Merchant of Venice.'

'Oh, ye of little faith.' He grins. 'Pretty sure that's from the bible.'

She grins back at him. 'Are you trying to impress me with your hidden depths, Nick Quenington?'

'I might be.' He puts down his drink and pulls her close, his breath fortified by the whisky. 'Thanks to your suggestion, Mrs Quenington, I reckon the evidence against Bernie and Lia is now more or less watertight. Roland knows exactly where I stand on the deal thing. I've just filled in Leon and Gil on what we have on tape. They're planning to meet with Roland tomorrow afternoon. So that's it.' He slaps his thigh. 'At least for now. This was such a good idea of yours, Evie.'

'I can't take the credit,' she tells him. 'It wouldn't have worked if you'd done thing's my way. So…' She searches his eyes. 'What happens next?'

He swings her around, dances with her despite the lack of music. 'That all depends on what you're referring to.'

Eve tries to stand her ground. 'Let's stick to the legal case.'

'Well, let's see.' Taking her by surprise, he dips her down then pulls her back upright again. 'I'd say right now it's in the lap of the gods, as some long-dead Greek once said.'

'I believe that's a quote from The Iliad,' she tells him. 'That chap Homer.'

He tightens his hold on her. In her ear he whispers, 'Always been a big fan of The Simpsons.'

Despite her reservations, his mood is catching. Having missed lunch, they go down early for dinner. 'Come on, Evie, have a proper drink to celebrate. The sun's probably over the yard arm at home.'

'Campari and soda, please,' she tells the hovering waiter.

'And I'll have the same,' Nick says. She can't remember him ever voluntarily drinking anything pink.

'It actually stays light till nine these days,' she tells him. 'Not that you'd know since you're normally holed up in the studio all times of the day and night. Sometimes I wonder if you've got a coffin in there.'

'Hmm. I might install one. My very own Twilight Zone with sound effects. What d'you reckon? Don't most girls get the hots for vampires?' Sticking out his upper teeth, he hisses at her.

'And you'd know all about what most girls go for.'

'Ouch.' He wrinkles his nose. 'You really know how to kill a bloke's buzz.'

Despite the bar being crowded, the waiter hurries back with their drinks. Nick looks around the room, his expression mutating into a wide smile as if he might be posing for an unseen photographer. For all she knows he could have arranged to have them snapped by a pap. *Embattled Queningtons on Romantic Getaway.*

She's swizzling her drink when Nick raises his glass to some people sitting across the room. Could they be his mysterious surveillance team?

Surrounded by glamourous women, a darkly handsome man echoes Nick's gesture with the glass then gets to his feet and starts to walk in their direction. It takes her a moment to recognise Jag Beckett – the movie star. Though she's fairly sure the two have never met, they go for the double-handed shake like old friends. Jag ends it with a tap to Nick's elbow. 'I'm such a huge fan of the band, man.'

'Good to know,' Nick says. 'This is my wife, Eve.'

Jag turns those famous dark eyes on her. 'Enchanté.' He lends the word a heavy suggestion. 'As they say here in Italy: piacere di conoscerti, Bellissima.' His pale chinos are teamed with a cream silk shirt and a light grey sweater knotted at the neck like he might have stepped straight off a yacht. The man's cologne reeks of wealth.

Turning back to Nick, he says, 'That yellow door song's one of my all-time favourites.' Then to her, 'It's quite an honour to meet the woman who inspired it.' When he bends to kiss Eve's hand, a volley of phone flashes light up the room like a heavy storm arriving.

'So great to meet you.' She hates herself for gushing.

'Love your work. I must have watched Cheating Death a dozen times,' Nick says. 'Such a brilliant film.'

'Not as good as Hanging on the Line,' Eve says. 'I have to say that movie is an absolute masterpiece. Lorenzo's one of my all-time favourite characters.'

Jag dips his head. 'Kind of you to say so.'

'But what made you agree to do Fine-toothed Blade?' she has to ask. 'I mean the plot didn't begin to hang together—'

'I guess we all make bad choices from time to time.' Before she can respond, Jag bestows a condescending smile. 'I should re-join my party. Just wanted to come over and say hi. You folks enjoy your evening.'

In a lower register she only just catches he says to Nick, 'Hang on in there, man.'

Eve recalls the acrimonious divorce Jag was embroiled in a few years back; his ex-wife's allegations of abuse were emblazoned over every newspaper. Is he showing solidarity with another wrongly accused man or is this one abuser recognising another?

Jag clasps Nick's hand again giving it a final enthusiastic shake. Big matching smiles. Her vision's strobed by another barrage of flashes from all directions.

Projecting his voice beyond their table, Jag adds, 'Good to run into the two of you.' A quick bow to Eve and then he heads back to his friends.

'Wow, that was a bit surreal,' she says. And then, 'Should I feel bad about what I said about Fine-toothed Blade?'

Nick shrugs. 'I 'spect it made a change from his entourage blowing smoke up his arse all day long.'

'Did you know that was once a standard medical procedure?'

Nick pulls a face. 'You're joking.'

'I kid you not. Back in the eighteenth and nineteenth centuries they tried to resuscitate dead people by sticking a tube into their rectum and attaching the other end to a fumigator and a bellows.'

'Enough.' Nick holds a hand up in surrender. 'I get the picture. And there was I thinking a coffee enema was about as bad as it gets.' He raises his glass, waits for her to raise hers and clink it against his before declaring, 'Here's to smoke and mirrors.'

'Bottoms up,' she says.

Chapter Thirty-Six

In contrast to the bar, the hotel's dining room is a lot more formal and surprisingly dark, its bare stone walls illuminated by flaming torches that manage to fool the eye only at first glance. Real burning candles are grouped together on the type of metal frames she associates with churches. They're giving off the distinctive odour of beeswax. On each table a lone candle illuminates the diners chiaroscuro style. Though smartly dressed, they're a dour-faced lot. She hears whispered disapproval every time laughter filters in from the bar area.

Despite the atmosphere, their food is refined and delicious, each course perfectly paired with wines recommended by the sommelier. She drinks very little while Nick keeps throwing it back. Even so, some bottles are cleared away hardly touched. A waste – or possibly a perk for the staff.

Nick is animated in a way she hasn't witnessed for months – almost his old self. He peers around at the other diners and declares, 'Why d'you think this lot look so sodding miserable?'

'Shh. They'll hear you.'

He laughs then leans across the table to whisper, 'You know

I still can't get over how we managed to outsmart Bernie and Lia today.'

'*You* were the one who outwitted them. My being there made no difference.'

'Listen, I needed your moral support. Always have done.' His smile lingers. She watches his eyes stray down to her cleavage. 'Besides, it was very much a team effort – I couldn't have pulled it off without all the tech stuff.' He shakes his head. 'You know you can even make calls on that phone. It had all kinds of working apps. But those sunglasses – man they were something else. I mean, you might not believe it, but they did a pretty good job just as sunglasses.'

'Like something Q might come up with.'

'Exactly. Might get myself a pair. These days you never know when a record of a conversation might come in handy.' He chuckles into his wine. 'Old Bernie must have thought he was beyond reach, safely tucked away on that farm of his miles from anywhere.' He digs a spoon into his panna cotta taking care to scoop up some of the boozy cherry sauce.

Toying with hers, Eve says, 'Few places on this planet are truly out of reach these days.' She recalls the drone that had hovered above their heads on the island. Had it simply been recording footage for Lachlan's website? 'However remote the location, spying eyes can still find you. None of us can escape surveillance for long.'

Eve looks him straight in the eye wondering if she'll see a giveaway flicker of something. He's certainly quick to look away, takes a long sip of his wine before he says, 'I wish I'd thought to leave a bug in Bernie's house. What wouldn't I give to see his face when he finds out he played right into our hands.'

After the meal they go up to their suite. Under brighter lights, Nick looks flushed, his eyes unfocused and bloodshot. The night they arrived she'd told him she was exhausted and needed time to think about how she felt about their relationship. Though she can't recall his exact words, he'd said he understood and respected her wishes. They'd shared a bed and, true to his word, he hadn't touched her – at least not in that way.

Nick kicks off his shoes. 'That was a great meal, though it was a bit like eating in a funeral parlour.' Balancing on one leg, he's struggling to remove his trousers. 'And fancy Jag Beckett, of all people, coming over to shake my hand.'

'He actually *kissed* mine.'

'Yeah, I noticed how his eyes were all over you.' He's slurring his words.

She scoffs. 'They were not. Besides, he wasn't exactly short of female company tonight.'

'Ah, but none of them half as beautiful as you, Evie darling.' His expression grows serious. 'D'you know,' he holds up a wavering finger, 'I still get a kick out of telling people you're my wife.' His slow smile is nothing short of lascivious. 'Hey, you know what would make a perfect end to a pretty near perfect day?'

'I think I can guess.' She turns towards the bathroom, but he steps sideways to block her way. 'Where're you off to in such a rush?' He grabs her around the waist. 'We've always made a great team, you and me, Evie.' His breath reeks of garlic and way too much booze.

For the first time it occurs to her he might not be willing to take no for an answer. 'I'm desperate for a pee,' she tells him. He most definitely hesitates before he lets her go.

Reaching the bathroom, she shuts the door, slides the bolt across though it's too flimsy to keep out anyone determined. After the usual ablutions, she wets a towel with cold water and holds it over her face. Looking at herself in the mirror, she wonders what to do. Through the door she can hear the distinctive sound of snoring.

Still in his socks and boxers, Nick is lying spreadeagle on the top of the bed, his mouth wide open. Out for the count as far as she can tell.

She grabs her night things and retreats to the smaller bedroom, slowly turning the key in the lock so the noise won't wake him.

It strikes her again how basic the room is. Both single beds are narrow with the type of hard metal frames favoured by disapproving Victorians. The jute rug in-between barely relieves the hardness of the brick-tiled floor. She thinks back to her loft bedroom in the cottage back on Fluraichean. Though similarly spartan, it always felt cosy. Rory could have taken to sleeping up there now.

This bed might have crisp cotton sheets, but the pillow is hard and the covers smell musty from lack of use.

It's a long time before she lets herself fall asleep.

She's woken by the sound of a woman speaking in Italian. She gets dressed before venturing into the sitting room. A continental breakfast has been formally laid out on the dining table. Nick is dressed though his feet are bare. 'Sorry about last night,' he says. 'I went out like a light.'

Does he think he's apologising for his insistence or lack of performance? 'Sit yourself down.' He pours her coffee with just the right amount of milk. 'I thought breakfast up here would be better than having it down there amongst the stiffs. I got them to bring those almond croissants you like.'

They do look good. She sits down, takes a sip of coffee. Pulling out the opposite chair, Nick rakes back his hair several times like he does when he's nervous. 'I guess you and I need to talk,' he says.

'Okay.'

He keeps fiddling with his cutlery. 'Goes without saying these last few months have been tough on us both.'

She puts down her coffee. 'They certainly have.'

'It won't be easy but, once all this the legal stuff is cleared up, we'll be able to get back to normal, leave all the bad stuff behind us.'

'I'm not so sure –'

'Hear me out, please.' More hair raking. 'I know this has been tough for you. Whatever you might think, the truth is that for me there's only ever been one woman and that's you.'

'I think we need to start by being completely honest with each other.'

'Okay well, I'll admit I've not been a perfect husband – not by a long shot, but I'm willing to try to be a better one from now on. More than just try.'

'You know when something gets broken, sometimes it just can't be mended.'

'Don't say that. I've been a selfish bastard, I readily admit. My dad once called me a self-centred hedonist and he was spot on. But things *will* be different from now on, I swear to you. You've always wanted a family and there's no reason why we can't have one. I was reluctant to take on all that stuff, but it's high time I grew up.'

'I'm sorry, Nick but it's not as simple as that. Things have changed.'

'Okay, but we can put whatever it is behind us. Leave the past in the past. Maybe this has been the wake-up call we needed. *I* needed.'

She shakes her head. Before she can say anything, he says, 'You have to admit we make a damned good pair you and me. Yesterday – well it was sort of fun in a way. Don't tell me you didn't get a kick out of it?'

'Okay, you're right. But the problem is the two of us have always wanted very different things. It's no one's fault. I've always wanted a settled home life. And a family…'

'And I want the same.'

'Right now you might think you do.' She reaches across the table to cover his hand with hers. 'Staying together is something we know – the safe option.'

'I'm not–'

'Shouldn't life be more than settling for what you know, Nick?'

'But that's exactly the opposite of what I'm saying. Look, I wasn't that keen on the whole having kids thing. My mum leaving us … you of all people know how that screwed me up. Things can be different. I'm up for us taking a risk, so I'm saying – what the hell, let's start a family.'

Removing her hand, she shakes her head. 'We'd be doing it for all the wrong reasons. A child should never be a sticking plaster for a relationship that isn't working. Especially a child who's already had a difficult start in life. Besides, after everything that's happened, I can't see any reputable adoption agency taking a risk on us.

'You know, Nick, what I can't figure out is why you agreed we should apply to adopt when you've never really wanted kids. What the hell were you thinking?'

He shrugs. 'I figured that if a kid was up for adoption, it was down to somebody else's major screwup and not mine.'

'What kind of half-arsed logic is that? I mean, we're talking about some poor child's life here.'

'What can I say – it made sense to me at the time.' He touches her arm. 'Eve listen, forget all that, what I'm trying to tell you is we have other options.'

'And I told you a long time ago, I'm not prepared to bribe a dodgy agency to acquire some poor infant who could have been snatched from its poor mother.'

'I'm not talking about going down that route – I'm talking about you and me having children of our own. Raising our own flesh and blood.'

She stares at him. 'Nick, the doctors already told us it's not possible…'

'Supposing it is.' He looks down at the floor for a while. 'Okay, I have a confession to make. Like the doctors told you, I'm effectively sterile.' He meets her eye at last.

'And you shouldn't feel bad–'

'Thing is, I persuaded them not to tell you about the

vasectomy I had years ago. Please don't look so shocked. What can I say – at the time it made perfect sense. I definitely didn't want kids and I sure as hell didn't want some girl rocking up asking for money to raise one she claimed was mine.'

'I don't believe this.' She stands up spilling coffee over the pristine white cloth. 'All those fucking tests I went through…' She's shaking from head to foot. 'And now you… you just calmly sit there and tell me that you already knew you were sterile.'

On his feet, he grasps her wrists. 'But that's the thing, Evie – these days they can reverse the operation. Apparently, it has an 80 per cent chance of success. And you know, even if that doesn't work, IVF is a viable option.'

'You've actually discussed this with a doctor, haven't you?' The extent of his duplicity astounds her. No wonder he didn't want her to use a donor sperm. She's tempted to slap his stupid face.

Instead, she strides into the bedroom, opens a couple of drawers and throws their contents into her half-unpacked suitcase. From the threshold Nick says, 'Look, I understand why you're mad at me right now, but once you've had a chance to calm down a bit, you'll see–'

'I'll see what Nick? That our whole relationship is built on lies and deceit?' She shakes her head. 'You are, quite literally, unbelievable.' She throws up her hands. 'I can't stay here with you. Not after this. And I'll never *ever* be able trust a single word that comes out that mouth of yours.'

He hits the bedroom door with his fist; the violence of the blow reverberates against the bare stone walls. 'This is all about that bloke, isn't it?'

Open mouthed, Eve stops what she's doing. 'What bloke?'

'You know exactly who I'm talking about. Think I don't know about that blond fucker you were so taken with back on that island?' A sly smile. 'Did you honestly think I'd let you go there without checking out what you were up to?'

Eve throws the rest of her stuff into the suitcase, then grabs her passport and handbag. She says, 'You know I ought to thank you for making this decision so simple.'

He comes towards her. As she pushes past him, he grabs her upper arm. 'Eve – think about what you're doing, everything you'd be throwing away if you walk out of here now.'

'Oh, I'm thinking about that alright.'

'I'm sorry but I can't let you leave like this.' His grip tightens.

'Let me go,' she spits, 'or so help me I'll scream this whole bloody place down. It's breakfast time – lots of guests up and about. It'd be all over social media within minutes. Quenington Abuses Wife in Luxury Italian Hotel. Great new twist to the story. Is that what you want, Nick? Yet another lawsuit to contend with because so help me...'

Eve sees the calculation in his eyes. She pulls her arm out of his loosened grip then heads for the door.

Chapter Thirty-Seven

Rory's on her doorstep clutching a bottle. 'Housewarming present,' he declares. 'A wee taste of the Highlands.'

Fighting back tears, Eve gives him a tight hug; awkward with the bottle wedged between them. 'Come on in.' She's quick to add, 'This place is just a temporary stop gap.'

'And a perfectly pleasant one.' He looks around. 'I suppose people imagine cream is inoffensive.' His expression makes his distain clear. 'Still, you've electric lights, mains water, central heating – what more could anyone's heart desire?'

'You're right. I've been thinking about my pursuit of perfection in the house, that it was really a kind of displacement activity. Fix the house – fix your life. I like to think I've moved on from there – from being that person.'

Smiling she pats his shoulders. 'Look at you – God, you're a sight for sore eyes.' She remembers how they'd parted – the sensation of watching him and his boat being swallowed in mist. 'I thought you'd be back ages ago. What made you stay on for so much longer?'

'Ah well, after you left, I started painting with a vengeance.

I was like a fecking man possessed. Borrowing Lachlan's computer, I sent a few images to Merton – my dealer – and he practically begged me not to leave while the muse was upon me, so to speak.'

'I'm not surprised you were so inspired, that island's an extraordinary place. I never thought I'd end up missing it as much as I did. As I still do at times.'

'Coming back's been a bit weird. Take our house – it seems so massive even though objectively I know it's only a cottage. I've been wondering around flicking light switches on and off just for the sheer hell of it.'

'You devil.'

'And you know I still can't get over simple things like the aga staying hot without me having to load it up with logs.' She's seldom seen Rory so animated.

He looks different in other ways. 'You've lost weight.'

'Aye, because once you'd left I kept forgetting to eat, which as you know, is not at all like me.'

'Tea?'

'That'd be grand.' He follows her into the kitchen and sits down at the table. Eve brushes a few crumbs from the vinyl tablecloth protecting the polished surface underneath. She's still learning to live with its insipid pattern.

'Eilean Fluraichean.' Rory sighs. 'The place gets under your skin after a while.'

'Almost like you've been enchanted.'

'Not sure I'd go quite that far, though I know what you mean.' He gives her a curious look. 'At the risk of sounding a bit hippy dippy, I guess I was able to reconnect with nature at a more fundamental level.' Rory chuckles. 'Will you listen to me – pretentious shite, or what?'

'What,' she says.

'Maybe you did well to escape when you did.' He gives her a long look she chooses to ignore. 'Since I've got back, I've also found it hard to adjust to the noise. It's everywhere. You know, I never noticed before how much fecking racket a proper sized fridge makes. Damned things keep whirring away night and day.'

They both pause to listen to the hum of hers. He says, 'Here, we're away from major traffic but there's always some eejit mowing a lawn or playing music with their windows open. And then there's aeroplanes… Such a fecking din we all make between us.' He grins. 'Jared says it's as well I left seeing's I'm already halfway to becoming a hermit.'

While she's occupied with making tea, he says, 'I hear your old gaff is set to become a boutique hotel.'

'We sold it off-market. I never asked about their plans. The sale went through so fast. They wanted everything including furniture and fittings. I heard talk in the shop that some people are up in arms. They've called a meeting in the village hall next week.' She lines up their two mugs. 'I'm glad to be well out of it.'

'And no second thoughts about…'

'Not really. It was high time.' She adds a plate of biscuits to the tray. 'I expect you know Lina Wolff's withdrawn her charges.'

'Aye. Nick told us.' He gives her a quizzical look though he certainly doesn't need her permission to stay friends with her ex.

'I don't know this for sure,' she says, 'but I have my suspicions the band might have bought off the other women.'

'Still, mud tends to stick all the same.'

'And in all fairness, maybe it should.' Eve decides not to elaborate as she drops the squeezed-out teabags into the bin.

After finding the relevant page, she pushes the newspaper under his nose. 'Have you seen this?' She taps the listing. 'The band have agreed to appear on the Jerry Bellingham Show. A brave move. The man's certainly no pushover.'

'Aye, the famous smiling assassin.'

'Kendra and their management team must have decided it was the best tactic. Fighting fire with fire and all that. One hell of a gamble all the same.'

Rory shakes his head. 'You're not wrong.'

Once they're settled with their tea, she hesitates then says, 'D'you mind if I ask your advice about something?'

Chewing a chocolate digestive, he mumbles, 'If it's a financial matter, I'm most definitely *not* your man. Jared's good with that sort of thing. Anything else, I'll take a stab at, though I'm not sure I'd be much of an agony uncle.'

'It's nothing like that.' The relief on his face is impossible to miss. 'The thing is,' she says, 'I can't decide what to do about this journalist who keeps emailing me.'

He swallows what's left of his biscuit. 'About what for heaven's sake?'

'He's not interested in gossip or anything like that. No, he's the investigative type; specialises in true crime and that sort of thing. He's been looking into what happened to my parents.'

'Oh, Eve darling.' He squeezes her hand, his fingers still

chocolatey. 'I would have thought that's the last thing you should worry about right now.'

'Which is why I've been putting him off for months. I know he won't have been doing all that research simply out of personal curiosity. He must be hoping for a book deal or even a Netflix documentary. Which means their personal lives and the state of their marriage will be picked over by people who never even knew them.'

'Sounds to me like you've already made up your mind.'

'Yes, but what if there's a chance... I mean, I sort of feel I owe it to Mum and Dad to at least try to find out more. As things stand – well you know as well as I do how they stand.'

'You think it's possible this fella could dig up something the police might have missed?'

She nods.

'And if you don't agree to meet him, you'll always be worried about passing up the chance to get to the bottom of what happened. Setting the record straight and all that.'

'Exactly.'

'Then, since you asked for my advice, I'd say you've no choice but to meet with the fella.'

'Oh.' She's a little crestfallen. 'I didn't expect you to be so definitive.'

He takes his hand away leaving chocolate stains on hers which he doesn't appear to notice. 'Only *my* opinion. Call it the clarity that comes from clearing your mind of so much everyday crap; though I'm sure the nonsense will creep back in soon enough.'

'Pr'aps I should have stayed on the island a bit longer.'

'If you do go ahead, I'd be more than happy to tag along, make sure the wretched fella's not about to swindle you out of your life savings.' He picks up another biscuit and waves it around to make his point. 'What harm can come from hearing the man out?'

'You're right, oh wise one.' She retrieves her laptop from where it's charging on the kitchen counter. 'I'm going to email him right now before I change my mind.'

Chapter Thirty-Eight

They meet in a café in her hometown, the sort of greasy spoon establishment patronised occasionally by the urban middle classes – always with the emphasis on *patronised*.

Chetwin Lange – 'Call me Chet' – looks considerably older than his profile picture. Late-forties, piebald beard trimmed to a wedge, his moustache flicked up at the ends like a small bird landing on his upper lip. He seems pleasant enough, except his heavy eyelids do a good job of shading his eyes. 'I need to meet him one-on-one, so I can see the whites of his eyes' she'd told Rory, who seemed disappointed not to be asked along. Ironic too, since she can't really see them – the white bits that is.

They order tea which arrives lapping at the brim of chunky mugs. It's around 11:30 a.m. and massive breakfasts are being consumed at every table. Middle-of-the-road music takes the edge off the fact that there's not much conversation around them, just the sound effects from lots of chewing and slurping.

The Boney M cover of *Rivers of Babylon* has just started up when Chet clears his throat. 'Thank you for agreeing to meet me today, Mrs Quenington.' His accent suggests a privileged background. Of course, she'd Googled him in advance. Second son of a minor aristocrat. Eton followed by Cambridge followed by a spell in Hong Kong. A smooth progression into journalism that temporarily ended when his pregnant wife was killed in a helicopter accident. The same accident left him in a coma with a head injury that would force him to re-learn how to talk and walk. Those last details had persuaded her: Two years ago, he'd received an international award for his sensitive coverage of the trauma experienced by victims and survivors.

'Believe me, Mrs Quenington, I understand your reluctance to re-open such a painful chapter in your life.' His narrowed dark eyes are at odds with the sincerity in his voice.

'D'you mind if I...' He extracts a small Dictaphone from his briefcase, placing it on the table next to his notebook. His index finger is poised on the start button.

'Go ahead.' She holds up a hand. 'By the way, I no longer use my estranged husband's name. Call me Eve, please.'

'Okay Eve, well I hope you won't mind if I jump straight in?'

'Feel free.' She braces herself.

'You've had a chance to read the series of attachments I sent you?' She nods. 'Good.' Chet smiles his approval that she's done her homework.

He takes a breath. 'Anyway, I thought we might have a bit of a chat and then maybe take a stroll down the road to your old home.' He makes it sound like the easiest thing in the world. 'I've already had a word with the current owners – Mr and Mrs Sullivan – and they've kindly agreed to give us the run of the place for a couple of hours or so.'

'You're saying you actually want me to go inside?'

'If you wouldn't mind. And, of course, I'll be right there with you the whole time. It's changed a lot, but nonetheless, being back there again may help to jog a few memories.'

She pushes her mug in his direction. 'I'm sorry but I'm not sure this was such a good idea.' Eve begins to gather her things. 'I never want to set foot in that place again.' How in hell had he won that award?

His hand tamps down the air in front of her like he's bouncing a ball. 'Of course, I fully understand and respect your wishes, Eve. Far be it from me to persuade you to do anything you're not entirely comfortable with.'

Leaning back, Chet sips his tea like he's no threat. 'Do you mind if I ask you a few questions?'

He starts with the easy ones. Relaxing a little, she tells him about her childhood emphasising how ordinary their lives were. 'I was an only child, but that wasn't intentional. And I was never lonely.'

'Your father, Gary, worked as a joiner for a local builder. He and your mother, Claire, met when she was at art school here. A strikingly beautiful woman. Remarkably like yourself in looks.' Surely, he can't be hitting on her at a time like this.

'She painted your front door bright yellow like it says in the song.' She winces at this reference to Nick and their shared past. 'Would you describe your mother as bohemian, a bit of a free spirit?'

'Only in some ways. Look, I can guess where this is leading.'

'Oh.'

'Artists are seen, almost by definition, as people who like

to question *the rules*, flout accepted conventions. Ergo, they're also judged to be the type likely to shun normal morality and shag around.'

He stays mute, opens his hands as an invitation for her to continue.

'The police kept asking me … they repeatedly suggested Mum might have been having an affair. That my dad found out about it and killed her in a jealous rage. I kept telling them that was utter bullshit. My mum loved my dad. And he loved her too. In any case, he was kind – a real gentleman in the true sense. A gentle man. I saw Mum's body… I can tell you with absolute certainty that my father would have been incapable of inflicting terrible wounds like that on her.'

Chet leans forward. 'Then help me prove it. Would you be prepared to take a look at the house just from the outside?'

'Possibly.'

'What about from the back garden? Like the house, it's changed a great deal since you lived there.'

'How do you know what's changed and what hasn't?'

'I've studied the police photographs, the ones taken at the scene. In fact, I have copies of them right here in my briefcase.' For one horrible moment she imagines him slapping them down on the table in front of her. 'And I have to say, Eve, to me the whole thing looks staged. Everything I've discovered so far tends to corroborate what you've just told me about your parents' relationship.'

'Wait.' She takes a moment to steady herself. 'Are you telling me you don't believe Dad murdered Mum?'

'Well, like I said in my email, I certainly think the police should have pursued other possibilities. To be fair, they did make a slightly half-hearted attempt to follow a few other lines of enquiry.' He makes a fist. 'A brutal murder in a respectable suburban area threw everyone into a panic.' His knuckles rap the table. 'They were under tremendous pressure to come up with a culprit.' Another rap. 'Murder followed by the murderer's fatal accident meant the case could be closed; the force could breathe a sigh of relief and get back to dealing with minor drug dealers and break-ins.' He opens his hand.

'Makes sense when you put it like that,' she tells him.

The roads are much busier than she'd remembered. 'There's no rush,' Chet keeps assuring her like she's a nervous horse about to bolt. 'Just take your time.'

Cars and vans race past trailing exhaust fumes and thumping bass notes. They have to keep stepping off the pavement to avoid pushchairs and dawdling small children. It's hot, the heat intensified by the many hard surfaces that surround them. Trees that used to offer shade have been cut back to little more than sprouting stumps.

The local shop now displays the strident blue and yellow logo of a national chain. Rounding the corner, she's abruptly standing at the end of the street – the one she once thought of as *theirs*.

The solid brick-built houses line up on either side. Cars are parked nose to tail along one side of the road. Tiny front yards that used to sport flowerpots have been taken over by recycling bins and padlocked pushbikes. Looking up she sees most of the houses have been extended into attics just like her dad had done; her mum's studio granted the best view, the best light.

Eve swallows down nausea. Each step takes her closer. She sticks to the opposite side of the road where it's easier to control her breathing. Lots of windows are open for the air; music and snatches of conversations drift out as they pass.

She stops two doors away. 'I can't.' Her legs won't budge. Head reeling, she tells him, 'It's no good. This is too much.' She leans against the railing of number 18 – the Turnbulls' house, though the family, including her friend Kimmy, moved away when she was twelve. Eve's tempted to sit down on their front doorstep like the two of them always used to.

On the other side of the road, the door of number 17 opens and an older woman in a blue floral dress comes out. Eve notices the ramp for the first time. Seconds later a wheelchair emerges. Slumped, his head lolling to one side, the man sitting in it raises a hand to shade his eyes from the brightness of the sun.

They look so familiar. Eve begins to walk towards them. Seeing her, the woman clutches her chest. 'Oh my Lord!' She manoeuvres the chair to take a closer look. Relief softens her face. 'For a minute there you gave me quite a turn, young lady.'

Chet's hard on her heels, 'I assume you mistook this young lady for someone else?'

Taken aback, she says, 'I did as a matter of fact.' She looks Eve up and down. 'You're the spitting image of someone who used to live two doors down.'

Chet persists, 'Might that have been this lady's mother, Claire Albright?'

The woman's expression changes again. 'You're the daughter, aren't you?' It sounds like an accusation.

Eve retrieves a name. 'And you're Mrs Wilson. I thought I recognised you.'

Self-consciously, Mrs Wilson adjusts her greying hair. 'That was an awful business. A terrible shock for all of us in the street. Thank God nothing like that's happened before or since.' Her red lipstick has been badly applied leaving a line on her teeth. 'I wouldn't have expected to see you back here. I mean, I should hardly have thought you'd be wanting a walk down memory lane.'

'You had a dog called Foxy who looked like a fox. Mr Wilson used to take him for walks all the time.'

'Yes well, our poor Foxy passed away a good five years ago. Liver cancer the vet said. Fourteen – so I suppose he'd had a good innings.'

Eve peers down at the invalid. 'Hello, Mr Wilson.' She pictures him with a full head of dark hair. Tall and broad-chested with a pot belly despite his obsessive walking. Hard to believe this wizened frame could hold the same man.

She bends closer to allow his watery eyes to pick her out. 'I don't suppose you remember me?'

Opening his mouth, he starts to wail – a peculiar animal howl that grows louder before the effort becomes too much for his frail body. Eve steps back. 'I didn't mean to upset him. Is he alright?'

'Oh, don't mind him,' Mrs Wilson taps her own temple. 'Jack's not right in the head these days. Early onset Alzheimer's I'm afraid.'

His lips come together in a struggle to speak. 'Cl... Cl... Claire.'

'Not Claire, Jack. This is her *daughter*, you remember young Eve?' Mrs Wilson begins to steer the chair away. 'He has an appointment with the chiropodist. We'd best be getting on our way.'

'I... didn't...' Mr Wilson turns his head; a bony finger emerges to point at his wife. 'Tell her, Mary.'

'Don't go taking any notice of his nonsense.' A poor attempt at a laugh. 'I never know what's going to come out of his mouth next.' She makes a point of looking at her watch before she wheels him away at surprising speed.

Chapter Thirty-Nine

The two of them exchange a look as they watch the Wilsons reach the end of the street and turn the corner out of sight.

'I've changed my mind,' Eve says. 'Let's go.' She strides off towards her old house.

The front door is painted dark green like it's in camouflage. After what happened there, it's no surprise. The letterbox has survived along with the two digits of the number 21. A thin yellow band is just visible on the inside the curve of the 2.

She says, 'Should we knock?'

'No need.' Chet fishes a set of keys from his briefcase. 'We have the place to ourselves for a couple of hours.'

He's right about how much the house has changed – the place is barely recognisable. The layout has been reconfigured so that an enlarged kitchen now leads straight through a set of glass doors to the back garden. Makes sense.

They tour the rest of the house but nothing is the same as the house that stubbornly resides in her memory. She makes herself go up into the attic, but she needn't have worried. They use it as an office. Eve can't find any trace of her mum in the room.

Disappointed, she walks back down to the kitchen. 'You know something that immediately struck me,' Chet says, 'is that, unlike most of the other houses, there's an alleyway running down this side here. I guess it's to give people street access to their gardens for wheelbarrows and such like. The only window that looks out onto it was, and still is, this one here.'

The kitchen area is now startlingly light making the side window redundant. She pulls up the heavy roller-blind and peers into the gloom of the alleyway. 'Mum loathed net curtains, so people sometimes used to look straight in when they went past. Let them look if they're that nosey, she used to say, we've got nothing to hide.'

'Did you ever see Mr Wilson looking in?'

Eve sits down on the nearest chair and shuts her eyes. 'The face at the window.'

'Excuse me?' Chet pulls up a chair beside her.

'I have this recurring dream,' she tells him. 'I see a face looking in at a window. Always the same man, although I can never make out his features. I sort of assumed I might have seen something in a film that set it off. But what if it's real? Half of me wants to believe it's Mr Wilson.'

'Did this dream occur before or after the murders?'

She notes his use of the plural. Eve shakes her head. 'It's really hard to be sure either way.'

She gets to her feet, walks out through the kitchen doors into the garden. Just as before, the alley terminates in a pathway that runs along the boundary, hidden by a two-metre boarded fence. The same fence turns the corner to run along the back boundary of all the gardens. A tall wooden gate leads into the alley from the garden. It won't open. 'Did they give you the key to this?'

Chet searches through the bunch. 'Looking at that lock, I think it might be this one.'

He's right. Through the gate they turn left past the gates to number 19 and then there it is – the gate to number 17 – the Wilsons' house. Chet begins to take photographs – the potential significance clearly not lost on him.

They retrace their footsteps. Standing in the back garden of number 21, she looks up at the house hoping for more clues, but on such a sunny day it couldn't look more innocuous.

'Mum would have loved this fishpond.' She sits down on the stone slabs that surround its raised sides.

Dogged in his pursuit, Chet sits down right beside her. 'Try to think back, Eve. You'd just returned from university. Aside from the obvious, did anything else strike you as out of place or odd in the house?'

'I suppose I'd have to see the photographs again.' Several large carp come up to the surface, mouths open, hoping to be fed.

'As I told you, they're right here in my briefcase. If I pick out the ones showing only the peripheral shots, would you be prepared to take a quick look at them?'

Alongside the others in various shades of orange and yellow, one of the carp is totally black – hardly visible in the depths of the pond. She remembers how they call them ghost carp.

'Okay.' Eve hopes she won't regret the decision.

'Why don't we go back inside,' he suggests.

'No. I'd rather stay out here.'

'Fair enough.' Balancing his briefcase on his lap, he sorts through the prints like someone preparing a magic trick. She looks away just in case.

'Okay,' he says, 'so these are some of the shots of the living room.'

He shows them to her one at a time. When he's done, Eve shakes her head. A big sigh and then he tries again. This time shots of the kitchen worktops and there it is again – the empty slot in the block of knives.

'Like I told the police, that pizza box there immediately struck me as odd. Mum and Dad never ordered takeaways. The Inspector – he told me they'd checked into it. A local pizza place remembered delivering a large margarita to the house the evening before.'

'Hmm. So why would they break with their regular habit and order in pizza?'

Chet is silent for a while. 'Thinking about it, could it be because their cooker wasn't working?' He checks the photos. 'Looks like a standard slot-in oven with a hob on top.'

'Yes, it was freestanding – the sort you slot into a gap.'

'Maybe they had a power cut,' he says. 'Or perhaps their cooker or its dedicated feed might have developed a fault? They can't roast anything, can't even heat stuff up on the hob. In which case, they would have to get somebody to fix it urgently.'

Heart thumping, she says, 'Mr Wilson – the initials on his van were W. E. S. Wilson's Electrical Services and then something about no job being too small. I remember that because they'd spelt too with only one o instead of two. Dad said I shouldn't point it out to him or he'd be upset.'

'Okay, we might be getting somewhere.' Chet is jotting down notes.

'They were cooking a roast when it happened. I remember stepping into the kitchen and smelling blood mixed with this burning smell coming from the oven. If it did have a fault, someone must have fixed it.' Eve hands him back the photos and stands up.

'Did Wilson make a move on your mum while he was fixing the oven?' Chet says. 'Was he enraged when she turned him down?'

She clutches her chest. 'The dahlias. I completely forgot about the dahlias.'

Chet frowns at her. 'I'm not following.'

'Mr Wilson grew these dahlias he was really proud of. He used to give big bunches of them to Mum along with some of his surplus veg. Dad even made jokes about him having the hots for her. But she couldn't stand dahlias, they were too artificial looking for her liking. Old ladies' flowers she called them. She told me on the phone she was worried Mr Wilson might have spotted them chucked out on our compost heap.'

'So, let's imagine Jack Wilson deluded himself about your mum, then found out she'd spurned his precious gifts.' He pulls a pained face. 'It's not enough, not by a long way. I'll need to look into the man's background – see if he might have any previous.' He sounds like someone from a movie.

They go back inside. 'Do you want to take another look around?'

She shakes her head. 'I've seen enough. Now I just want to put this house, this street and this whole town behind me.'

'I might just take a few more photos for reference.' He's already flashing away.

Eve looks at the framed family photos, the handwritten reminders pinned to the fridge. 'Are you sure the Sullivans won't object to you doing that?' When he takes no notice, she says, 'Please stop. That's way too intrusive.'

He grins. 'It's fine.' She follows him into the hallway. How could shots of the staircase be of any use? 'Don't look so worried, Eve. They're being well rewarded for this.'

'Oh, I see.'

Chet is unabashed. 'Right – well I think I have everything I need for now. After you.' He holds the front door open. 'I said I'd drop the keys through the letterbox when I left.'

'Keys.' She covers her mouth with her hand. 'I totally forgot – Dad gave the Wilsons a key so they could pop in and feed our cat when we were away. I remember him saying how kind it was of them to offer. For all I know, they could still have it – the key that is, not the cat. Misty came to live with me. She died two years ago.'

Chapter Forty

As she drives south, Eve is glad to see the town's landmark buildings recede in the rearview mirror. There is nothing especially remarkable about the place. Around seventy miles from the capital, it nestles amongst floodplains and low hills with few noteworthy features. Her mother had moved to the town drawn by the excellence of its art college. Her father's family had for generations worked in the building trade. If Claire hadn't bumped into Gary on a narrow-boating weekend, it's doubtful her parents' paths would ever have crossed. And if Claire hadn't decided to paint their front door bright yellow, Eve would never have known how Nick felt about her. People's lives can be changed by random events or decisions which, in retrospect, appear to be coincidences but aren't really.

Chet had been fired up, could hardly drag himself away from his phone to say goodbye. 'I'll be in touch,' he'd promised, or threatened, in a tone that made her think of Arnie's famous line: 'I'll be back.'

As she walked away from him, she'd felt the weirdest sensation of lightness at having completed her part and passed on the baton.

Reaching the motorway, she's faced by starkly alternative directions. A fork labelled: "The North" or "The South". Such a binary choice. Thirty-three years old and about to divorce, her life would take a different path with the slightest turn of the wheel. Running out of tarmac, she heads back the way she came, drawn by ease and familiarity.

Waking, Eve stares at the pale cream ceiling above her head. She scans the room taking in the watercolour still-life with fruit. A tiny oasis of colour, it hangs on one side of the window with its plain beige curtains. Her mum would have something to say about the décor in here – none of it good.

Her mother – a vibrant and opinionated woman who'd been so much more than the lifeless body Eve habitually sees whenever she thinks of her. And her poor dad forever lying there with that dark halo around his head and a bloody kitchen knife in his hand. She'd faced down her demons by going back there, doing her best to get them justice at long last. And now all of it is out of her hands, though not exactly in the lap of the gods but in the computer files of Chetwin Lange. She can't imagine a more unlikely avenging spirit.

At the kitchen table, piece of toast in hand, she makes a decision. Her lease will be up for renewal soon. She won't be staying here because it's high time she moved on in every sense.

Opening her laptop, she clears her mind before typing "conservation jobs" into the search line. The resulting list is too long and quite bizarrely diverse. She'll need to narrow her terms. On impulse, she adds the words Wildlife and Scotland on either side and then scans through the results.

The most interesting jobs are the ones she's woefully underqualified for. Should she study for a higher degree? The divorce settlement will take care of any financial concerns, but what she really wants is to get out there and *do* something. A job that involves getting her feet wet and her hands dirty. In any event, it's clear that what she needs first and foremost is up-to-date, relevant experience.

Lachlan's landline number is right there on the Eilean Fluraichean website. She feels a pang looking at so many beautiful shots of the island. Also on the Home Page, a head and shoulder shot of Lachlan, smiling face staring back at her.

Eve's fingers hover undecided. Nine o'clock – he's probably outside doing something. The last thing she wants is to leave a could-he-please-call-me-back-sometime message with his mother.

Before she can decide, her phone vibrates, and Chet Lange's number pops up on the screen.

Is she ready for this? She could let it go to voicemail.

'Hi,' he says. 'How's things?' Then, not waiting for an answer, 'I'm sending you a copy of the background check I commissioned on Wilson. As you'll see, it includes a detailed criminal record check.' This time she notices the momentary pauses that could be the legacy of his near-fatal accident.

An email drops into her inbox. Frowning into her phone, she asks, 'Isn't that sort of thing illegal?'

'Not if you use a bona fide firm of investigators. People do it all the time. Honestly anyone can check out a potential spouse, or maybe a nanny they're about to employ. It's in the public interest.'

'But shouldn't we hand everything over to the police?'

'I understand why you might think that, but I have a fair amount of experience in these matters and believe me, it's far better to build our case before we even think of involving them.'

Is he right, or is he only interested in sensational headlines?

'Okay, I've downloaded the document,' she tells him. 'Before I open it, could you summarise for me?'

'So, it turns out Wilson has a record for violence. It's all in there. In his teens, he broke a man's nose after a drunken scuffle outside a pub. There was a road rage incident that also came to blows though that got written up as a tit-for-tat with a caution for both parties. Couple of years after that, the police were called to his home – this was when they lived in Henley Avenue. Mary was taken to hospital badly bruised with a broken wrist. The neighbours told the police it wasn't the first time. Mary dropped the charges before it got to court. That's when the Wilsons moved across town to number 17. Fresh start in a new neighbourhood.'

She hears rustling as he turns the page. 'Here's where it gets really interesting. Six years ago, a woman named Gloria Davis succeeded in getting a court injunction against Wilson. She worked as a barmaid at The Falcon on Inkerman Street. Sometime after they closed, Jack tried to waylay her in the street. Frightened the life out of her by following her all the way home. Gloria was worried about involving the police – she had a couple of drug convictions. But when it happened again, she finally called them to make a complaint.'

'Wow!'

'There's more. About a year after that, he verbally abused some poor woman in a supermarket. The security guards detained him until the police arrived. After his arrest, it came to light he was suffering from early onset dementia, so they let him off with a caution.'

Eve feels sick. 'I don't know what to say. Do you think it's enough?'

'To be honest with you, Eve, I don't see this ever getting to a criminal court. As you saw with your own eyes, the wretched man's far too sick now to be able to defend himself. Potential witnesses for either side will be hard to find. Personally, I think the new information throws enough doubt on the evidence against your father. But it's not an easy matter to overturn a coroner's verdict – especially after all this time has elapsed.'

'Then what do you suggest?'

'I have a few more leads to follow up. Once I have, with your permission, I'd like to run the story. Shake the tree – as they say in the movies. See if it jogs a few memories. You never know. I'll do my best to keep your name out of it – assuming that's what you want. Although the grieving daughter needing closure angle is a very effective way of getting the reader's sympathy.'

Before she can respond, he says. 'The point being, if we can cast enough doubt, get a few prominent people to line up on our side, we'll have more support when we apply to get the coroner's verdict overturned.'

'I can see that makes sense,' she tells him.

'The Sunday paper I freelance for will run it past their legal team. Fortunately, I'm rather adept at finding ways around their objections.' There's a pause before he adds, 'Do I have your blessing?'

'I owe it to my dad to clear his name. So yes, you have my blessing – not that you need it, right?'

'All the same, it's good to know I have it.' She can hear someone speaking in the background. 'I'll be in touch.' The line goes dead.

Chapter Forty-One

The programme is getting top billing; terms like *No holds barred* and *explosive* are being bandied around. They repeatedly show a trailer that ends with the punchline: *Jerry Bellingham stares down Twin Barrels.* An obvious pun and yet the eyeball-to-eyeball confrontation it conjures up is making her nervous.

As their publicist, Kendra must have sanctioned the whole thing. Presumably the band's management team must be fully onboard. All the same, given the fickleness of the viewing public, they're about to take one hell of a risk.

Eve tries to busy herself in the hours leading up to the scheduled 10:00 p.m. start. Well after the watershed. The listing in the paper makes it clear that Jerry will be interviewing the three of them live. No chance for anything they say getting cut in the edits. They're likely to need that built-in, tiny delay to bleep out any expletives.

After their morning ride, Jared had cleared his throat. Hands on hips, he waited until she'd more or less finished grooming Brandy. 'So, we were wondering if you'd like to watch the interview at ours. Maybe have a spot of supper beforehand…' He did his best to make it sound casual, like they'd be watching an England game or Eurovision.

'Thanks, but I'm actually busy tonight.' An outright lie. To avoid his eye, she'd carried on grooming Brandy, tried to act like none of it especially interested her, although faced with his incredulous stare, she conceded a little. 'I'll probably, you know, catch the end of it if I'm back in time.' Who exactly was she trying to fool?

She's not sure now if it was the right call. The familiar intro music is perky enough; she'd never noticed its deeper undertones before. With everything on the line, all three of them must be bricking it right now. God – what if they're about to do a Prince Andrew?

After a wide shot of the studio and its clapping audience, Jerry Bellingham's grinning, avuncular face fills the screen. His swept back hair has a well-judged amount of grey at the sides. Having said they need no introduction, he introduces 'the boys' – a crazy way of speaking when two of the three are well into their forties.

They're sitting in a row on the big blue sofa. In front of each, a drink of their choice aimed at loosening tongues, making answers less guarded.

The applause fades. All things considered, Nick looks pretty good in his well-pressed shirt and clean jeans. It reminds her of that interview with Leanora from the adoption agency.

Eve shifts her attention to Leon. He's dressed head to toe in black; his plain t-shirt and black jeans carry a tiny red designer logo you could easily miss. Not quite to toe – under the glass table his scarlet trainers stand out like they don't quite belong to the rest of his body.

Whilst Jerry's talking, Leon adopts a supercilious smile he really needs to lose. Pronto.

Gil is wearing his customary waistcoat and hat. His tight jeans terminate in a pair of scruffy cowboy boots. The camera zooms in on his face. Oh God, it looks like he might be stoned.

Jerry sips his wine – a non-verbal invitation for them to do the same. In the wider shot that follows she can see Nick's hi-ball glass is already half empty. She hopes it contained more mixer than spirit.

Turning to the audience and a different camera, Jerry begins to list the band's achievements – their extraordinary tally of record sales and track downloads. The specifics of their Aria, Brit and MTV awards, along with the formidable list of countries they've toured.

His face grows serious. 'And then, this spring, everything changed for Twin Barrels. Their upcoming tour was cancelled, radio stations refused to play their music, sales and download figures plummeted. For want of a better word, the three of them became pariahs almost overnight.'

After a heavy sigh, he swivels his chair to face the band. 'Been a tough old year for you lads.' He plasters on a concerned expression.

'You're not wrong,' Leon tells him. The others nod with enthusiasm.

'Absolute *bleep* nightmare,' Gil adds. 'A total shit-show. And right in the middle of it all, just when I thought things couldn't get much worse, me mum died of breast cancer.'

'My sincere condolences.' After a beat, Jerry drops his sad face. 'How did it make you feel when those allegations began to surface?' A question aimed at no particular target.

Leon's about to answer when Nick talks over him. 'We knew from the start the young woman in question had to be mistaken.'

'You're saying you knew Lina Wolff was lying from the offset?' Jerry shoots back.

'I prefer the word mistaken.' Nick sits forward elbows on his knees. 'Look, the poor woman has mental health issues and deserves our sympathy.' He sits up as if someone in his ear has told him to look more upright. 'In all probability, I think she genuinely believed what she was describing had actually happened.' He looks straight down the camera lens. 'However, let me be crystal clear on this, it did not. We were all completely mystified when she made those allegations. I mean, none of us had ever even met the woman.'

'So how do you explain the lurid footage that was doing the rounds at the same time?'

'Deepfakes.' Leon lets the word sink in. 'All doctored. Our heads planted on other people's bodies.'

'Yeah,' Gil interjects, 'by some little arsehole, some total knobhead with a fancy computer program tryin' to get in on the act.'

'You see the same sort of fake footage all over the internet,' Leon tells him. 'They graft well-known people's heads onto porn actors' bodies with no thought to what the person whose identity has been stolen might suffer.'

'Take yourself, for example.' Gil hesitates as if his train of thought has just pulled out. He rallies. 'I mean, you, the famous Jerry Bellingham, could wake up tomorrow morning and find there's pictures of you riding a donkey or an alpaca.' He grins. 'When I say riding, I don't mean you're sitting on its back–'

'Thank you, Gil, I think we all understand what you're suggesting,' Jerry tells him.

'All joking apart,' Leon jabs a finger at an imaginary opponent, 'something really needs to be done about these fakes. We need new legislation not just here in the UK but internationally.'

'Little *bleep* should be strung up,' Gil says.

'Well, let's not get carried away.' Nick lays a hand across Gil's lap as if to restrain him. 'The thing is, people talk about victimless crime but these deepfakers are directly harming the people whose identity they steal. Film stars, politicians, chat show hosts like yourself – no one's safe. Aside from the profound humiliation, these images can damage people's lives – their whole careers. Their closest, dearest relationships…'

Jerry narrows his eyes. 'Talking of which, Leon, you recently broke up with top model Medora. Tell me, was that due to–'

'Medora and I reluctantly decided to go our separate ways.' Leon throws his hands up. 'Sorry, but I really have nothing more to say on that subject.'

'Yes, but was the split due to the strain Nick here just referred to?'

Leon shakes his head. 'Like I said, I've got nothing to add.' He glances behind like he might be contemplating walking off.

'Nick – it's no secret your marriage also recently broke up.'

'But not as a direct result of those allegations,' Nick's quick to point out. 'Although of course all our families have been put under tremendous strain by these events. And we're not alone. It's easy to make wild allegations – intentionally or not. Anonymity is so often given to the accuser but not the accused. You can't begin to imagine how it feels to be wrongly accused of such dreadful things…'

'We might be a bunch of aging rockers,' Leon says, 'but first and foremost we're human beings, you know.'

Head on one side Jerry rubs an eyebrow, 'At one point it looked as if you were going to face a me-too style class action. Now that all seems to have melted away.'

Leon raises a finger to signal he wants to address the point. 'Those allegations have all been withdrawn.'

'So, were the claimants simply opportunists jumping on the bandwagon?'

'Thing is,' Nick says, 'taken out of context several years afterwards, actions can sometimes be completely misinterpreted. When you're rehearsing a video shoot with dancers, for example, you're playing a part just like actors do. None of it is real.'

Shuffling his notes, Jerry tries a different tack. 'Fancy lawyers cost big money, and at a time when your income must have fallen through the floor. Let's turn to the financial impact of all this.'

'Let's not.' Gil's looking even more belligerent. 'If we wanted to talk money, we'd go and see our *bleep* accountants.'

Hand to his chest, Nick intervenes again. 'I think we'd prefer to talk about the human costs of the experience. We've all suffered exactly the same as anyone would if they were unfortunate enough to find themselves in a similar situation. Our hearts can be broken, just like the people in this audience or the viewers watching at home.'

Someone takes this cue to clap. A consummate performance though that last bit seemed a tad over-rehearsed. Like rainfall, the applause turns into a deluge accompanied by cheering. When the camera pans around to the audience, Eve spots Kendra and Lance sitting side by side in the front row clapping with undiminished enthusiasm; an unlikely pairing to say the least.

After a minute or so the applause subsides. Jerry waits for it to peter out before raising his wineglass in the direction of the sofa. 'Well said, Nick. I'm sure we can all agree that none of us should rush to condemn others without being in full possession of the facts.'

Jerry's softened expression shows he's aware of the mood music – the need to back off. 'So, let's move on to the new Twin Barrels' album,' he says. 'Have to say it's quite a departure. You're going to perform a track from it in a moment, but first let's just talk about the inspiration behind it.'

Gil stands up. 'The music says it all, man.' He strides over to the stage area leaving the other two with no option but to follow. The camera operators have a job keeping up.

They switch to a shot of Jerry's taken aback face.

The band are in position, Leon centre stage. Backing musicians move into the shadows behind. No dancers tonight. The lights dim and a twisting road is projected onto the backdrop. A rain-soaked windscreen is superimposed across the three of them. The intro builds as their faces fleetingly fall between darkness and the sudden glare of oncoming lights. At times their features appear to be melting.

Not ready to hear Nick's words, Eve mutes the sound and watches the performance in silence. It's a strange experience scrutinising them from afar. Noticing the way even Gil comes alive in front of an audience.

When it's over, the camera pans back to the host who slaps on a genial expression as he stands to applaud. She flicks the volume back on. 'Great stuff,' Jerry says. 'My thanks to Nick, Leon, and Gil.' One outstretched arm encouraging another burst of applause.

Jerry sits down, swivels his chair to a new angle. 'After the break, we chat to one lucky woman who, against all odds, has just won a six-figure sum on the lottery *for the third time.* What's her secret? What are her plans for all that money? Perhaps we'll find out.'

Before they cut the feed, Leon, Gil and Nick grin and wave to the audience from the stage – their natural home.

Eve continues to stare at the screen, at the noisy eye-jangling ads that follow. Jerry re-appears. The band have been replaced on the sofa by the lottery woman; her pink dress a nightmare of flounces and frills – proof, if needed, that money and taste don't always go together.

Eve turns it off. She sees her own reflection staring back at her from the blank screen. Grabbing her phone, she presses the Twitter icon. #twinbarrels is already trending. The comments seem divided. Before she can read them, her phone vibrates. 'Were you watching?' Nick demands.

'Yes, I was.'

'And?'

'And you all did very well. A great performance. The donkey stroke alpaca part was a bit of a low point, but you turned it around at the end. Took the audience with you.'

'Does that include you?' Music is playing somewhere in the background.

'How do you mean, exactly?'

'What Jerry asked me tonight, well, it's got me thinking. If I ask you a question, do you promise to answer it honestly?'

'Okay.'

'I'm serious, Eve.'

'Okay yes – I promise I'll give you an honest answer.'

'What I want to know is – did you leave because you still don't believe I'm innocent?'

Eve shuts her eyes. Into her inner darkness she says, 'If we're talking specifics, of course I believe Bernie was behind the whole Lina Wolff thing.'

It's tempting to stop right there – let him enjoy his moment of triumph if that's what it proves to be. She says, 'The problem is more general, I'm afraid. The sad truth is that I lost my trust, my faith in you. In *us*. For a long time, I was able to fool myself about a lot of things in our marriage because I wanted so badly for it to work. I'm afraid the blinkers are well and truly off now.'

'Ouch.' She can still hear him breathing. Almost as a mumble he says, 'Well I suppose I asked for it.'

Chapter Forty-Two

He tells her he wants to see her. 'Why don't we meet halfway,' she suggests. And so they rendezvous in the car park of a motorway service station. A location only ever on the way to somewhere else.

After an awkward greeting, they take their coffees outside to sit at a picnic bench set on a narrow verge surrounded by manoeuvring cars and whining infants.

'First of all,' Chet says. 'I wanted to tell you the Sunday newspaper I mentioned has agreed to carry some lengthy extracts from my book in next month's supplement. As always, I've amassed way too much material, so I've decided to concentrate on three specific cases where I believe there's been a clear miscarriage of justice; your parents' deaths being one of them.'

This is both a relief and a concern.

'I need to ask you something, and please think very carefully before you answer.' He waits for her nod. 'Was your father right or left-handed?'

'That's easy – he was left-handed like me. He called us

southpaws – we're like the queen, he used to say. I don't see how that helps.'

'Because, although the knife was found in your father's half-open left hand and his muscular development strongly suggested that was his dominant hand, the pathologist's report on your mother raised the distinct possibility that her killer could have been right-handed. Unfortunately, Dr Tarrant wouldn't or couldn't be definitive about it and so DI Digby simply chose to ignore the possibility because it didn't fit with the version of events he'd already decided on.'

'Wow – I had no idea.' Head bowed, she covers her face with her hands. Finally shaking her head, she tells him, 'This is really hard to take in.'

'Since the vast majority of people are right-handed, it doesn't exactly narrow the field when it comes to alternative suspects.' A note of triumph in his voice, Chet adds, 'However, I've also managed to track down and interview some of the neighbours who lived in your street at the time.'

He takes out his notebook and flips through the pages until he finds what he's looking for. 'Before he was incapacitated, several people told me they'd had their suspicions about Jack Wilson. One woman by the name of Mrs Helen Silver–'

'Mrs Silver – I remember her. She had this Golf convertible that was always badly parked.' To his quizzical look she adds, 'I tend to notice people's cars.'

'Where was I? Ah yes, Mrs Silver. She told me she always found Wilson, and I quote, "creepy as hell". She said he was: "What I call a lurker. I'd see him hanging around for no obvious reason." She remembers warning her visiting niece there was something fishy about Wilson and she should give the man a wide berth.

'Another neighbour – Reginald Linsey – told me Wilson was: "Always mooching about in the dark. Jack must have walked the legs off that poor old dog of his." Reg couldn't be sure, but he thinks he remembers seeing Wilson standing in the dark, looking up at your mother as she worked in her studio. Was she in the habit of not pulling the curtains?'

'The windows in her studio never had curtains.'

'You're quite certain of that?'

She frowns. 'Of course. She was always fully clothed so why would she need them? And besides, in daytime they'd have got in the way, blocked out some of the much-needed light.'

He flips to another page. 'I managed to trace a woman who used to work in the corner shop. A Mrs Ivy Freemantle.'

'Oh, I remember her – she had this peculiar hairdo – long grey plaits wound around her head, almost Princess Leia style. She was nice though. If she was changing over a box or a jar, she'd sometimes give me and Kimmy a handful of free sweets.'

'Mr Wilson popped in regularly to buy cigarettes. Marlboros apparently. Ivy said he had an annoying tendency to leer at her cleavage. With a bit of prompting, she also remembered your mother telling her about their oven not working. She's not sure, but she thinks that was only a couple of days before it happened.'

'Did Mrs Freemantle mention that to the police?'

'She didn't,' Chet says. 'She told me she didn't think something like that would be relevant.'

Finishing his coffee, Chet's fingers smooth his moustache back into place. 'I haven't been able to discover whether Jack Wilson is right-handed. Also, I should warn you, Eve, all of this new information proves nothing. In some countries – France for example – they take into consideration the sheer *weight* of circumstantial evidence against a suspect. If there's enough, they take it seriously. Here in the UK, the law's much stricter. We'll need hard evidence implicating Wilson before they're likely to consider revisiting the original coroner's verdict.'

'So, what next?'

'Let's see what happens after they run the story. Of course, the newspaper won't be keen to get embroiled in a defamation case so…'

'You'll have to leave a lot of this out.'

'Of the article, yes. But it'll all be in my book. My publishers are already demanding cuts. Understandably, they're also nervous about being sued. If need be, I'll publish the book privately. Once it's all out there, if Mrs Wilson or any of her family decide to sue me for defamation on Jack's behalf – well, let's say I look forward to the court case.'

A banner across the top promises: exclusive extracts from *When Justice is Blind* the upcoming book by award-winning journalist Chet Lange. Turning to the relevant page, Eve sees they've given it a three-page spread under the banner headline:

GETTING AWAY WITH MURDER?

The first part deals with the unsolved killing of a mother and daughter in Wales. It shocks her to think of other people going through what she's been through.

Eve runs her eyes down the columns on the second page and there it is:

A Bungled Investigation?

Surrounded by cardboard boxes, she sits down to read with more care. Chet manages to make a compelling case about the shoddiness of the investigation, the staged nature of the scene and police failure to explore alternative interpretations of what might have happened.

Under a smiling photo of her mother, his text drops heavy hints about a different scenario involving a delusional admirer. There's no mention of Mr Wilson by name. She can only hope the publicity prompts more witnesses to come forward.

'Fingers crossed,' she says closing the supplement and folding it with care. For a moment she imagines her parents restored to life and health, standing right behind her, both smiling.

A daft thought – it's not like she believes in ghosts.

The van carrying her possessions shrinks to the size of a toy before it disappears over the crest of the hill. Once they've reached the storage unit, all the boxes she'd carefully labelled will be piled up and locked away. If a fire destroyed the lot tomorrow, she's not sure she'd care very much.

Eve takes a moment to admire the long line of cottages that make up the main thoroughfare of the village. Tucked up against each other, their yellow stone walls are glowing in the new day's sun. People are beginning to emerge in ones and twos, mostly getting into cars and driving away. Probably off to work somewhere else.

She's always loved the chestnut trees that line the raised pavements on either side of the road. Their leaves are losing grip, they float to earth every time the wind shakes more of them free. Eve kicks at the fallen ones simply to hear the crunch and rustle.

Some people consider autumn a gloomy time of the year; to her it's always been magical. For obvious reasons, Americans call it the fall – a biblical turn of phrase. How could so many startling colours ever be sad?

Rory and Jared had wanted to be there to wave her off. 'Can't have you sneaking away from us like a thief,' Rory had said.

'I'm not sneaking away,' she insisted. 'Like Bilbo Baggins – I'm setting off on a new adventure outside the shire.'

'So, I'm to imagine you shouldering a bag on a stick and whistling a perky little tune as you go?'

Laughing she'd said, 'Something like that.'

At Rory's insistence, there'd been a rowdy piss-up in The Feathers. Inevitably she got hammered; still has the hangover as proof.

Linda, the owner of the stables, had shown up with a few of the girls who work for her. Worse for drink and slurring her words, Linda had repeatedly assured her Brandy would be well taken care of. The woman seemed a bit thrown by the sizable donation Eve had made to her riding for the disabled program. She'd been tempted to tell her it was only money but that would have seemed crass.

Various people from the village had pressed drinks on Eve, their words overly sentimental. A couple of hours in, Amber had made her entrance. Dressed in flowing shades of green, her purple hair was adorned with artificial roses like some strange woodland nymph. Her opening line, 'Thought we'd better stop by to wish you luck and all that bollocks.' Her wide smile had mitigated that sting in the tail. By *we*, she'd meant she and Jermaine their former security guard – a hook-up that didn't surprise.

Eve had heard that they'd both been taken on by the new owners. 'Course it's not the same without you and Nick.' The girl gave her an enigmatic look. 'It's totally, you know, different now.'

'Yeah, it is,' Jermaine confirmed. Eve found it impossible to tell if they considered this good or bad.

Before setting off, she takes a long swig from the water bottle she'd filled at the last minute. Given the amount she's drunk this morning in an attempt to rehydrate, it won't be long before she needs to pull in for a pee.

Her all electric Fiat 500 is already a complete mess inside – piled high with randomised clothes, toiletries and books. She'll have to stop a couple of times to recharge, but that's fine. No rush these days.

She takes one last look around before climbing into the driver's seat. Instead of the sadness she'd anticipated, as she pulls away from the curb, a sensation of weightlessness over-whelms her.

She's approaching the dual carriageway when a Twin Barrels track comes on the radio. Leon's distinctive voice fills her ears. Though hard to make out over the pounding, hypnotic beat, the lyrics are about bumping into a former lover.

'The boys are back with a vengeance,' the DJ informs her. 'That was their brand-new single: 'Regret Me Not.'

Eve smiles. 'Couldn't put it better,' she tells him out loud. At the first major junction, she heads north.

Chapter Forty-Three

It's usually dark well before five these days – sometimes earlier if the weather closes in. Most afternoons Eve arrives back chilled through despite her protective gear. She's still besotted by the sight of all those pregnant grey seals, so lumbering and awkward on land compared to how sleek and agile they are in water. She's learnt to call them cows, though why call the breeding colony a rookery?

It's a privilege to watch the mothers haul themselves out of the water to give birth. It takes a couple of days for the pup's coat to turn from yellow to fluffy white – which makes it easier to count the new-borns. The pups' round dark eyes hold such a molten appeal. Seeing their mothers' dedication and protectiveness never fails to stir her emotions. Other cows ignore their pup's heart-rending cries and won't allow them to suckle. She's witnessed far too often how this failure to bond means the pup won't survive. Watching from a distance, Eve has to fight the urge to intervene.

"Home" for the time being is a large comfortable if rather spartan room in one section of a converted outhouse. She enjoys the relative luxury of mains electricity and a small en-suite shower room. The days are long and demanding; all the same Eve can't recall ever being happier or more herself. Who would have predicted a year ago she'd be in her element living up here observing seals and recording pup numbers?

Her laptop is in her storage locker in the main building – a conscious choice on her part. Turning her mobile on, she finds a WhatsApp from Rory sharing the latest gif of Jerry Billingham with a pair of red-lipped, pouting alpacas. His comment – 'Poor guy's never going to live it down' – makes her smile.

In return she sends them a close-up shot of one of today's newborn seals. 'Those eyes!!' Jared pings back. Rather rashly, she'd promised to send them weekly updates with photos but she's finding it hard to say anything that's different to the last one.

She checks her emails. Amongst the spam, two messages vie for her attention – one is from Chet Lange, the other from Lachlan.

As the one from Chet promises '*Further Updates*' she opens it first.

Dear Eve,

I sincerely hope this finds you well and in good spirits.

I've just heard the sad news that Jack Wilson has finally passed away. I use the word 'sad' because I deeply regret the fact that while he lived we weren't able to satisfactorily link him to the murder of your parents. I'm sure your lawyers will have informed you that, once they've finished re-examining all the circumstances surrounding your parents' deaths, the coroner's court will almost certainly overturn the original verdict on your father's death. An inadequate, partial victory, but still a victory nonetheless.

I sincerely hope that you can find some measure of peace in the knowledge that your father has, to all intents and purposes, been exonerated. It may not go nearly as far as we both had hoped but remember that anyone reading my book – and I'm delighted to report it's selling very well – will undoubtedly share your dismay and regret at the injustice your family received at the hands of an incompetent police force.

I've also been approached by a certain streaming company. They've expressed interest in making a docudrama series, so their story may well reach a wider audience in due course.

I remain disgusted that Detective Inspector Digby was able to retire to the Isle of Wight on full pension with no official criticism of his appalling leadership in this case and several others. I'm sure you share my hope that lessons have been learnt by the force.

As for yourself, please excuse me if I speak to you from my own personal experience. I'm sure your parents would want you to move on with your life and not dwell on how things could have been different. Bitterness is a terrible thing, Eve. When they finally informed me that my wife and unborn child had died, I was eaten up by the injustice of it – along with the predictable survivor's guilt. Uncovering miscarriages of justice has been my way of moving forward in the knowledge that my late wife would have wanted me to embrace the future and not always be looking back with sadness and regret. I hope you're able to do the same.

Best regards for your future,

Your friend Chet.

How dare Jack Wilson die peacefully in his comfortable care home, no doubt with his loyal wife holding his hand until the end. Overcome by despondency, Eve shuts her eyes, cradles her head in her hands. The law might dismiss it as conjecture, but there's no doubt in her mind that he murdered her mother and then her father when he tried to intervene. Did Wilson's wife know or guess? He must have arrived home with his clothes covered in blood. Did he or his wife wash them like he'd simply spilt a cup of coffee down himself? Remembering the look on Mrs Wilson's face she's sure the woman must have had her suspicions. Had she been covering up for him for years? The Wilson family haven't yet announced any plan to sue Chet for defamation. In a way that was an admission of his guilt.

'Everything alright, Eve?' Raising her head, she plasters on a smile for Shona's benefit.

'Yeah, I'm fine. Just a bit knackered.' She does her best to sound casual.

'You've gone really pale.'

'Have I?' To avoid the girl's curious stare, she turns her attention back to her inbox and that email from Lachlan.

She exits the screen; right now she hasn't got the bandwidth to process anything else.

After supper – some sort of greyish lentil concoction which tasted a lot better than it looked – she puts on several layers and ventures outside. It's a clear night and, with no light pollution, the stars are astounding. All those other galaxies might look serene and timeless, but once you're able to look deeper, it's all violence and beauty up there. As always, such a sight puts the smallness of her life into perspective. Chet's advice was well meant and clearly from the heart. Being here, leading this simple, uncomplicated life, has been therapy enough. Every day she passes the remains of an ancient abbey; It's easy to see why those isolated religious communities found spiritual peace in a place like this. Tomorrow she'll email Chet and thank him. She'll also reassure him that she has no intention of letting bitterness dictate her future.

Along with the other volunteers, Eve's up early next morning. It's taken her a while to adjust to the regime. They're a nice bunch – though one or two can be a bit too earnest and preachy; she's tempted to point out that they're amongst the converted. She hasn't been part of a team since she played netball at school.

Despite increasingly chilly temperatures, the healthy seal pups are growing at an impressive rate, putting on around 2 kg a day. It saddens her to think that their mothers will abandon them after only three weeks or so when they go off alone to mate with the bulls who are already fighting for supremacy. The young pups will shed those cute fluffy coats. Once they've used up much of their fat reserves, hunger will drive them towards the sea and its abundant larder. Their mothers won't have shown them what to eat or how to survive. On their own, the poor things will have to take their chances in a wild unforgiving ocean.

Eve always looks forward to this free time before supper. (Or tea – as some insist on calling it.) She turns her phone on. After sending Chet a thank you, she checks her inbox once again and of course it's still there – emails don't delete themselves overnight.

In the subject line he'd written: "Greeting from Fluraichean."

Dear Eve,

I've been wondering if counting all those seal pups every day is making you sleep better at night? How are things? Still enjoying yourself, I trust.

Here we're now in the off-season – the last of our visitors left almost a month back. I'm working my way through a long list of chores. Outside I'm trying to clear some of the scrub the ponies have missed. At home I'm teaching Breac his times tables amongst other things. For various reasons he's lost a lot of schooling this past couple of years. But he's a quick learner.

By the spring I should have finished work on

another of the old croft houses – it's just a stone's throw from the farmhouse so reserved for special guests only. This time, we're not going to name it after the previous inhabitants. Instead, we'll let Breac choose a new name – though definitely not Crofty-McCroftface.

I really hope you're not so heartily sick of counting wildlife that you've changed your mind about helping us with our seabird survey in the spring. I also hope you'll be the first person to try out the new cottage – free of charge of course. To tempt you further, I should mention that, along with the usual kittiwakes and fulmars, we spotted a handful of storm petrels and skuas earlier this year. Maybe a few puffins will be blown off course and be persuaded to nest on the West Cliffs here.

I often think of you. Do let me know how you're getting on.

Breac sends his love. See attached picture of him with Bounty who, by the way, follows him everywhere these days.

All best wishes,

Lachlan.

In the photograph Breac is head up lying on his front in the grass with Bounty balancing on his back: the two a picture of happiness. In the background the view of the island is as seductive as ever.

Neil comes in to tell them the food's ready. As it's Shona's turn to cook, it's bound to be a curry of some sort. Her empty stomach growls at the prospect. Smiling, Eve types a hasty reply.

Hi Lachlan,

Great to hear from you again. Loved the photo – so glad Bounty's made a full recovery. Pleased to say I haven't changed my mind about the survey.

Can't wait to

No. She deletes those last three words. Better not sound too eager.

Looking forward to seeing you in the spring.
Love to Breac.
Eve x

She's sends it without thinking about that x and what he might imagine it implies. For goodness' sake, she's a thirty-four-year-old divorcee not some lovestruck teenager.

Next evening, after a hot shower and a change of clothes, she checks her emails to find he's already replied. She scans through the text pleased and then disappointed that it contains nothing aside from the normal sort of stuff. Until the last line. And then there it is:

Lachlan xx

Two kisses – he's most definitely raised the stakes.

About the Author

Before becoming a writer, Jan Turk Petrie taught English in inner city London schools. She now lives in the Cotswolds area of southern England. Jan has an M.A. in Creative Writing (University of Gloucestershire) and, as well as her published novels, she has written numerous, prize-winning short stories

As a writer, Jan is always keen to challenge herself. Her first published novels – the three volumes that make up The Eldísvík Trilogy – are Nordic noir thrillers set fifty years in the future in a Scandinavian city where the rule of law comes under threat from criminal cartels controlling the forbidden zones surrounding it.

By contrast, her fourth novel – 'Too Many Heroes' – is a period romantic thriller set in the early 1950s. A story of an illicit love affair that angers the mobsters controlling London's East End at that time.

Jan's fifth novel: 'Towards the Vanishing Point' is also set primarily in the 1950s and depicts an enduring friendship between two women that is put to the test when one of them falls under the spell of a sinister charmer.

'The Truth in a Lie' was her first novel with a contemporary setting. It is the story of a successful writer who has a complex and often difficult relationship with her mother and her own daughter as well as with the men in her life.

'Running Behind Time' was Jan's first time-slip novel. Written during the unprecedented events of 2020 and the new social norms arising from the pandemic, she was inspired to imagine a time-hop back to the early 1980s.

Jan is a big fan of Margaret Atwood, Kate Atkinson, Philip Roth, Kurt Vonnegut and Jennifer Egan – authors who are always prepared to take risks in their writing.

Dear reader.

I really hope you've enjoyed reading 'Still Life with a Vengeance'. Thank you so much for buying or borrowing a copy, the book means a lot to me. If you would like to help readers discover the book, please consider leaving a review on Amazon, Goodreads, Bookbub, or anywhere else readers are likely to visit. It doesn't need to be a long review – a sentence or two is fine.

Many thanks in advance to anyone who takes the time to do so.

If you would like to find out more about this book, or are interested in discovering more about my other published novels, please visit my website: https://janturkpetrie.com

If you'd like to follow me on Twitter, my handle is: @Turk-Petrie

Twitter profile: https://twitter.com/TurkPetrie.

Facebook author page: https://www.facebook.com/janturkpetrie

Contact Pintail Press via the website: https://pintailpress.com

Acknowledgements

This is my eighth novel and writing it was certainly not without its challenges. As always, I have to begin by thanking John Petrie, my wonderful husband, for reading and commenting on the various drafts of 'Still Life with a Vengeance'. As always his feedback was absolutely invaluable. I'd also like to thank him for his unfailing support and encouragement during the long process of writing this book.

As always, I'd like to thank my lovely daughters Laila and Natalie for their unwavering love and support. Thanks also go to my wider family and in particular my mum, Pearl Turk, for her constant encouragement and those highly individual 'Pearls of Wisdom'.

Writing is a solitary occupation and so feedback from my fellow *Catchword* writers during our zoom meetings was especially helpful. Comments and suggestions from members of the highly talented *Wild Women Writers* and the feedback from Stroud's *Little George Writers Group* were extremely valuable.

Special thank you to Debbie Young and everyone in the Alliance of Independent Authors (Alli) group in Cheltenham for their impressive knowledge of indie publishing and their sound collective advice.

Lastly, I'm once again grateful to my editor and proofreader, Johnny Hudspith, and to my cover designer, Jane Dixon Smith, for their consistently excellent work.

Printed in Great Britain
by Amazon